Unfold You

By C.L. Knopf

Text copyright © 2017 C. L. Knopf
All Rights Reserved

Book Cover: Everpage Designs

Prologue

Ben

I come to a stop. It's hard to believe that I drove over 600 miles. My back is killing me; this was easier when I was in my twenties. I rest my arms on the steering wheel, staring at the house in the distance. Chills come over me thinking about my last memory there. Damn, it's been twenty years since I took off.

This used to be the place I called home; well for at least six months out of every year. My family owns a circus, so home was everywhere. We would travel from city to city every other week, business was always pretty good. Dad sure knew what he was doing in that aspect; besides being the owner he also acted as the ringmaster. Mom has always been more of a behind the scenes person, helping with whatever she could. My brother James and I performed in the 'Globe of Death' act, god I loved it. The smell of the exhaust fumes, the thrill that shot through my body knowing that one wrong turn and it could all be over. We were obsessed with our bikes and really did live that lifestyle. James is two years older and I looked up to him. The globe was a very popular act; it always got the crowd going.

Our show had everything you could imagine ranging from trapeze and knife throwing to clowns. During our off season most of the performers lived with us. Our place was overrun with trailers, quite the eyesore but with our next neighbor being miles away, it never bothered anyone. So many different people and cultures, it was a melting pot. I was young, happy and in love. Sarah was my everything. She was a contortionist and I loved watching her perform. We dated two years before getting engaged. Life was perfect.

I still can't believe I'm about to come home. That memory just won't go away. It is so vivid in my mind as if it just happened. I was completely caught off guard. Never in my wildest dreams would I have thought that dad could have betrayed me in that way. I ran out the door with my bag packed, telling him I would never come back as long as he was alive. I kept my promise. My biggest regret was leaving my mom, brothers and one little girl who had a very special place in my heart. I still see her in my rearview running after my bike screaming my name.

I left my life, everything I knew and started over. After many failed attempts and countless rocky relationships I finally thought I was settled. So why am I sitting here in the middle of rural Georgia? I chuckle, after all this time I am about to return home, my life a bigger mess than when I left.

I take a deep breath and drive toward the house. It's Friday, late afternoon. Of course I'm unannounced. I have had zero contact with anyone over the years. I didn't want to make that awkward phone call begging to come home. I figure if I just show up my chances could be better. I step out of the truck and take a look around. Where are all of the trailers? Where are the people? The season hasn't started so why is it so dead? I feel my whole body shake as I walk up the steps that lead to the porch. Well, no turning back now, I ring the bell. Footsteps approach, this is it.

"Ben?" My brother James stares at me like he's seen a ghost.
He sounds ecstatic so it puts me at ease. James still looks the same, just older. His brown hair is still tied back in a ponytail. I notice a few tattoos which throws me off a bit. I remember his stance on them when we were young and I got my first one.

"Yeah, it's me, I'm sorry to just show up like this. I just didn't -"

"I can't believe it! Oh my god, I thought I would never see you again. You're here, you're home! It's been god knows how long." Before I can answer I see two familiar faces peeking from behind the door. Alex and Mason; my two little brothers. They were just young kids when I left, now they are men. The look of surprise is written all over their faces.

"You recognize him don't you? It's Ben! You guys were about six when you last saw him. Man, get in here," James says pulling me in the door. I look around the living room, it has changed quite a bit. Different furniture, new pictures on the wall with faces I don't recognize. It seems much bigger than I remember.

"Ben, you probably don't know, "he pauses, "dad died about five years back."

"I know," I reply looking down, "I found his obituary online. I had to make sure the bastard was gone before I would even think about coming here. I would have never been able to face him again after –"

James interrupts me. "Nope, I totally understand. What he did was unforgivable. Unfortunately, he learned nothing from it. Still continued doing what the hell he felt like."

"Hey James, where's mom?" I ask nervously.

James laughs, "Oh yeah, Mom. Well after Dad passed she decided she needed to get out of here and travel on her own. She met this guy on her trips and now lives Canada with him. She usually visits twice a year," Wow, I was not expecting that.

"You know Ben. I'm happy for her though. All of the shit Dad put her through over the years, she deserves to be happy."

"Dude, I totally agree with you. I don't know how she did it. It just sucks that she's so far away, I really hoped to see her."

"You're actually going to get the chance here in a little less than two months. I'm getting married in July so Mom and Gerald will fly in for the wedding," James says excitedly.

"Wedding? You haven't married Cheryl yet?" I ask stunned.

"We did get married. It just didn't work out. We divorced about two years ago."

Mason starts giggling, "No, he's marrying Carmen. They met online on one of those dating sites. They're madly in love." The way he drags out Carmen's name makes me wonder.

"Oh shut up Mason. At least I have somebody that loves and cares about me and yes we are in love. She's amazing."

Alex butts in "Yeah, amazingly rich."

"Anyway you'll meet Carmen next week. She's flying in for a visit." James adds.

"Right on, that's great. Looking forward to meet her."

I'm amazed how easy this conversation has been, like no time passed. It's comfortable, natural.

"Hey I wanted to ask, where is everyone? I didn't see any trailers outside," I ask, I've never seen this house so quiet.

"Oh that's right, you wouldn't know. Well after dad died and mom left it was up to me to keep things going but I was in over my head. I had no idea how much work was really involved. I had to shut it down, sold everything and most people left and got hired on with other shows. Some stayed local, but not many. I actually opened up an auto repair shop on the property so Rick, Carol and Shane work for me." Damn, everyone's gone. In the back of my mind it's what I suspected.

James continues, "But here it's really just us. Carmen is moving in after the wedding so that will be nice and," he pauses and his eyes widen with excitement. "Do you remember Sam's little girl Layla? She lives with us. She's still at work but should be home in a bit. Layla is going to lose it."

How could I forget? I thought of her many times over the years, wondering what became of her. When James' said that everyone had left, sadness came over me knowing I may never see her again. Now the feeling has changed to pure panic. What do I say to her? Will she recognize me?

Chapter One

Layla

Gosh, what a day. I always told myself working at 'The Bull' was temporary but now we are going on year number three. At least I only work Tuesday through Friday. I'm happy to be employed though, this town is so small and jobs are very limited. Most people work in Macon about thirty minutes west but I like being close to home. My Boss, Randy loves to keep things interesting. He's been hosting karaoke on Friday nights for a while but now he's adding line dance lessons. We have our regulars and a great deal of outsiders that come here for the small town vibe. The décor is typical country with lots of wood and exposed brick. The bar has a few saddle stools; they look really neat but are awkward to sit on. One of the walls is covered with license plates from all over the United States. The Bull would not live up to its name if it weren't for Diablo, our mechanical bull, usually reserved for drunk girls trying to show off and look cute. I'm a bartender here, started as a server and now I'm with the big dogs. The pay is good, so I'm not forced to search out something new. I keep checking my phone for the time. Yes, only one more hour to go.

"Hey Layla, hand me that bottle opener," a voice calls from behind me. It's my friend slash ex-boyfriend. Layne and I still get along very well. We were introduced about four years ago through our friend Alex and sometime last year we thought it would be a good idea to take our friendship to the next level. Actually alcohol was the trigger and the result was a hookup. It only lasted about six months and it wasn't a bad breakup. The relationship was just awkward and too familiar. The attraction is there but I never felt a bond. It has nothing to do with his physique. He is tall, muscular, I'm talking six pack and all, has sky blue eyes and a deep sexy voice. He wears his blonde chin length hair tucked behind his ears and walks around with that *'I haven't shaved in three days'* look. That's what gets the women hot and bothered, that and his charm. Sounds like a dream, but just not mine. Sexually we were in sync, but emotionally there was no connection.

Yes, finally it's 8 pm. I'm so happy I switched with Layne. I usually have the late shift Friday nights but he's been eyeing this girl that has been coming in right around the time he normally leaves. Lucky for him, she just showed up. As I'm leaving I remind him that safe sex is the best. He asks me if I happen to have anything for him. I roll my eyes, dig in my purse and hand him a condom. He gives me a kiss on the cheek and his famous *'love ya Layla'*.

I head out, get into my car and drive home. I live in a massive house right on the outskirts of town. I believe it was built sometime in the late 1800's and sits on about 3 acres. It's quite an unusual living situation if you're an outsider looking in. I live with James and his two younger brothers Alex and Mason. The connection? James' father Paul and mother Norma ran a circus that we were all a part of. After Paul's death, Norma decided she needed a change and opted out. James tried his best to keep things going but within two years it was over. I wasn't sad to see it go. Performing was never my thing. My *'biological'* family are acrobats; they do everything from aerial silk to trapeze. I performed very well but have severe anxiety when it comes to heights. So in the last few years we added the Acro Dance act. What a relief that was, at least it was on the ground. Mason was my partner from time to time, he loves to dance.

Unfortunately, after it ended everyone was out of a job so people had to move. Some stayed in the area; others got jobs with other shows or carnivals, my family was one of them. That lifestyle just wasn't for me and I am so lucky that James offered that I could stay with them. It wasn't hard to watch my family go, I grew up with so many different people that everyone was my family. My parents and I aren't particularly close, we really only talk on birthdays and

Christmas. As a couple they were perfect but as parents they failed miserably. You'd think they would have gotten it right at some point after having seven kids.

Turning left onto the long bumpy driveway I notice an unfamiliar truck sitting in front of the house. The back is jam-packed with duffle bags and boxes. My first thought is Carmen, James' fiancé, is moving in before the wedding but then I come to my senses. First of all she would have her things in an actual moving truck and second, she would not disrespect her family's wishes in moving in before they were joined in holy matrimony. Even though Carmen is forty, she comes from a very religious Italian family. She's been married before and has an adult son but I guess the whole sex before marriage thing reset for her father when she became a widow. She moved back in with her parents after her husband's death and respects their wishes. I must say she is quite trustworthy, according to James they have only fooled around a bit, but she always stops him before it gets too far. Different strokes for different folks I suppose.

I make my way to the front door, unlock it and walk inside. Immediately I hear James calling "Layla, is that you? Come in the living room I have a surprise." I hear Mason and Alex snickering. I roll my eyes; I am so not in the mood for this tonight.

Sluggish I make my way toward the living room sighing, "It was a long day and I'm tired can we just-"

I am at a loss for words and feel as if I've just been hit by a truck, standing in living room is someone I never thought I would see again. He looks slightly different than I remembered. His hair is longer, darker, messy and covering his eyes a bit. He no longer has the baby face and now wears a goatee, a bit lighter than his hair. He's wearing loose blue jeans and a black V neck shirt. I was four years old when he left but I would have recognized him anywhere.

"Oh my god! Ben?" I shriek as I throw my hands up covering my mouth in shock.

He stands there a bit shy and uncertain but then smiles, "Wow, you do remember me. To tell the truth I really didn't believe James. I don't think I would have recognized you though, you're not that little girl anymore."

I want to run up to him, hug him and never let go but I'm frozen in place. The four of us sit on the couch and talk for what seems like hours. After a while, Mason goes up to his room to play video games, typical.

"So where have you been all these years? Do you have any interesting stories?" Alex asks.

"Nah, nothing too exciting. I pretty much stuck with the nomad thing for a while. I ended up settling in Missouri, St. Louis actually."

"Wow, big city! Do you have any kids? A wife?" I notice he's not wearing a wedding ring but it can't hurt to ask.

"Ha-ha, nope, I never had kids. Been there, done that with the marriage thing, realized it's not for me."

James slaps Alex on the leg, "Well, brother, I guess it's up to you and Mason to expand the family tree since our ship has pretty much sailed."

I just sit there quietly in awe, studying his movements, taking in every word he says. I've noticed he uses his hands a lot while talking, James does the same. There is something about the way he keeps his hair covering his right eye ever so slightly, like he's hiding, doesn't want to be exposed. I don't know how he can stand it, I would go insane.

Alex addresses the elephant in the room, "So I saw your truck is loaded with boxes, does that mean you'll be staying?"

"Um, I'm glad you brought that up," Ben says looking in James' direction, "I was wondering if it was okay for me to stay here for a while. I need to work through some stuff and just had to get away. I mean, if you have room."

I butt in, "Are you serious? We have like six bedrooms here, of course there's room."

James smiles, "You know this is your home right? Stay as long as you want. Take the room that's by the kitchen. We set it up as a guest room with its own bath. That's where mom and Gerald normally stay when they visit."

A look of relief comes over Ben's face., I can tell it was a difficult thing to ask. I am stoked that he is staying. He is a total stranger and I can't wait to get to know him again.

It's 4 am and I have been tossing and turning all night, still in disbelief. For years I swore he would come back but as time passed I stopped hoping. I went through so many emotions, sadness, anger, resentment and then nothing. I actually told myself I would never want to see him again. If I ever did, I wouldn't care. His piercing blue eyes are not leaving my mind. They reflected a sort of uncertainty and pain, like he's been through hell and back. I wonder what really made him come home. He was very vague about it, like he didn't want to disclose any more than was necessary. I don't care, he's here now.

I get up a few hours later and head to the bathroom down the hall to brush my teeth. As usual, no one is awake. Heading downstairs I make my way into the kitchen. I hear the guest room door open and slip into the pantry. Great, hair is in a ponytail, I have mascara remnants under my eyes and wearing a tank top and shorts. God I don't want him to see me like this but on second thought, explaining why I am in the pantry with the door half shut is probably even more awkward. Before opening the door, I grab the first thing in my reach and step out to see Ben standing at the kitchen island.

"Good morning Layla"

"Oh, good morning. How did you sleep?" I answer with a grin.

"Awesome actually. I was exhausted from the drive so I was out cold," Ben grins. I just stand there and smile. After a moment of silence he points to what I am holding in my hand.

"You like coffee?" Shit. I didn't pay any attention to what I was grabbing, I hate coffee. What am I going to say? Why would I be holding a bag of coffee if I didn't like it? Total fail.

Not wanting to look like an idiot I reply, "Oh yeah, totally love it! How about you? Would you like some?" What is wrong with me?

"Sure, that sounds awesome," he replies. Oh hell, I never make coffee, have to come up with something fast.

"Do you mind making it?" I ask, handing him the coffee, "I'm just going to jump in the shower and I'll be right back." He gives me a funny look but agrees. Score! After showing him where everything is I race up the stairs. Hurrying into the shower I jump as soon as the water hits my skin. It is freezing cold but I don't want to keep him waiting so I finish in record time. I don't bother drying my hair, it is too long and it will take forever, so I decide to braid it to the side. I throw on some faded blue jeans with rips and tears, the kind my mother would discard right into the garbage, and a flowy dark blue tank top. A little eyeliner and mascara and I'm back in business.

I rush down the stairs and hear voices, James and Alex are awake. It's no surprise that Mason is still asleep, the sounds of a first person shooter game went on until the wee hours of the morning. Walking into the kitchen I'm greeted by Alex with a huge grin.

"So since when do you drink coffee? Ben here said you told him you love it so he was nice enough to pour you a cup."

Wish I could smack that smirk right off his face. "Like you know everything about me," I roll my eyes and grab the cup thanking Ben. Alex tries to reply but James stops him. Taking a sip of my coffee totally confirms yet again, I hate coffee. Oh well, I suppose I got myself into this so now I'll have to grin and bear it.

We move to the dining room and sit at the enormous table. It's an heirloom made of beautiful mahogany that has been in the family for generations. It seats twelve but most of the time it's just the four of us. Once in a while Brittany, Alex's girlfriend, will join us.

Brittany is beautiful but a little bit of a spitfire. She's twenty-six, same age as Alex and works at the Bank in town. She has wavy brown hair with perfectly placed blonde highlights and amber eyes. She is uncensored and will speak her mind at any time, even when it is not appropriate. I guess Alex is happy though. They've been together for about eight months. There has been talk of moving into her apartment but he likes to change the subject every time it's mentioned. I've always been very close with Alex. Years ago I found myself swooning over him. Nothing ever happened though. He is handsome, curly brown hair, olive skin and deep brown eyes, also a bit of a flirt. Mason and Alex are twins; they look very similar but are fraternal. Mason is creative, smart and a bit reserved. Even though their parents were a disaster they sure did something right. All four of the Parker men are gorgeous, each in their own way.

Sitting at the table trying to finish my coffee I get lost in the guys' conversation. After a while James gets up, "Hey Ben, do you want to check out the shop?"

"Yeah, I wanted to ask you about that. I have my mechanics license and I can totally help out, you know, earn my keep," Ben offers.

James just chuckles and pats him on the back, "Earn your keep, are you serious brother? I will take you up on that though. We can always use the help and it will keep you busy. Come on let's go. The guys are off today."

The guys! It gets me every time. I guess Carol is just one of the guys now. She does carry herself in a very masculine way. We joke that she probably has more testosterone than all of the men combined. The shop is literally only twenty feet away from the house. It's probably the best idea James has ever had. We all pitch in when we can. I usually end up going in there on Sundays to straighten the chaos left behind. Rick,

Carol and Shane make a great team. Back in our show days they were part of our mechanic's crew.

The shop is open Monday through Friday but you can usually find James and Mason tinkering on things over the weekend too. Alex has no interest in getting his hands dirty, he's more of a suit and tie kind of guy. He works as an assistant loan officer at the same bank as Brittany, that's actually where they met.

As the guys are walking toward the shop, I join them. It won't hurt to get a look at what's in store for me tomorrow. As usual the place is a total mess. I sigh, turn around and start walking back to the house when I hear James calling, "Hey Layla, could you please stop by Al's and grab a case of beer on your way to the grocery store?" James turns to Ben and asks, "You still drink beer, don't you?"

"I sure do", Ben answers laughing.

Saturday is my grocery shopping day. On my days off I cook dinner for everyone. James is a really good cook but I like to help out since he already lets me live here for free. Walking through the aisles I'm kicking myself for not making a list. I've already been here twenty minutes and have three things in my shopping cart. It's time to pull out my phone and search for meal ideas. Before I can press the link for *'Tastiest*

Meatloaf' I hear a high pitched voice and I just want to close my eyes and disappear.

"Layla, I am so happy to run into you." It's Bailey Moore, one of Layne's recent ex's, "So I was just wondering if you talked to Layne lately."

I try to hide how annoyed I really am and say, "Bailey, you do know I work with him right?"

She flashes a smile, "You're so silly, of course I do. I just wanted to see if he was okay. You know, since I broke up with him. I've tried calling several times but haven't heard back. I know I must have broken his heart. Has he mentioned me at all? Does he seem depressed?"

I'm amazed that Layne actually found someone vainer than himself. It's no surprise their relationship didn't work out. "Nah, he's totally fine Bailey. I wouldn't worry about him. I think he's actually hooking up with this blonde he recently met at the Bull, but don't quote me on that. I'd say he's moved on." That was a little catty but I tend to believe Layne's story of him breaking it off with her.

"Oh my, okay, well that's great," she starts backing off, "So, I have a hair appointment to get to, sorry but I'll have to run. It was nice seeing you Layla."

"Oh, you too Bailey. I'll give your best to Layne," just had to say that. She gives me a fake smile and she's out the door.

Okay back to shopping. This took minutes off my life I'll never get back. Instead of browsing more recipes I decide to wing it. Stir fry, grilled chicken and beef stew will have to do. At the checkout I run into Donna, Randy's wife, and we talk for a while. You really can't go anywhere without running into at least one person you know, the charm of a small town.

When I get home, Alex comes out to get the groceries. In the kitchen I tell him all about my run in with Bailey and he gets that little boy grin on his face. He loves to hear about Layne's crazy women, one story better than the other.

"Hey, can Brittany come to dinner tonight? I want her to meet Ben. Do you think we'll have enough food?"

"We definitely have enough food. Are you going to tell Brittany to tone it down a few notches tonight?" I ask.

"What are you talking about?" his voice bleeding sarcasm, "yeah I will, don't worry. She'll be on her best behavior." For some reason I doubt it, Alex probably doesn't even notice it anymore.

"Who's going to be on their best behavior?" James asks while walking in the door with Ben.

"Brittany. I wanted her to come over for dinner tonight so she can meet Ben," Alex says optimistically. James throws his hands up jokingly and walks out to the living room with Alex right behind.

Ben looks in my direction, "Who's Brittany?"

"Alex's girlfriend. Overall she's nice but she doesn't know when to keep her mouth shut. She will probably ask you a lot of questions and you'll feel like you're being interrogated, yep, that pretty much sums her up."

"Awesome, I can't wait," Ben says sarcastically.

I'm just finishing up in the kitchen and Mason is pulling the chicken off the grill as the front door opens and Brittany walks in. "Hey everyone, sorry I'm just a little bit late."

I peek my head into the living room, "Hey Brit, you're good I'm almost done. I think everyone else is in the dining room."

Walking into the dining room I hear Brittany interrogating Ben, "So why St. Louis? Did you want to live in a bigger city?"

Ben replies, "I don't know it's just where I ended up. Had a good job there and yeah it was cool living in a big-"

Brittany interrupts "But why come back to this place? I mean there is nothing here. Certainly no jobs."

"Well, obviously my family is here, so that's a good reason. I have some stuff I need to work out and a small place like this is perfect, "he replies.

"What do you need to work out?" she asks curiously.

I look in Alex's direction and he's just staring at the ceiling. Then I glance over at Ben, he's starting to look uncomfortable so I intervene "Brit, he just got here and I think that's something private that he may not want to discuss with everyone."

"Oh, okay," she backs off.

After dinner Alex and Brittany take off. As I'm washing dishes Ben comes into the kitchen. "Man she's a bit brazen isn't she?"

"Oh yes she is. Took me a while but I figured out that if I don't want to talk about something I just tell her and she's totally fine with it. If I would have known that right away it would have saved me a lot of frustration."

Ben smirks and asks, "So what did she want to know about you?"

Catching me off guard and causing me to blush, I reply, "Mainly if I was attracted to Alex. She also wanted to know why I live here and not with my real family."

"Well sounds like she didn't really like you Layla," he says grinning.

"Oh I'm sure she didn't. Once she figured out I wasn't a threat everything was fine. We're friendly now but not friends, if that makes any sense."

"Sure does," Ben replies.

The four of us spend the rest of the evening lounging on the couch binge watching reality TV, my guilty pleasure. "Layla, "James mumbles, "You know this crap is all scripted, don't you? I can't believe you watch this."

I roll my eyes looking at him, "Says the guy asking me to hit the pause button while he goes to the kitchen."

Ben starts to laugh, "Damn, looks like she told you."

"No, I just like to keep tabs on what the youngsters are watching here," James replies thinking he is being clever.

"Youngsters?" Mason responds, "Who are you calling youngsters? Heck Layla and I could be married and have kids."

I sit up and look at Mason "To you? You've got to be kidding," I think I hurt his feelings a bit. "No, I meant in general but you'd be lucky to land someone like me, I'm quite the catch," Mason boasts.

I look over in Ben direction and he's cracking up. About thirty minutes later we decide to call it a night, I go into the kitchen to grab a bottle of water out of the fridge. Ben walks by on the way to his room and tells me goodnight.

It's Sunday so it's time to tackle the shop. Trash bags and cleaning products in hand I make my way over to find the door open. Suppose they forgot to lock it up yesterday. I walk in and find Ben inside working on a bike. What a sight, he looks really hot. You can see the definition of his biceps through his shirt.

"Morning Layla, what are you doing here? Cleaning?" he asks. All I can think is, great here I am again looking like shit.

"Yeah, I come in here on Sunday's and straighten up a little but I can do it later so I'll just come ba-"

He stops me, "You want to stay and keep me company?"

I think, *'God yes!'* but end up replying, "Sure, I can do that."

"Cool, I'm going to run to the house, made coffee earlier so I'll grab you a cup too. Cream and sugar, right?"

I smile and nod as he walks out the door. Damn it, I dug myself a hole with this coffee thing that I don't know how to get out of. I hope this won't become a daily gesture. I start to pick up all the water and beer bottles and put tools back in their places. I smell the coffee before he makes it in the door. As he hands me the cup he says, "So Mason told me you guys used to do Acro Dance together. I just assumed that you would've done the silk thing."

"Aerial Silk; I did that for a long time but being scared of heights didn't help. I seriously thought I was about to die before each show. How you rode your bike in that globe thing is beyond me, way too dangerous."

"Yeah, it was dangerous but the high was so worth it. Never felt anything like that again, "he says as his face lights up.

I raise my eyebrows, "I'm not really a thrill seeker I guess. Pretty happy with my normal boring life, or mostly normal."

"So, how are you parents doing?"

I completely forgot that they used to be friends, "My parents are doing good. We don't talk very much; they are busy with their life. They found another small family owned circus so they're still traveling all over. Come to think of it I haven't actually seen them since they left here."

"Did all of your brothers and sisters go with them?" he asks.

"Yep, everyone but me. Guess I'm the oddball. I have to tell you I was so happy when James said I could live here, just always felt closer to your family, especially your mom. She's so sweet and just wants to take care of everyone. I was so sad when she moved away," I pause, "Have you talked to her yet?"

"No," he replies, looking down.

"I have an idea, when I talk to your mom I usually use video chat. Would you like to talk to her? I can call her tomorrow; I know she would be so ecstatic to see you," I suggest.

"Man, I don't know, I haven't talked to her in so long I wouldn't know what to say," He replies looking a little on the worried side.

"Ben, it's your mom. She loves you; I know that for a fact. No pressure at all, just think about it. She's going to be here in a couple months, it would probably be more awkward at that time plus she would strangle us for keeping a secret like that."

"Alright, I'll think about it," he smiles.

The rest of the day seems to fly by. James and Ben went out to the lake to do some fishing. The lake is on the property, maybe about 150 feet away from the house. Years ago their dad made a pathway through the little forest area so it would be more accessible. It's really peaceful there, a great spot to just sit and let your mind wander. Sometimes I grab a book and my mp3 player and spend what seems like hours out there.

After dinner Ben comes up to me and says he would like to take me up on my offer of calling his mom tomorrow. I'm so excited; I send her a quick email to set up a good time to call since she is always out and about. I can imagine how anxious he must be. Norma has never stopped talking about him and it was through her stories that I got to know him when I was younger. I told him I would initiate the conversation to make it a little easier on him.

After waking up I immediately check my email. Norma replied and said 3 pm would be great. We talk about every other month and email in between. Sometimes I think it's really sad that I am closer to her than my own mother, but it is what it is. I get up and want to rush down the stairs but I stop on the second step. No, I will not go down there looking a mess again. I turn around, head to the bathroom to take a shower. After getting dressed and finishing my makeup I look in the mirror. Alright, looks good.
Its 9:30 am so I know Alex is at work and everyone else is already in the shop. As I walk outside I hear loud voices coming from that direction. I bet the guys were surprised to see Ben too. Glancing in the door, there's more talking going on than work.

"Good morning everyone."

"Oh hey Layla," Carol says looking me up and down, "You look really nice today, going anywhere?"

"Um, no. Wasn't really planning to, why?" I say awkwardly.

"I think Carol just figured you probably had a date or something," Shane adds.

"Sure, like that happens a lot," I snicker. I look over in Ben's direction and he has the tiniest smile on his face.

"Girl, you are just too picky," Rick starts, "You know that's your problem, right? If you ju-"

James puts his two cents in, "Now, being picky is not a bad quality to have. I prefer that over her bringing countless guys here. I mean, not that she couldn't, can't tell her what to do."

Wow, he really just said that. I am kind of feeling uncomfortable with me being the center of this topic. "Okay, well then. I'm heading back in the house and you all can continue what it is you're doing or not doing here."

"Ouch!" Carol yells as I turn around and walk off.

I head out the door and then it dawns on me why I went there in the first place. I turn around, "Hey do you think I can borrow Ben at around three today, have something he needs to help me with." Ben looks in my direction and smiles.

"Oh, I'm sure he does. Didn't your momma teach you to stay away from older men?" Rick says taunting me.

James steps in, "Rick, shut the hell up. Yeah, Layla that's fine. We don't have a whole lot going on today anyway."

There wasn't really anything unusual about what happened there. Rick is quite perverted; he's the typical dirty old man. I don't think James would have hired him but the three come in a package deal, they even live together.

I keep myself busy with things I didn't get around to this weekend like laundry, checking social media and updating the playlist on my mp3 player. As I'm downstairs grabbing the last load out of the dryer, Ben walks in the back door, "Hey Layla, I'm just going take a quick shower and then I'll be ready."

"Sounds good," I reply, "Just come up to my room when you're done."

There's a knock at the door just as I'm putting my clothes in the dresser. "Come in," I say and Ben opens the door. I grab my phone and sit on my bed, signaling him to come over. For a moment he just stands there and looks at me nervously but then makes his way over to the bed.

"Man Layla, I don't know if I can do this, I'm freaking out, right now." Noticing his hand trembling, I instinctively grab it and tell him it will be okay. It seems to put him at ease just a little bit.

"Alright, are you ready?" I ask, still squeezing his hand. He nods and I press the call button, she picks up on the first ring.

"Layla, how are you sweetie? I can't wait to hear about this big surprise you emailed me about. Did you meet someone? "Norma asks. As she speaks I notice Ben's hand stops shaking but I continue to hold it.

"Well, I'll let you see for yourself, hold on one second" looking over at Ben asking if he's ready. He takes a deep breath and nods. I hand the phone over to him.

"Hey Mom," he says softly. I can't even make out what Norma is saying between the happy crying and screams.

"Hey I'll give you two some privacy, take your time." I let go of his hand and walk out, shutting the door behind me. Downstairs I sit on the couch and organize my bag a bit; it's like a black hole. About forty-five minutes later I notice Ben coming down the stairs.

"Thank you so much," he says, handing me my phone with a big smile on his face.

"So," I ask impatiently, "What did she say?"

"Well she talked about you a lot, said that you keep her up to date on what's going on around here. She also said she can't wait to see me and that she's happy that I came back home. I also met Gerald; he seems like a really great down to earth kind of guy."

"Gerald is very nice and so good to her, treats her like a queen," I say.

"She should be treated like a queen, she deserves all the happiness in the world," he pauses "Oh I wanted to ask you, is that an App that we used to call her?"

"It is. Do you have your phone on you? I can install it for you if you'd like," I offer. He hands me his phone and I pull it up for him. "Ok, so it wants your password to install. After that you just start a new account and create a username and password. Then you can search usernames, hers is JBAMParker," I say handing his phone back to him.

"She used all her boys' initials, "he chuckles, "Again, thank you so much Layla. I'm going head back to the shop to see if there's anything left to do so I'll see you later," he says winking at me. This is the happiest I have seen him, and god that wink, he really is a sight for sore eyes. He may be seventeen years older than me but hey I can still appreciate that he is attractive.

I notice it's already 4 pm; I need to start the beef stew if we want to eat tonight. As I put the pot in the oven Alex comes walking in.

"Geez, work sucked today. Seems like half the town came in for loans."

I chuckle, "Well, you know James is always accepting applications."

Alex looks at me like I'm crazy, "No way, Layla look at these hands, perfectly manicured. Besides, can't live and work with James, we would kill each other. By the way, what are you cooking?"

"Beef Stew and garlic bread," I reply. Alex loves my beef stew.

Ben offers to do the cleanup after dinner, I don't argue and decide to go outside and relax on the porch swing. The sun is just starting to set and there is a slight breeze in the air. Inside I hear James on the phone with Carmen; he will be occupied for at least the next hour. The door opens and I turn to see who it is.

"You mind if I join you?" Ben asks.

"Not at all, come sit," I say removing my legs from the other seat.

"Man, it's really nice out tonight and so quiet, I'm not used to that anymore, "he says as he sits down, "In St. Louis I lived in an apartment, so the complete opposite. You always heard people, traffic, horns blaring."

"Do you miss it?" I ask curiously.

"No, not really. At least not yet," he replies.

"Well, I guess you've only been here for a few days. I'll ask again in a month, by then you may have had enough of us," I laugh.

"Nah, I highly doubt that. Anyway, I have to stick around since I told mom I'll see her in July," he pauses and looks at me "So I hear you were pretty heartbroken when I left."

I start to blush and look away, "Um, yeah I was really sad, you were always so nice to me and yeah, I was pretty much crushed, like I lost my only friend."

"I'm so sorry Layla, I had to, just didn't see another way. I had to start over."

"Please," I say, "You don't have to apologize. I know why you had to leave."

"You know? Who told you?" a look of complete surprise takes over his face.

"Your dad actually, "I reply.

"Are you serious? What exactly did he tell you?" he looks really interested.

"Well, he told me that he'd been having an affair with Sarah when she got pregnant. After telling you about the pregnancy she tried to convince you that it wasn't a good time and she wanted an abortion. Your dad supported her decision, for obvious reasons, and tried explaining that it was best for her career to not have a child right now. When he noticed that you weren't buying it he came clean about the affair and the possibility of the child being his."

"Damn," pausing, he leans back in the swing running his hands through his hair, "At least the asshole told the truth. I figured he probably would have tried to spin it in his favor, you know so he's not the bad guy. He always did that. Please tell me you were older than eight when he told you?"

"Don't worry, I was sixteen. He was sitting on this porch one day and wanted to talk, think it was weighing on his conscience. He always had this tough guy attitude but that day I saw a different side of him. I know he was sorry for tearing the family apart, even though he never said it."

We sit in silence for a little while. "Hey, can I ask you something?" he says looking down, "Do you know if Sarah ever got the abortion?"

For some reason that wasn't a question I was expecting, "Your dad told me she did, he went with her." He lets out a sigh of relief.

With that out of the way he seems relaxed. I suppose the possibility of him having a child out there has crossed his mind more than once. We spend the rest of the evening on that porch just talking and joking around with each other. I tell him all about what he's missed since he's been away, the funny stories mainly, and there are plenty of them.

Chapter Two

Layla

It's Tuesday so I'm back at work and waiting for Layne to come in. Tuesday and Friday are the only days we work together. I can't wait to tell him about what happened over the weekend. I texted him Saturday but never heard back. I assume things went well with the young woman he had his eye on.

"Hey Layla! How are ya?" Layne says as he walks through the door.

"I'm great. How did things go with you know who?" He steps behind the counter giving me a hug.

"Oh, you mean that blonde chick? It was alright. We ended up at my house and things were getting hot but then she played the *'I'm a virgin'* card." I shoot him a confused look, that girl looked like anything but a virgin. "So anyway, I was a gentleman and drove her home."

"What about her car?" I ask.

"She came here with friends so she didn't have one. Had to drive her to Macon, so almost another hour of my life wasted with the back and forth. She gave me her number and said she wanted to hang out again. I said of course but threw that shit out as soon as I could."

I roll my eyes, "You are so bad Layne, what if she comes back in here?"

He grabs me and hugs me really tight, "Well, Layla, that's where you come in. I'll say I accidently lost her number and now I have a girlfriend. Let's just hope she comes in on a day you're working too." Typical Layne; always has a backup plan.

"Hey," I say, wiping down the counter, "I ran into Bailey at the store on Saturday. She wanted to see how you're holding up after she left you."

"Are you joking? She didn't break up with me. God she is such a – I'm not gonna say it." Layne growls frustrated.

"I know. Don't worry, I set her straight and she took off pretty fast," I laugh and he gives me a high five.

"So something else happened this weekend. When I got home from work Friday there was a truck parked in the driveway with Missouri plates. I walk in and it's James' brother."

Layne looks at me like I'm crazy, "So, Mason bought a car and had it shipped from Missouri?"

"No, no, no. Gosh I don't think I ever told you. James has another brother, Ben. There was big family feud years ago, he took off and no one had seen him since. I was about four years old back then. When the circus was up and running there were always so many people around and I was always overlooked but he took the time to talk and listen to me. He was my favorite person and when he left my world fell apart."

"I thought I was your favorite person," he jokes, "just kidding, but why haven't you mentioned him before?"

"I don't know. I suppose as time went by I just didn't think about him anymore. I was shocked when I saw him, totally caught me by surprise."

I must have rambled on all night, but Layne being the good friend that he is just listened. I decide to keep the *'I may have developed a slight attraction to Ben'* to myself. He doesn't have to know all the details; it's probably just a little crush anyway.

I don't know where time has gone; this whole week's been such a big blur. It hasn't really been that busy at work but we are down a bartender so Randy asked if I could stay late a few times. The new hire is starting Saturday and Layne is supposed to show him the ropes. I haven't really had time to hang out with anyone at home, I really hope the new guy catches on quick and things will be back to normal next week.

Carmen flies in today and James is on his way to pick her up. I'm getting ready for work, luckily Randy doesn't have any strict rules on attire; it just needs to be appropriate. I usually wear blue jeans, cowboy boots and a dark shirt so if I spill anything it won't be too noticeable. Over time I've learned the secret to better tips, just *'doll'* yourself up. It is not a problem for me now. Ever since Ben got here I ensure I'm always made up, especially after those first two mornings where I'm sure I looked like hell.

I walk through the front door and find Ben on the swing looking at some old car magazines. Needing an excuse to talk to him, I ask if there is anything he needs before I go to work. He grins and shakes his head. My God, something about him drives me crazy. I give him a quick smile and walk toward my car. I turn the key and it won't start, it's just making a weird clicking noise. I don't know a thing about cars, never had to, someone is always there to fix it. I get back out of the car.

"Is everything okay?" I hear Ben yelling from the porch.

"My car won't start, it's just clicking." I answer.

"Here, I'll take a look," he smiles, "It might be the starter. I'll try to jump the battery first just in case."

"Could it be the alternator?" I'm totally just throwing terms out there; I don't know what I am talking about.

"Nah, I don't think so," he says, "let me get my truck."

In the meantime, I text Randy to let him know I will be a little late. After a few attempts to jump the battery, I text Layne to see if he can come get me. Alex still hasn't made it home from work and I'm not sure where Mason is.

"Did you get a response?" Ben asks curiously and I shake my head.

"Hey I'll drive you to work, no problem at all, I'm not doing anything anyway." He closes the hood of his truck and walks over to the passenger side top open the door for me. Wow, totally wasn't expecting that.

We pull up to the Bull and he shoots me a confused look "Layla" he pauses, "you work at a bar?" It dawns on me that I hadn't told him what

I do for work. We've talked about lots of things but I guess my job never came up.

"Yeah, I'm a bartender. It's not like a dive bar or anything; it's actually pretty nice inside."

He chuckles "I used to be a bartender, hated every minute of it. You have to be a people person for that job. Anyway, I'll let you go but I'll come pick you up after you're done."

"Don't worry about it. I can catch a ride with someone, you don't have to drive back out here," I insist.

"Layla, it really isn't an inconvenience, let me give you my number. Just text me when you're about to get off and I'll come get you. I'll take a look at your car when I get back to the house."

Handing my phone over, he adds his number to my contacts. I get this giddy feeling, like a teenager getting the hot guys number. Snap out of it Layla. He gets out of the car and comes around to open my door. I could definitely get used to this, feels kind of nice.

Work is pretty slow, but that's typical for a Thursday night. Tomorrow will be a different story. Randy is planning to give line dance lessons to get more people on the dancefloor. I know Carmen said she was interested, so I think she will be there with James. I finally heard back from Layne but I told him Ben drove me. I check my phone and its 10: 50 pm, ten minutes left before my shift is over. I feel a little weird texting Ben but he told me to so it's not like I'm trying to come up with something to say. I write ***Hey! Getting off in about 10 min if you're still able to come get me =)***. Before I can put my phone on the counter he responds ***K! Be right there***. Maybe I shouldn't have put the smiley, his message was kind of short, maybe I'm just thinking too much.

I check my makeup in the mirror behind the bar and reapply some lipstick before heading outside. Ben is already there, getting out of the truck to yet again open my door. While driving he asks how my evening was, I tell him it was boring and slow.

"So I was able to fix your car, it was just the starter, like I thought. I put a new battery in for good measure."

"Oh wow, thank you so much. You have no idea how much I appreciate you doing that and driving me." He just looks over at me and gives me the most beautiful smile I've seen. His hair isn't covering his face and his eyes are just mesmerizing. Well I guess I won't be sleeping tonight, there is no way I will be able to get that image out of my head, nor do I want to.

Waking up the next morning I remember that Carmen is here. I start my morning ritual with brushing teeth, shower and makeup before I head downstairs.

"Layla!" Carmen runs up to me and gives me a hug. As usual she is dressed chic from top to bottom. I can see why James fell for her; she is very warm, classy and feminine. She has beautiful brown hair that curls a bit at the ends and sage green eyes. Her lips are her best feature. They look as if they have been filled with collagen but she swears they are all natural. Everyone else is sitting on the couch with the exception of Alex, who already left for work.

"Look at you, all put together already," Carmen observes.

Mason grins, "Oh yeah this is the new Layla, all dressed up with nowhere to go." I give him a death stare but out of the corner of my eye I'm watching Ben. He has a big smile on his face and looks down.

"So I was thinking, since the guys are working in the shop all day maybe you and I can do some shopping in town," Carmen suggests, "I wanted to go to that little gift shop on the corner by the fountain. My mom's birthday is coming up and I wanted to get her something unique. Oh and maybe we can do lunch too."

"Sure, I'm pretty much free all day. I have to be at work at 7 pm but that's about it."

James walks up and kisses Carmen, "You guys have a good time. I need to get to the shop and get to work on these cars. The rest of the crew took the day off today so we will be busy."

I knew we weren't just going to the gift shop. We stopped at the florist, the bakery and nail salon; I guess I shouldn't complain since I didn't have plans and I do enjoy her company. She and her sister do a lot of girly things together. I'm always around guys and I never was close to my actual sisters before they moved. I don't ever paint my nails but I have to say these French tips look pretty awesome; I can't stop staring at my hands.

We decide to have lunch at Betty's diner. Not very original since the woman who owns it is named Betty. Carmen is probably used to nicer places being from New Orleans but she has never said one negative thing about this small town. She will be moving here after the wedding and it makes me wonder if she is going to miss her old life. Her parents are very well off and I bet they didn't want their daughter falling for an ex-big top performer turned mechanic. I suppose you can't control who you fall in love with.

"Betty sweetie, how are ya?"

Carmen perks up, "Hey Layla isn't that the guy you used to date, Layne?" Without looking I say yes. I can recognize his voice anywhere, especially when he is being flirtatious. He comes up to our table

"Hey ladies, how's it going? Ma'am, it's nice to see you again."

"So aren't you supposed to be at work already? "I ask.

"Well yeah, I got up late and Betty was nice enough to fix me some lunch to go," he says winking at Betty standing behind the counter. She is in her sixties but when Layne comes in she turns into a silly fifteen-year-old. It's actually kind of cute to watch.

"Alright, I really have to get going before I lose my job," Layne mentions, grabbing the Styrofoam container off the counter. I can hear Betty in the background, "You can always work here sweetie!"

"Awe, thanks hun, I'll keep that in mind," he says with his sweetest smile. He leans down to give me a hug and flashes Carmen a flirtatious smile as he walks out the door.

Carmen watches him as he gets into his truck, "He sure is something isn't he? I can't believe you guys broke up, you look really nice together and you get along."

I smile to myself, "Yep, he sure is. It just didn't work out but on a positive note now we are closer than ever." She doesn't need to know everything; from the way she was following his every move next she'll ask me how he is in bed.

Changing the subject I ask, "So, what do you think of Ben?"

She turns back toward me, "Ben seems nice. He comes across as very quiet and reserved, but that may be because we only just met. James seems overjoyed to have him back. I can tell they were close when they were younger." We sit and talk for a little while longer before heading home.

After arriving back home, we decide to stop by the shop to check on everyone before heading into the house. They are all filthy and sweaty. James runs up to Carmen and playfully tries to give her a big hug but she refuses.

"Oh no you don't. You need to shower first." Ben and Mason start laughing. It looks like they have been having a great time. They are rocking out to eighties music and evidence shows that a few beers have been consumed.

They finish up working just as I'm about to head out the door to go to work. I pass James, "Hey, we're having line dance lessons tonight. I know Carmen wanted to go. It starts at 8 pm" He throws his head back and sighs but says they will most likely be there.

When I get to work I notice it's very crowded. I guess word got out about Randy's event. I wonder how many people are actually going to get up and dance. Personally I think line dancing looks silly, you definitely won't find me out there.

Layne bumps me with his hip, "Wow, Layla you got James to come out? Be right back, gotta get some more ice." I turn around to see James, Carmen, Mason and Ben coming towards the bar. God, why am I feeling so nervous?

"Layla," Carmen yells, "I'm so thrilled James finally brought me here. I can't wait to dance."

I smile, "Well it starts in about half an hour, can I get you guys anything?"

"Yeah I think three beers will do and whatever Mason wants, he's nice enough to drive us tonight," James says patting Mason on the back.

"Carmen, would you rather have a girly drink? You just don't look like the beer drinking kind of girl to me," I ask knowing exactly she will agree.

"You're right; I would love a Pina Colada."

As I garnish the rim of the glass with a pineapple slice, Layne comes back to the bar, "Hello again Ma'am, James, Mason," he pauses, "and you must be Ben! I've heard a ton about you already. Feel like I've known you for years." I think to myself, why did he have to say that? I give him a swift kick to the leg. "Layla, what the fuck? Anyways, my name's Layne, I'm Layla's friend, it's great to finally meet you." They shake hands and Layne continues rambling. Mason wanders off to join a few of his friends.

The music stops and Randy is on the mic "Okay ya'll, is everyone ready for some line dancin'? Come on don't be shy. Donna and I will be showing ya'll the steps so come on up. Hey Layne! You're shifts over, come on up here. Girls if ya'll want a chance to dance with him, here he is." Randy used to be a car salesman; he knows exactly what to say to get people to do what he wants. As soon as Layne gets on the dancefloor, four girls are already in tow.

"James, come on let's do it, "Carmen pleads.

He agrees and turns to Ben saying, "If I have to go up there I'm dragging your ass along with me."

"Hell, no man. I don't dance, you two have a good time though," Ben smirks.

The lesson starts and it's quite entertaining to watch. Layne is having a great time; he is in his element with all the women wanting a chance to dance with him. James and Carmen look really happy even though they are stepping on each other's toes. Ben is just shaking his head laughing, "This is exactly why I don't dance, don't want to look like an idiot." I don't think anything could make him look like an idiot.

He turns to me, "So you talk about me a lot?" Oh my god, I never thought he would say that. He's been pretty shy and reserved, maybe it's the alcohol.

I can feel my cheeks burning and reply, "Well, just a little, Layne is known to exaggerate at times," I try to play it off. He just stares at me, his eyes are intense.

"Layla, another beer." We are interrupted by the voice of a patron. Timing couldn't have been better, my heart was about to jump out of my chest. Since he came home I have had this weird feeling in my stomach that I couldn't figure out until tonight. Butterflies!

Chapter Three

Layla

The sound of thunder rips me from my dreams. It felt as if the whole house shook. Great, now I won't be able to fall asleep again. I grab my phone and decide to send Layne a message. I write **Ugh I hate thunderstorms!!! They scare me.** My phone buzzes, but it isn't Layne, its Ben. His message reads **Ha, I love them =)**. I realize I sent the message to the wrong person. Oh my god I am such and idiot, but hey, I got a smiley. I reply **Wrong person, I'm sorry if I woke you.** His next message makes my jaw drop **And here I thought I was on your mind…..jk! Good night Layla.** What is that supposed to mean. Is he being flirtatious or just funny?

I wake up very early the next morning and can't find anyone in the house. Bedroom doors are open so I know everyone is awake, even Mason. Opening the front door, I find Mason, Alex, Carmen and James sitting on the steps and Ben leaning against the column.

"You guys are up early," I point out.

"Hey Layla, come sit," Alex signals with his hand, so I sit down next to him.

"Last night's storm did some damage to the shop's roof. We were just talking about what all we need to fix it. Luckily the inside is ok but we really need to get the shingles replaced in case there is more bad weather on the way. Ben, lets run to the hardware store and pick up what we need." Ben hasn't really looked my way once. Is he embarrassed about what he said?

After lunch the guys start working on the roof, even Alex is involved. It's only May but today is a scorching hot day, so I feel for them. I guess it has to be done though; the equipment in the shop is too valuable to get damaged.

Carmen asks if I could help her dry the dishes. I grab the dish towel and stand next to the sink, there's a big window overlooking the yard. I notice Ben and James on the roof, already drenched with sweat, the sun is brutal. They seem to be having a good time joking around and laughing. It's so nice to see them interact, they get along great.

"Hey," Carmen's voice pulls me out of my daze, "I think that plate is dry enough, you'll rub the gold rim off, silly." I put it to the side and grab the glass she hands me. I look back up to find Ben removing his shirt, that's all it took for the glass to hit the floor.

"You must still be tired, I know you got in late last night," Carmen comments. We finish with the rest of the dishes and I manage not to break anything else.

As Carmen dries her hands she takes a look out of the window and suggests we bring the guys some water. We each grab a few bottles out of the fridge and head in the direction of the shop. Ben is making his way down the ladder skipping the last five steps and jumping down. He's looking in my direction, it's more than just a look, he is glaring straight at me with those eyes that haven't left my mind since last night. The right side of his mouth rides up a bit, a perfect devilish grin. I feel my heart beating faster and faster. There is something different about him; I noticed it last night, almost like a new found confidence. Maybe he's just getting comfortable.

"Here, you guys need to take a break and hydrate, "Carmen says handing a bottle to each one of them. We brought a few extra so I set them on the old wooden picnic table. I am actually quite surprised that it survived the bad storm. I sit on the table, feet propped on the bench. Carmen dominates the conversation with their upcoming nuptials. James really lucked out; Carmen's father will be handling the financial aspects of the wedding, even our plane tickets to New Orleans. Every once in a while I feel Ben's eyes on me but when I return the glance he turns away but not in a *'oh no I got caught kind of way'*, it's intimidating.

"Hey Layla," he says in his raspy, rugged voice, "Can you throw me another one of those waters?" I pick one up and toss it his way, thinking right about now I'd rather throw myself at him. He opens it and pours it over his head moving the hair out of his eyes with his other hand. Little streams of water run down his body flowing across his tattoos. I count three overall. His right shoulder reveals a motorcycle with the grim reaper lurking behind. On the same side, a huge dragon is crawling down his ribcage. That must have taken hours, maybe even days. Lastly the one I remember, his mother's name written above the left side of his chest. I recall tracing the letters with my finger when I was little. I watch in admiration. Get a grip, what the heck is wrong with me. His last text pops back in my mind, that combined with the grin and I come to the conclusion that he is being flirtatious.

The roof is finished by dinnertime; after everyone cleans up we sit down at the table to eat. Carmen and I made an authentic creole jambalaya, it smells delicious and I can't wait to dig in.

"Hey Ben, you know our wedding is coming up here pretty soon, I wanted to ask you if you'll be my best man, "James asks anxiously awaiting his response.

"Really? Man, that would be awesome, I'd be honored to," Ben replies smiling. You can tell James is ecstatic and Carmen mentions that her father will be taking care of his plane ticket.

"Carmen, he doesn't have to do that, I can buy my own," Ben mentions.

"Oh no no no, he insists," she says.

"Well, please tell him thank you and I appreciate it," Ben replies.

Carmen continues, "So James and I are going to Atlanta tomorrow, I've never been there and he's booked us a nice bed and breakfast to stay at overnight. It's an old Victorian house that was built in the late 1800's."

Before she can say anything else Mason snickers, "If you're looking for historic charm, you're sitting right in the heart of it. This place was built in 1856."

Annoyed, James looks at Mason, "You know, maybe we just want to get away for a night, just the two of us. Anyway we are leaving at 9 am tomorrow morning so I think I'm going to head upstairs, pack and go to bed early, I think I got much sun today."

I was fairly quiet during dinner, was lost in my thoughts. Carmen asks who wants to help with cleaning up so I volunteer and follow her into the kitchen. "Layla, you've been really quiet all day, everything alright?" Carmen asks.

"Me? Oh yeah, I'm good. Just didn't sleep much last night, you know with the storm and all. Anyway, how did you like the line dancing?" I ask, changing the subject.

"Oh, "she starts, "I loved it, so much fun, but it's much harder than it looks. I knew it wouldn't be James' thing but he was a good sport. Layne is really good at it; I can't believe he had a line of women just waiting to dance with him."

I chuckle, "Yeah he's quite the charmer, you should hear him sing, he has a great voice."

"Who has a great voice?" Ben asks bringing in the remaining dishes from the dining room.

"Layla's friend Layne, you know the guy who said he knew so much about you," Carmen smiles. Oh great! Here we go again with the exaggeration.

Ben grunts, "Yeah I remember, he seems kind of full of himself doesn't he?"

With a surprised expression Carmen replies, "You really think so? I think he's just confident and very outgoing, I like him."

"Yeah, you're right, that's probably it, "Ben replies to put an end to that conversation.

"So Ben," Carmen begins, "You're not much of a dancer?"

"Hell no, I don't dance. Never has been my thing," he says leaning on the counter.

"Oh I'm sure I can get you on the dancefloor at the wedding," I tease.

"Layla, you don't want to dance with me, I'm a freakin' mess," he replies laughing.

"Well, I figured it was worth a shot," I respond with a playful frown.

"Who knows, maybe if I'm drunk enough, but then again, I highly doubt it. Goodnight ladies, I'm going to catch some Z's, I'm beat," he says smiling, heading to his bedroom.

"I think he just likes to play hard to get," Carmen remarks, looking at me, "I have a cousin that is just like him. Well I think I'm going upstairs too, have to pack a few more things for tomorrow. Goodnight Layla, sleep good."

I walk into the living room and Alex is sitting on the couch, I decide to join him. "Watching anything good?" I ask.

"Nah, not really. I'm debating on going to the Bull." I look at him like he's crazy, he never goes there. He says Brittany is having a girl's night and he doesn't know what to do without her on a Saturday anymore.

"Well, if you want company I'll go with you," I tell him.

"Really?" he asks eagerly, "Okay, let's go!"

It's not as busy as I would have expected for a Saturday night. We walk toward the bar and I see Layne trying to teach the new guy how to make a Cosmo.

"Hey Layne, what's up man," Alex asks as he sits on one of the saddle stools.

"Alex? Holy shit! Man I haven't seen you in months; I see you got yourself a new girl here," Layne smirks as he winks at me.

"Shut up Layne," I say sounding annoyed.

"Ah, you know it's all in good fun. But yeah, I'm really surprised to see you here but even more shocked that you got her to come in here on her day off. Looks like hell froze over twice."

"Well Layne," I start, "I just didn't get enough of you last night, I mean having to share you with all those women you were dancing with just about killed me," I joke.

"Oh babe, I never thought you were the jealous type. You know, I get off in about three hours, come home with me and I'll make it up to you. Or if you're not too picky there's a storage closet we can sneak off into," Layne says with his smartass grin. After knowing Layne for four years I should have known that he would have a comeback, so I just roll my eyes at him while the new guy is looking at us like we are crazy.

"Where are my manners?" Layne suddenly says, "Josh, these are my friends, Alex and Layla. Guys, this is Josh from California."

"California?" Alex asks, "What the heck are you doing in this cow town?"

Josh smiles, "My grandpa lives here and he's getting older so I'm here to help out a bit. Layla, you're a bartender here too right? Layne's told me a little about you."

"Oh he has, well hopefully only the good stuff," I say staring at Layne. We end up staying until closing time; I haven't been out like this in a little while so it was a nice change.

I set my alarm so I could say goodbye to James and Carmen, but end up hitting the off button instead of snooze and sleep another two hours. When I wake up I realize it's eleven and jump out of bed. I get myself together and head downstairs but come to a stop at about halfway. I hear a familiar song playing, Mason and I used to perform our routine to it. Slowly I walk into the living room to find Mason and Ben sitting on the couch staring at the TV. They are watching one of our recorded performances from 2007.

"Mason, seriously?" I say as I try to get the remote out of his hand.

"What? I just wanted to show him, it's a really good one too," he replies holding the remote like his life depends on it. I sit on the other side of the sofa, lean back and cover my face.

"Mason, this is embarrassing, I can't believe you're showing him that, "I mumble through my hands.

"Layla, what are you talking about? I loved watching it, it was beautiful, no reason to be embarrassed," Ben says as he sits down next to me. Suddenly I feel his hand on my arm, I feel my pulse increasing, he pulls my arm down so my hand no longer covers my face and looks straight at me.

"I'm serious, I thought it was amazing, also I had no idea Mason had moves like that," he grins.

I give him a little smile and look over at the TV, gosh that was eight years ago and I had just turned sixteen. The act is beautiful to watch, every move tells a story accompanied by the song.

"Well I'm going to the kitchen to get a drink, are you guys just going to sit here and watch these videos all day?" I ask, hoping I didn't just give them an idea.

"Nah I think we're done, Ben made some coffee earlier, it should still be warm so you don't have to make a new pot," Mason grins.

"Great, thank you for letting me know, so thoughtful of you," I reply giving him a bitchy look. As I come back into the living room with my coffee I take a sip and think hey, maybe I can get used to this, heck I may end up loving it, enough sugar covers up everything.

"Morning everyone," Alex says as he plops himself on the couch, "Oh my god kill me now, I have a headache from hell."

"What's up with him?" Mason asks curiously.

"We went out last night and he had some drinks so I'm guessing a hangover, "I explain.

"Where did you go? Why didn't you tell me?" Mason asks sounding a little upset.

"We just went to the Bull," Alex mumbles, his face on the pillow, "Mason, you never go out to bars."

"What are you talking about, I was just there on Friday. I would have gone with you guys," Mason frowns.

"Okay," I say setting my coffee on the table and giving him a hug, "the next time we go out we'll check with you."

Ben goes into the kitchen and comes back with Ibuprofen and a glass of water for Alex and hands it to him. Later in the day we decide to have lunch at the diner. As we pull up in my car I notice that it's very quiet for a Sunday, we walk in the door and Betty starts screaming, "Oh my lord, Benjamin Parker is that you? I don't even remember when I saw you last and look at you now."

"Hey Betty, yeah it's been about twenty years, good to be back. Diner still looks the same." I think Ben is trying to change the subject.

"Well, we try to keep as original as possible. Well ya'll go have a seat wherever you want. It's dead right now since the church is having a potluck today."

I head to the booth in the corner and the guys follow, we keep it pretty simple and order burgers. While waiting for our food Betty comes to the table and chit chats for a little while telling Ben about her grandkids. I completely forgot how big the burgers are and can only finish about half of mine, I decide to get a box and take the rest home.

The waitress brings the check; Ben grabs it and takes it up to the counter to pay. I chuckle as I leave a five-dollar bill on the table. The diner is cash only and I wonder if he carries cash, most people don't.

"Oh Sweetie, I'm sorry we're not high tech here, cash only," Betty explains.

"Oh my god, I never have cash," Ben sounds a little worried so I step in, "I got it, that's the upside of being a bartender, you always have cash." He smiles but you can tell he's a bit embarrassed.

When we get home Alex says he's going to Brittany's which means we will probably not see him until tomorrow afternoon. I go to the shop to start my weekly cleaning ritual but to my surprise there's nothing to do. I walk back into the house to ask Mason about it and he said that Ben spruced it up this morning when he got up. I did most of the laundry and cleaning yesterday and since it's such a nice day out I want to spend it outside.

"I'm going to the lake to soak up some sun if anyone's looking for me," I mention as I grab my bag.

"Alright cool, Mason and I are going to work on the car that came in Friday, if you get bored you're welcome to join us, we may be able to teach you a few things," Ben smirks.

On my way to the lake my phone rings and it's Layne asking if I can cover his shift tomorrow. He pulled a muscle while working out and is in a great deal of pain. I ask if he needs anything else and he mentions he feels as if he's starving. I walk by the shop as I head toward the house.

"Hey Ben, looks like Layla does want to learn about cars," Mason yells.

I shake my head, "No, Layne called and said he got hurt while working out, he asked if I can bring him some food. I'm just going to bring him the rest of my lunch so I'll be back in a little while."

I noticed Ben's interest peaked once he heard Layne's name, I get the feeling he is not a fan. Mason shakes his head, "So none of his little girlfriends are available right now?"

I roll my eyes, "I'll see you guys in a bit."

I pull up to his apartment complex; it's fairly small with about twelve units. It's a bit old but the interior was renovated about two years ago. I get out of the car and knock on the door, I hear Layne sighing, telling me to come in. I walk in to find him on the couch, his face in agony.

"Oh my god you don't look good at all, have you taken anything?" I ask a little worried.

"Yeah, I took a few muscle relaxers, they're starting to kick in," he groans. I ask if he's used ice and he shakes his head no, I walk into the kitchen and grab a plastic bag, fill it with ice and wrap it in a towel. He sits up and I lift his shirt and place the ice on his back.

"Thank you Layla, and thanks for the food, you're awesome," he moans.

"Layne, if you need me to stay longer I can, it's no problem at a-" he interrupts me, "No, no, no I'll be fine. I've done this before, I'm just gonna get some sleep. Besides, I know you, you'll be cleaning this whole place while I'm sleeping and then I won't be able to find anything." Yep, that's exactly what I would do, it really needs it.

"Okay, but if you need anything at all call me, doesn't matter what time, okay?"

"Of course, love ya Layla" he says with a grin. I lean in carefully to give him a hug before walking out the door. It's weird seeing him in pain like that, hopefully he starts feeling better. I think I may stop by before heading to work tomorrow.

I don't think I've ever worked at the Bull on a Monday, I'm guessing it will be slow. When I get back home Mason's car is gone and the house is really quiet, wonder where they went. I go up to my room, lie on my bed and surf the web for a while. I can feel myself dozing off and eventually gravity wins. I wake up with my head on my laptop and it's 8 pm. I glance out my window and his car is still gone, I decide to send him a text. I walk downstairs to the kitchen to have a bowl of cereal for dinner, no need to cook for just myself. I open the fridge, grab the milk jug and right at that time I hear a voice, "Hey Layla, didn't think you were home." Startled I drop the milk on the floor and it explodes, splashing everywhere.

"Oh my god Ben, you scared me," I say my hand gripping my chest.

"I'm so sorry, here let me help you clean that up," he says grabbing the paper towel roll off the counter.

"I didn't see Mason's car here and it was so quiet I figured you two went somewhere," I remark while picking up the plastic jug discarding it into the garbage.

"One of his buddies called and he went to hang out for a while. How's Layne doing?" Ben asks, wiping up the last bit of milk from the floor.

"He's ok, will probably take a day or two to recover," I say. The last thing I want to do is talk about Layne with him, it just feels weird. Ben offers to make us some sandwiches and we eat outside on the picnic table for a change of scenery. We sit there for a while and he looks up into the sky.

"Man, the stars are so clear here, so beautiful," he comments.

"Can you see any constellations?" I ask curiously.

"Yeah right," he laughs, "Don't even know what to look for."

"Hold on, I'll be right back," I say as I get up and run to the house.

I come back with a blanket and Ben gives me a puzzled expression, "You cold?"

"No, come with me," I signal him to follow me to his truck. Lowering the tailgate, I spread the blanket over the truck bed and hop up, he looks at me like I've completely lost my mind.

"Come on, lie down, we are going to look for constellations," I say sitting down. For a moment he hesitates and shakes his head laughing but then climbs up anyway. We lie down and stare up into the night sky. Okay, this is a little harder than I imagined, I can't find anything. I've seen the big dipper and Virgo before, Layne taught me how to find them, but no luck tonight so I pull my phone out of my pocket and search for a map.

"Alright," I say as I hold the phone for both of us to see, "Let's see what we can find." We lie quietly for about ten minutes; this is a lot more difficult than I imagined.

"Here, let me see that map a minute," he says and I hand him my phone, "Look," he points, "I think that's Libra, it's not very bright but the spots add up to the map." I follow his finger as he draws an imaginary line in the sky.

"Oh my god you're right, that's totally it," I grin turning towards him, "I'm glad you found one I was starting to feel really stupid coming up with the idea." He turns to look at me, those eyes are just hypnotizing and I could really lie next to him forever, just staring.

"No way, I'm having a great time, definitely not stupid," he pauses, "I could lie here all night, it's so peaceful and the company isn't so bad either." I playfully nudge him with my elbow and he starts to laugh.

"Hey, I wanted to ask you, do your tattoos have any special meaning to them? I mean with the exception of your mom's name because obviously that one definitely does."

"Look at you missy, checking out my body art," he says real smooth, my eyes widen in embarrassment.

"You should see your face, I'm just kidding. Well the bike and reaper on my shoulder symbolize my love for motorcycles and how dangerous they can be. Honestly the dragon just looked really cool so I just did that for the heck of it."

"How long did the dragon take?" I ask curiously.

"It took four sessions, about two hours each time. It hurt like hell but I'd do it again in a heartbeat. Do you have any tattoos?"

"Me? Oh god no. I'm too much of a wuss for that," I admit.

"It's really not that bad at all, depends on where you get it," he says, "If you ever want one I'll go with you and hold your hand, how about that?" All I can think right now is 'yes please, let's go right now', I totally want an excuse to hold his hand.

"Hmm you know, I may take you up on that one day," I answer looking straight into those beautiful blue eyes of his.

"You know, I'm really happy that I came back. When I was away I always felt this void that I couldn't explain. I met some amazing people over the years that I got really close to but that empty feeling was always there," he pauses for a second, "And now it's gone. I know it probably sounds crazy but-"

"No, not at all. I completely understand what you're saying Ben. I know you said you have things you need to work through and you don't have to tell me what they are but I want you to know that if you ever want or need to talk, I'm here for you."

"Thank you Layla, that really means a lot to me. I think it's just going to take some time for me to figure this shit out. I just thought at forty-one I would have my life together, one day at a time I guess," he smiles.

Ugh, why did he have to mention his age? That number brought me back to reality quickly, I guess this will only ever be a crush, damn it why can't I be a little older.

My thoughts are interrupted by an annoying voice I recognize all too well, Mason. It looks like he just made it back home and is having a grand time making fun of us.

"Are you guys seriously looking at stars? That is so lame man, Layla made you do it didn't she? She always comes up with this off the wall crap," Mason explains giggling.

We get up and I jump off the truck. "Whatever Mason, tell it to someone who actually cares," I snap back and walk to the front door.

"Layla, geez I was just messing around, sorry," he yells after me but I go in and shut the door.

I go up to my room and throw myself on my bed. God, if there wasn't that age gap between Ben and I, just thinking of him makes me happy. The noise of my phone buzzing rips me out of my thoughts, I check to see who it is. Seeing Ben's name sends and instant smile over my face, I'm curious what he has to say. I swipe to open and it reads **Had an awesome night, we should do that again sometime =) Don't let Mason get to you.** Can he be any more perfect? I say fuck the age; this is 2015, anything goes nowadays. I try to think of something to write back but I settle for a simple **Yes! I'd love to.**

It feels really weird getting ready for work on a Monday, I'm lacking motivation but decide I better get moving if I want to check on Layne on my way to work. James and Carmen haven't made it back from Atlanta yet and Ben has been working on cars most of the day. I walk into the kitchen and make a sandwich for Layne in case he still isn't up and moving, grab my bag and head towards my car. Ben and Shane are taking a break lounging on the picnic table; Ben is looking sexy as ever in his black sweaty sleeveless tank.

As I open the car door Ben looks my way, a little smirk and a wink from him and my knees become weak. I have about thirty minutes to kill when I get to Layne's apartment. I knock on the door and to my surprise he answers.

"Hey Layla, what are you doing here?" he asks.

"I just came by to see how you're doing. Made you a sandwich in case you still couldn't get around but I guess you're doing better," I reply handing over the sandwich.

"Awe you are too sweet. Hey come on in and hang out for a bit, I know you still have a little time before you have to go into work," Layne offers.

I sit on the couch and see a fresh bag of ice on the table, looks like he has been following my advice. Layne takes a seat next to me and gives me a funny look.

"What?" I say.

"Nothing, you just look really happy. Anything happen?" he asks.

"Why did something have to happen? Maybe I just woke up in a good mood. I'm glad to see you're feeling better, I've never seen you in pain like that before," I say.

"Yeah I just kept icing it and popping anti-inflammatory meds. Woke up a new man," he gins looking at me.

"That's great. Maybe you should use your day off to maybe clean this place up, you know, since you're feeling better, "I tease.

"Boy, time sure did fly didn't it? I think you may be late for work if you don't leave right now," he says jokingly. His apartment looks like the typical bachelor pad now, when we dated I used to keep things nice and tidy for him. We talk for a little while longer, I would really like to tell him about everything going on in my head but I choose to keep it to myself. When I get to work I'm greeted by a puzzled Randy, "What are you doing here Layla?" Great, obviously Layne hadn't informed Randy of our shift switch.

"Layne pulled a muscle the other day while working out so I said I'd cover for him today, he will take my shift on Thursday," I explain.

Randy just shakes his head laughing and says that Layne is lucky to have me. Just as I assumed Mondays are really slow, I got to know Josh a little more. He has some interesting stories about California, used to be quite the partier but said getting married made him settle down. I check the time and I have about two more hours to go until my shift ends. I'm bored out of my mind so I text Layne and ask him if it's always like this. He's never been great at replying to messages in a timely manner so it is not surprising that I don't hear back. I decide to take a selfie with empty tables in the background titled *So boooooooreeeed* and I send it to Ben, my chances of hearing back from him are about one hundred percent better.

Within a minute I get a reply, a picture message. I open it and it's Ben, James, Carmen and Mason at a restaurant, the message underneath reads **Could have been here with us**. I enlarge the picture a bit to see Ben's face a little better; I could stare at this all night.

When I get home Alex and Brittany are sitting on the couch watching a movie and ask if I want to join them, I figure why not. It's a romantic drama so my guess is that Brittany picked the movie.

"Alex, why can't you do stuff like that?" Brittany asks while pointing at the TV.

"Brit, it's a movie. Guys don't do that shit," Alex sighs.

"Layla, come on tell him there are guys out there that are romantic and will stop at nothing to get the girl." Before I can answer the front door opens and James, Ben, Mason and Carmen come walking in.

"Oh my god I wanted to see this movie, how is it?" Carmen asks as she comes to sit on the couch.

"It's really good, we were just having a discussion on men and romance, I suppose I didn't find myself a hopeless romantic," Brittany says staring right at Alex

"Oh really? So you want me to line the tub with lit candles and have fresh rose petals all over the bed?"

"Okay Alex, that's TMI. Don't need to know what you guys do when you're alone, "James protests with a little hint of smile.

"Okay, let's ask Ben," Brittany suggests and Ben raises his eyebrows in surprise, "Is it really so farfetched for a man to do something so sweet for someone he loves?" Brittany asks in anticipation.

"Oh boy, how did I get roped into this one," Ben starts as he takes a seat next to me on the couch, "I'm sure there are some guys that may do this, but speaking for the majority, probably not. Hell, it's never crossed my mind."

"You guys all suck," Brittany pouts while crossing her arms, Alex grabs her and gives her a kiss on the cheek and she's all smiles again.

"So did your night get any better?" Ben asks nudging me with his shoulder.

"Nope, it was dead, tips were nonexistent. Nice picture you sent back, was that at O'Malley's?" I ask.

"Good eye, it was O'Malley's. A little far but definitely worth the drive, I remember that place from years ago, was stoked to see that it's still there," he replies. I haven't been there in years but the big Irish flag in the background gave it away.

Things went back to normal over the next few days, Carmen flew back home and the guys have been really busy with incoming cars. James is a little down since Carmen won't be back until our 4th of July party. It's only a month away, but I guess when you're madly in love it seems like an eternity. Ben and I have made it a habit of sending funny selfies back and forth to each other. One of the best ones so far was Ben giving a confused expression as Mason straddles a bike in the shop posing like a badass. Once in a while James joins in too; he's still learning the ropes on how to pose.

I'm on my way to work when I get a call from my mother, which strikes me as odd since we never talk. When I pull into the parking lot I call her back. She informs me that their show will be passing through Georgia on the way to South Carolina; they have an extra day so they want to visit next Sunday. She said she spoke with James a few minutes ago and he told her Ben was back in town and they are excited to see him. Wow, this is going to be so awkward, I haven't seen them in years. Oh well, it's just for a day I guess I can handle that.

I walk inside and see Layne onstage in full karaoke mode with 'LOVE YOU LIKE THAT', the crowd is cheering and he's eating it up. He gives me a quick wave and I head behind the bar. When the song ends Layne makes his way over to me, "You look lost in thought, what's up?" he asks me inquisitively.

"It's nothing really, just got off the phone with my mom, they are coming to visit next weekend," I mumble.

"Holy cow, all eight of them?" Layne asks.

"Hell no, just my mom and dad, thank god. I guess my brothers and sisters are doing their own thing. I would die if they came along. Layne, I'm really not looking forward to this, I haven't seen them in years. You know we aren't close," I say playing around with the seam of my shirt.

"Well you never know, distance makes the heart grow fonder and maybe they miss their little girl. Just promise me that you're not gonna run off with them to join the circus, no pun intended," he laughs.

I smile, give him a quick hug and tell him that would never happen. Layne's shift is over but as usual he sticks around for a few more hours, he's trying to convince Randy to give him the late shift on Fridays and I think Randy is about to give in,

Layne can be very persuasive when he wants something.

The next day I wake up early and make my way downstairs. I'm greeted by James in the kitchen.

"Morning Layla, how was work?" he asks while looking at the newspaper on the counter.

"It was alright, tips were good and I sang a few songs. Anyway, so my mom called me on the way to work yesterday and told me about their plans," I mention while grabbing some orange juice out of the fridge.

"Oh yeah, guess they are passing through, I can't wait to see them how long has it been?" James asks.

"Three years," I answer quickly.

"Wow, time sure does fly. You know years ago Ben, your dad and I used to hang out all the time, we had some really good times," James reflects.

As he continues down memory lane Ben walks into the kitchen, "Morning, you guys talking about me?" he asks smiling.

"Hey," James begins, "yeah, I was just telling Layla about the time you, Sam and I raced our cars outside Greenville about twenty-five years ago."

"Oh my god, we were so stupid back then, lucky we didn't get hurt or die. I think your mom was pregnant with your brother Adam at the time, she was so pissed when she found out," Ben chuckles, looking at me.

I wish I could share in their enthusiasm but I didn't even exist when most of these stories took place. Damn, I feel like I'm on a rollercoaster with my emotions. Even though I told myself to screw the age difference it seems to be thrown in my face every so often so it's really making me question my judgment.

I decide to change the subject, "Well I need to go dress shopping, still haven't found one for your wedding."

"Carmen said you already had one?" James asks confused.

"I just said that so she wouldn't worry," I reply looking sideways.

"Great, I'm taking Ben to get fitted for a tux at the mall so come with us and we'll see if you can find something there. We're planning to leave in about an hour so make sure you're ready," James insists and walks into the living room.

"Don't worry, I'm about as excited as you are," Ben says patting me on the shoulder. I've been prolonging this because I hate dresses and now I have two guys coming with me to find one. Shoot me now.

We get to the mall and head directly to the tux store; it's really quiet so Ben is taken to the dressing room to get measured. James and I are sitting on a small sofa when Ben comes back in a black tuxedo, vest and tie and a grey shirt. I can't stop staring, he is stunning, a completely different look. "So what do you think?" Ben asks looking a bit uncomfortable.

"Amazing," I blurt out, "I mean, yeah it looks really nice. Where's the jacket?"

James chuckles and walks up to Ben taking a closer look. "Carmen wants the groomsmen to lose the jacket and just go with the vest," James explains, "Alright, that was easy, you comfortable Ben?"

"Well this isn't my usual look but I think I can pull it off," he jokes, "Alright, Layla's turn."

We head to one of the bigger department stores and the search begins. Not having a clue what looks good on me, I just grab a variety of dresses. I'm already on dress number four and hate them all. Standing in front of the large mirror in the middle of the dressing room, the attendant notices my frustration and asks if she can help with anything. I tell her that I need a dress for a wedding and I'm clueless. She asks my size and tells me to wait for a moment and disappears. She returns holding an emerald green dress with a scalloped overlay. I'm already put off by the color but decide to try it on anyway. I'm amazed the way it looks on me, the bodice is fitted and the bottom half reminds me of a pencil skirt, it fits perfectly. I decide this is the dress and thank the woman for helping me.

"Alright guys, I found one," I say walking toward Ben and James my new dress in hand.

"And we don't get to see it?" James asks.

Holding the dress up I respond, "Here you go, what you think?"

Ben laughs, "I think he meant on you."

"Nah, you'll see it at the wedding," I say, walking toward the counter to pay.

The rest of the weekend was uneventful. Ben, James and Mason went to check out a car show on Sunday, they invited me along but I passed, I can't share their passion for cars. Most of my evenings are spent outside on the porch with Ben, once in a while James and Mason will join us for a bit. Little by little Ben seems to be opening up by sharing stories of prior jobs and different places he's lived.

"I can't see you working in an ice cream shop Ben," I point out giggling.

"Well, that was when I was much younger. Yeah, it was this little shop by the Santa Monica pier. Whatever paid the bills, I did that during the day and at night I was a bouncer at a nightclub. I loved living in Cali, but even having two jobs it was really hard to get by, at least in that area."

"Where did you go after that?" I ask inquisitively.

"My roommate at the time was moving back home to New Mexico and I figured what the heck, so I went along. Found out the desert isn't really my thing," he replies leaning back against the column.

"Wow, I've always wanted to see California. Your dad never took the show out west, never knew why."

"Hell if I know, I remember him having offers but he always turned them down. Maybe one day I'll take you there, I can be your tour guide," he says with a twinkle in his eye. He never fails to make my heart skip a beat.

Chapter Four

Layla

It's Sunday, the day I've been dreading all week. I haven't seen my parents in so long and I'm really nervous. I'm in the kitchen with Ben getting the last few things together for the cookout James has planned.

"So, you excited to see them?" Ben asks, slicing the tomatoes.

"Oh, yeah totally. It's been a while so it's nice that they are able to stop by," I say trying to sound believable, he cocks his head to the side and gives me an *'I don't believe a word that's coming out of your mouth'* look but doesn't say anything else about it so that works for me.

A little while later the doorbell rings and I suppose I should be the one to answer. Taking a deep breath I open the door and to my surprise my older brother Adam is standing there. Now I really want to die, growing up he always pushed me around and pointed out my flaws.

"Layla," my mom screeches as she steps in to give me a hug, "Looking beautiful as ever."

"Hi Mom, Dad it's so good to see you," I pause, "Adam."

"Oh come here, I don't bite," Adam says as he pulls me towards him. This is so awkward; I don't remember ever being hugged by my brother.

The next thing I hear is my mom shrieking, dropping her bag on the floor, "Ben oh my God! I knew you would be here but it didn't sink in until now. It's been too long." You can tell my dad is overjoyed as well, giving Ben a big hug. James and Mason walk in and once all the greetings are out of the way, we get comfortable in the living room.

"So how are things?" My mom starts, "I hope Layla hasn't been too much trouble." I turn to the side and roll my eyes; seriously am I five years old and she's come to pick me up from my babysitter? Ben caught on to my irritation and just gives me a sly grin which in turn sends a smile to my face.

"Oh God no, Layla is a blessing, we absolutely love having her here." James exclaims which was really sweet of him.

"Yeah, she's really good at keeping this place clean and she's a good cook too," Mason broadcasts with a grin.

"Well, that's awesome," Adam begins and I turn to look his way, "at least she found something she's good at, sure as hell wasn't performing." I knew as soon as he opened his mouth that it wasn't going to be anything nice. Nothing has changed, Adam makes fun of me and my parents think it's hilarious and start to laugh.

"Yes, we always joke that she was switched at birth. She's always been the total opposite of us, never could understand that," my dad adds.

"Now I don't agree with that, Layla always did a great job with her routines, they were perfect. She just didn't enjoy it, that's all," James declares.

"Well, I guess we can argue about perfection, at least she got the job done and the audience didn't know the difference, but we sure did," Adam claims looking straight at me. I don't understand why he hates me so much, not sure what I've ever done to him. Sitting there not really knowing what to say I glance over in Ben's direction. His eyes are fixated on me, full of concern. I need to get out of here right now before I fall apart.

"Well," I begin, "I suppose at least I realized my shortcomings and found my calling being a bartender. If you'll excuse me I'm going to get the grill started," I say in a playful kind of way to disguise the hurt I am feeling.

As soon as I step outside I feel relief and I make my way to the shop to grab the charcoal and lighter fluid. Once inside, I close the door, lean against one of the cars and close my eyes. I feel a tear rolling down my cheek; maybe they aren't so far off with me being switched at birth. What loving parents enjoy making fun of their child? I am startled by the door opening and I quickly wipe away evidence that I had been crying. I can just imagine if it were Adam, he would prey on my weakness the rest of the day.

"Layla, are you okay?" Ben asks as he walks toward me, at least it's not Adam but I don't need Ben seeing me like this.

"Oh, I'm alright. Just have to grab the lighter flu-"

Before I can say another word Ben interrupts and puts his hand on my shoulder. "Layla stop! It's me! You don't have to put on a show. What went on in there was unacceptable and you have every right to be upset, don't just play it off like it's nothing," he pauses, "remember when you told me you'd be there if I ever needed to talk? Well I want you to know that I'm here for you, I mean it."

I'm feeling very exposed right now so I just stare down at the ground. I feel his fingers on my chin lifting my head, my eyes meeting his. "Listen, you're going to go out there and not give two shits about anything else that they have to say. Just know that you are important to us and we love you, even if we're not really family," he adds, making me blush and smile.

"Come here you," he wraps his arms around me, I was not expecting that but I hug him back and for a moment time stands still. This feels right, easy, comfortable. Feeling his arms around wrapped around me makes me squeeze him tighter. When we pull away from each other he wipes my smudged mascara away with his finger and smirks, "I'll grab charcoal, you get the lighter fluid and let's get this party started."

We pull the last four burgers off the grill and take them inside to the table. While eating, my parents share stories of their travels and new adventures. They have been rather busy touring across the entire United States with an off season of only three months. It makes me appreciate my life, if it weren't for James more than likely I'd be living that nightmare.

"So where's Alex? Does he still live here?" Adam asks.

"Yeah he does, he's out of town with his girlfriend this weekend, and they're visiting her parents in Tennessee. I'm sure he'd rather be here," Mason jokes. I'm really happy to be sitting next to Ben, he makes things so easy and I could literally talk to him all day long. My mom interrupts our conversation.

"Hey Layla, I've never seen your room. You need to give me a tour," she demands. We've finished eating a while ago so I figure now is as good a time as ever. She follows me upstairs, we walk in and she shuts the door. Oh boy, I don't think she actually wants to see my room, wonder what this is about.

"Listen," she starts, "I know we've never been close and sometimes your dad and I cross the line a bit," she pauses, wow is she actually owning up to it? Is she apologizing? "You're an adult now and you can do whatever you want but I just wanted to ask you something."

"Okay, what is it?" I ask kind of disappointed seeing this isn't leaning toward an apology.

"Is there anything going on between you and Ben? I know it probably sounds absurd but seeing the way you look at him, makes me wonder."

All I can think is *'I wish'* but I am also startled by her question. "You've got to be kidding me. Oh my god no. I can't believe you would say that. We're just good friends," I reply aghast, hoping that she will buy it. The last thing I need is for my mother to know that I'm enamored with him; she would probably tell me that I'm an idiot.

"Thank goodness," she takes a deep breath, "You have no idea how relieved I am to hear that. He could almost be your father. Also, with him just coming back home after such a long time, the last thing he needs is for you to cause problems. Now I feel silly for asking, I'm sorry," she replies sincerely. Great, the age is pointed out to me yet again, this must be a sign for me to just give it up. I just want to curl up in a ball and forget today ever happened.

Finally, it's time for them to leave so we say our goodbyes at the door. I let out a big sigh of relief as I shut the door. Hopefully I won't have to see them for another three years.

"Layla, I'm really sorry about what happened earlier," James utters.

"It's not your fault, they're my family," I chuckle.

"I didn't know Adam would be coming along. I just figured if it were just your parents it wouldn't be so bad. I should have known better, hell I watched it all those years," James says shaking his head. Ben gives him a look like *how dare you* but doesn't say a word.

"I'm just glad you let me live here," I respond giving James a hug.

Ben

What a day. I was really looking forward to seeing Sam and Beth but after witnessing the shit they pulled, it really left a bad taste in my mouth. How could they do that to Layla? God I felt terrible seeing her in the shop like that, trying to act so strong but falling apart inside. No wonder she never mentions them, her parents are not the people I remember. It took serious self-restraint not to grab Adam and beat the shit out of him; he has bully written all over his scrawny little ass.

For a moment I was pissed off at James too, thinking how dare he invite them knowing that things would possibly turn out this way. Then again, what reason would he have not to; it's between Layla and her family. I'm just glad that I was able to make her feel better, her tears nearly killed me. While holding her she squeezed me so tight and I thought she wasn't going to let go. Hell, I didn't want to let her go, being that close to her was intoxicating. I know we've flirted around here and there but just for fun. There is no way in hell she would actually be interested in me, that's just wishful thinking. I try to force myself go to sleep but I can't get her out of my head.

The next morning I get up, go to the kitchen and make a pot of coffee. James comes in and it looks like he had a rough night.

"Morning Ben," he mumbles.

"Morning, didn't sleep well?" I ask.

"Not really, I was on the phone with Carmen half the night, she was freaking out about our wedding rings. She went to the jewelers to pick them up and they weren't there and apparently no one knows where they are," he pauses, "I told her we still have about a month before the wedding and everything will work out, told her we could use rubber bands if push comes to shove."

"How did that go over," I inquire.

"Nah, couldn't sell her on that. I got her to calm down and I said I would give them a call today. Oh by the way, how's the bike coming along?" James asks.

"It's getting there, hoping to finish it maybe in a week or two. I can't believe you didn't want it anymore."

"It's been sitting for a while, I know you'll enjoy it," he says.

I can't wait to get it running. I was really bummed that I had to sell both of my bikes in St. Louis before coming here; at least I made a great profit.

It's noon and I've been working non-stop it seems, always in great company though. Shane and I have become friends, he's a cool dude. I swear there is something going on between Rick and Carol, everyone else disagrees but I have a great sense for those things. Haven't seen much of James since this morning, I'm sure he went back to bed as exhausted as he looked. I've just realized I haven't seen Layla yet, she normally stops in here every morning.

I decide to take a quick break and walk to the house. Before I make it to the steps the front door opens. "Hey Ben. I made some sandwiches and was about to bring them over to you guys," Layla says with a smile on her face.

"Awesome, I was just coming in to check on you, missed you at the shop." She starts to blush just a little and asks me to grab the pitcher of ice tea on the kitchen counter.

Shane, Layla and I sit at the picnic table to eat our lunch. "I tell you man, this girl is gonna make some guy really happy one day," Shane remarks pointing at Layla.

"Oh stop it Shane," Layla giggles, rolling her eyes. Hearing Shane say that sends shivers down my spine, I can't imagines seeing her with someone in that way, I don't want to. Why the hell am I feeling this way?

"Thanks for the sandwich Layla," Mason steps out of the shop, "Don't care what your brother says, you're awesome!" That was such a cool thing for him to say, I know he likes to pick at her once in a while too but it's never malicious.

Layla mentions that she has to run into town to grab a few things from the store and Rick asks if she could stop by the hardware store to get a new multi-meter. She gives him a deer in the headlights look and Carol grabs the old one to show her what it looks like.

As she leaves, a small pickup truck drives up to the shop. I never would have imagined that Betty would be driving a pickup. "Hey ya'll, was on my way to my daughter's house and just wanted to see if ya'll had time to change the oil in my truck, it's way overdue, really embarrassing," Betty confesses.

I pull the truck into the shop and we get to work, this is probably the easiest thing I've done all day. About an hour later my phone chimes, I go to the counter and see it's a message from Layla. I swipe to check the text and notice four picture messages, all of multi-meters. A huge grin comes over my face, there is something totally adorable about her being so clueless, I let her know which one to get and she sends a smiley back.

A little while later Layla pulls up, gets out of her car and hands the multi-meter to Rick, "Here's your multi-reader."

"Layla, it's not a multi-reader, it's a multi-meter. Sometimes you really crack me up," Rick laughs. We continue working and Rick is over the moon with the new meter, checking every battery he can find just for fun.

We finish just in time for dinner, I'm a little bummed I wasn't able to work on the bike at all; I may just go back after I eat. At the table, James shares his success story with the wedding rings; they have been located and should be at the store tomorrow. He looks so relieved knowing he won't have to go the rubber band route. After helping to clear the table I head back out to the shop.

About thirty minutes later there's a knock on the door and Layla comes in with a smile. God, she looks so hot right now, I just want to grab her, back her against the wall and – damn it, I need to stop this.

"You still have work to do?" she asks walking over to the bike.

"Well, I didn't have a chance to work on her today so I figured I would do it now," I reply, wiping my forehead.

"That's James' bike, isn't it? It's been sitting forever, are you fixing it up for him?" Layla inquires while grabbing the handlebars; I'm never going to get that picture out of my head.

"He said I could have it. I had two really sweet bikes back in St. Louis, wasn't feasible to bring them so I had to let them go. Can't wait to get his one running, I miss riding."

She walks over to the workbench and hops up onto it, her sitting on the bench like that seriously gives me some bad ideas and a sly smile comes over my face.

"What?" she asks scrunching her forehead. Shit, what am I going to say? I can't tell her what I'm actually thinking about so I just end up blabbing more about what I need to do to the bike, I'm sure I'm boring her to death but she just sits and listens.

"So, once I get it running I'll take you for a spin."

"Oh my god no, I can't get on that thing. I'm too scared to even think about it," she laughs.

"You'll be fine, I wouldn't let anything happen to you, I swear."

"Oh I'm sure you'd be careful but I'm a coward, you wouldn't enjoy riding with me," Layla states and all I can think is that I would enjoy it too much. She ends up hanging out with me for the rest of the night, playing music and helping out a little.

Layla

I'm at work waiting for Layne to get here and my thoughts are still at the shop with Ben. I really don't care to learn anything about fixing bikes but if that means spending more time with him, why not? Trying to imagine myself on the back of his bike, so close to him makes me feel tingly inside. Then my thoughts go back to the shop and watching Ben work, I'm learning a lot about tools at the same time too.

"Hey Layla, what's going on?" Layne shouts in a very good mood.

"Not much. You're really chipper today. Let me guess, you got laid," I say sarcastically.

"Nope, didn't have the pleasure to provide my services to anyone. Actually, it's been a little while now that I think about it. Anyway, I got my Friday shift changed, so it will be me and you against the world."

I give him a wide smile and hold my hand up for a high five; Terri must have switched with him. I know she didn't care for the late shift and I didn't really care to work with her, she's really boring.

Layne asks about my parents visit and I tell him about that disaster so he gives me a big hug and kiss on the cheek.

"Do you remember that old bike that's been sitting in the shop forever?" I start and Layne nods, "Ben is fixing it up and thinks he'll have it running pretty soon."

"Well that's cool. I was starting to think it was just a decorative piece," Layne jokes.

"Yeah I know what you mean; I was thinking the same thing. You know I've never really had much to do with the shop besides cleaning it but Ben's been teaching me a few things when I'm in there."

"Let me ask you, this Ben guy kind of has your head in different places doesn't he?"
I'm a little stunned that he can tell, but also relieved because now I may be able to share my thoughts with him.

"Maybe a little," I smile, "It's probably just a stupid crush, I don't know what it is Layne, he's sweet, caring and when I see him my heart pounds like I've just run a marathon," I explain.

Layne opens up a few beers and looks my way, "Layla, isn't he a bit old for you? I mean, I've seen him and he's definitely not twenty-five or anywhere near that."

"Yeah, he's actually forty-one but-" I'm interrupted.

"Holy shit Layla, that almost twenty years older than you. You can't be serious!"

"Yeah, I know how to do math Layne, thank you. It's seventeen, not twenty. He doesn't seem that old though, I have a great time hanging out with him. Do you think I'm crazy?" I ask.

"Well, yeah. Honestly I think you are a little crazy, but if you're attracted to him I guess he must have something. It's quite a gap but it's not like it's never happened before and I think you are a little more mature than most people our age anyway. What do you think James would say?" Layne asks.

Oh my god, I've never even thought of that, I actually have no clue what he would say. I know James very well but I'm sure he would be shocked, maybe even appalled. I'm getting way ahead of myself here and ask Layne to keep everything I tell him to himself.

During my work week I don't catch much of what happens at home, I barely even see anyone. I still stop by the shop every morning to say hello and to get my daily dose of Ben.

Friday creeps up. It's karaoke night and it should be a full house. I'm happy that Layne is working with me now; Terri seriously was like a sleeping pill. I just told Randy I would be going up next to sing and right at that time James, Ben, Alex and Brittany walk through the door. Complete horror comes over me, there is no way I can go up there now that Ben is here.

"Hey Randy, scratch that I can't go up right now," I say nervously.

"What the hell are ya talkin' about? Layla, we gotta get people up there so you just gotta get it started," Randy demands.

My anxiety hit me right in the face and Layne walks over and offers to go up instead, he understands my predicament. I walk back to the Bar and Ben finds an empty stool, sits down and looks directly at me.

"I'm surprised to find you guys here tonight, are you here to sing?" I ask Ben in a joking kind of way.

"No way, I don't do karaoke," he chuckles still staring at me with those piercing eyes.

"Man, you don't dance, don't sing. What do you do?" I ask a little too bold.

"Wouldn't you like to know," he responds in an instant. I think to myself, *'yeah I would like to know but maybe someplace else'*.

"So what can I get you?"

"Just a soda, I volunteered to drive tonight," he answers with a little bit of a frown.

"So Layla," Ben says scratching his goatee, focusing on my eyes, "Am I finally going to hear you sing tonight?"

"Oh no, not tonight, sorry," I respond with a fake smile.

Another seat opens up at the bar so James joins Ben and asks if I will be singing.

"Nah man, just asked her," Ben answers looking a little disappointed.

"Come on Layla, you have to. I told Ben you have a great voice and now he's waiting to hear." I have a decent voice but having Ben sitting there watching I won't be able to sing a verse.

The music starts up and Layne is on stage singing *'DRUNK ON YOU'*. Those lyrics with his animation will drive the women nuts for sure. It doesn't take long until you can hear the cheering and screams. Ben and James watch the entire performance and Ben actually says that he's impressed. Layne makes his way back behind the bar, "Hey James, Ben, nice to see you here. Where'd Alex go?"

James points to the corner near the restroom, Alex and Brittany found some of her friends and are sitting with them. Those were the girls screaming the loudest when Layne was onstage.

"Layne, it's your lucky night," I say with a smile, "don't even need an excuse to go over there."

"Hell yeah, so Layla are you thinking the blonde or the brunette?" Layne asks jokingly. I playfully shove him with my hand and he quickly tickles the side of my waist before making his way over to the girls. I give Ben a quick glance and he doesn't look thrilled at all, I could be misreading his expression since I assume he doesn't care for Layne.

"He's pretty smooth, huh," Ben says with a hint of sarcasm.

"Well, he has no trouble in the picking up women department, just keeping them is another issue," I respond. Ben raises his eyebrows and rolls his eyes. The next song starts and I'm surprised to see Brittany and her friend on stage. Makes it easy for Layne, process of elimination and now he's flirting with the brunette.

"Fourth of July party is sneaking up," James begins, "I think we are just about set with everything. Betty will be supplying the sides. I've got the meat in the freezer and the tables and chairs are reserved. Layla, can you double check with Randy about the drinks or is he around right now?" James asks.

I go to the back and grab Randy, I hate being the messenger. Randy takes James in the direction of his office which leaves me with Ben, just the way I like it.

"So this party is a pretty big deal?" Ben asks, "James seems to be stressing about it."

"Most of the town shows up, everyone contributes something. It's a blast, he's probably stressing because Carmen's parents are coming to visit during that time. You know him, everything has to be perfect," I explain.

Layne comes back to the bar with a smile on his face, proudly showing off the phone number written on his arm. I know he will never call her though, he's more into instant gratification and doesn't like to work for it, poor girl. That will be another one that we may never see at the Bull again.

I just finished my Saturday grocery shopping accompanied by Mason. He's going camping with his buddies over the weekend so he wanted to pick up a few things. As we pull up to the house his friends are already there waiting. After putting up the groceries I walk to the shop to check on Ben and James. Being that it's the last week of June it's no surprise to find them a sweaty mess. The shop doesn't have central air, just window units that don't give off nearly enough cool air.

"Do you need some water?" I ask, startling both of them.

"Please," Ben replies panting. I walk back to the house and grab the pitcher of water out of the fridge along with two glasses. When I get back the scene has changed just a bit. James has taken his shirt off and Ben is in the process. Dear god please kill me now, just watching him removing his shirt sends me over the edge. I walk over to the counter and set the glasses down, pour the water and hand them each a glass. James is standing with his back toward me checking his phone and Ben is facing him. Those tattoos make him look a little badass; he could actually have a few more. While I stare in admiration, Ben looks my way and throws me a wink. It is at that moment that I notice I'm biting my lip. I close my mouth tightly and turn around, flirting around is fun but this is too intense.

"Okay, I just got a text saying the bounce houses are also reserved. They will drop them off in the morning on the fourth," James says relieved. I know he was a little worried since he forgot all about them when reserving the tables.

"I told Layla I'm taking her for a spin on this thing as soon as it's done," Ben says looking in my direction.

"Ha, good luck with that," James laughs, "I doubt you'll get her on it."

"Well," I start, "I still have some time to think about it, I may need to overcome some of my fears, you know."

"Well Layla, then I suggest you get over them in your sleep because the bike will be running tomorrow, it's actually already running, just a few more adjustments," James informs me. Shit, I thought it was going to be another week; I must have a horrified expression on my face.

"You'll be fine, I'll take care of you," Ben ensures. All I can think is *'I'm sure you will, just not the taking care of I'm looking for'*.

I walk back into the house and look for my phone, great nowhere to be found. I empty my entire bag on the living room floor, still nothing. Trying to retrace my steps isn't helping much either, the last time I remember actually holding it was at the Bull. I figure I better give Layne a call in case he may have picked it up for me; it wouldn't have been the first time. Damn it, I don't have Layne's number memorized.

Walking back toward the shop I notice Layne's truck parked right next to it but no sign of him. It's Saturday and he has to be at work in about fifteen minutes, but since he's here I can ask him about my cell. As I walk through the door I see Layne, Ben and James deep in conversation.

"Hey Layne," I start, "I was just about to ca-"

"Looking for this?" Layne asks holding up my phone. I nod with a smile and he hands it to me. "You know Layla, as much as you lose this thing you may want to consider putting a passcode on it," Layne advises with a mischievous grin.

My eyes widen in horror, "You didn't go through my phone, did you?"

"Layla, it's me, of course I did. Are you serious?" Oh my god, I'm sure he read through all of my messages and looked through pictures. Throwing my hands up to my face in embarrassment, I can't look at Ben or Layne right now, I feel stripped. Damn technology. I am definitely setting a passcode. I'm startled as I feel someone giving me a big bear hug, recognizing the cologne I know it's Layne. "No worries Layla, didn't find any nudes or anything like that," Layne scoffs, giving me a quick peck on the cheek before releasing me.

This can't get any worse, ever since telling him about my infatuation with Ben he seems to be invading my personal space a bit more than usual. Ben certainly doesn't look excited; he turns around and continues to work on his bike.

"Man, you two," James shakes his head, "You could be siblings the way you go at each other sometimes."

"Well, I better get to work, If I leave right now I may only be about ten minutes late," Layne says as he walks out the door.

I spend the rest of my afternoon at the lake with a book I've been meaning to finish, being alone is just what I need right now. As I lie on my blanket, legs propped up holding my book against my knees I hear faint voices behind me. I prop myself up and see Ben and James walking on the path.

"Hey, what are you guys doing here?" I ask since I don't see any fishing rods.

"We're jumping in the lake to cool down," James answers throwing two towels next to me, "Why don't you join us?"

"No thanks, I have a few more chapters to go, don't mind me though, have fun!" I reply.

"Alright," Ben says and next thing I know he starts to unbutton his jeans; my eyes sink right back into my book. No they aren't going to get naked here in front of me, I must be hallucinating. As I glance up for a second they are both walking into the lake with their boxers, phew what the hell was I thinking?

"My god, this is fucking amazing!" I hear Ben enjoying the cool water.

"Remember when we did this as kids right before dinner? Mom used to get so upset with us," James reminisces.

I change position to get a better view by rolling over on my stomach and propping myself up on my elbows. I have my book in front of me even though I'm really not reading anymore. After a little while they get out and grab the towels next to me, I take a mental picture of Ben standing there, wet with a towel around his waist. My eyes are back on my book and then I feel little drips of water on my shoulders so I look up to find Ben standing above me.

"Hmm reading upside down, is that a new thing?" Ben smirks raising his eyebrows. I look down and feel myself start to blush, I guess I just threw the book in front of me and didn't notice the direction, now he definitely knows I was watching them.

I manage to talk my way out of the bike ride. Must say I am very proud of myself for being honest saying I wasn't ready to hop on yet. Lying only gets me in trouble; Ben still makes me a cup of coffee on my days off.

Chapter Five

Layla

James is ecstatic because Carmen is flying in with her parents today. She was hoping to bring her son along but he already had plans with some of his college friends. James won't be picking them up at the airport. Her parents hired a driver that will take them to the hotel they reserved in Macon. I won't get to meet them until tomorrow when they arrive at the party. James and Ben will be making a trip to Macon tonight to have dinner with them. Mason and Alex are staying behind to pick up the house and get things organized for the party since I'm working tonight.

It's 3 am and my shift is over but I still can't go home. Randy and Layne are loading up my car with the alcohol Randy is supplying for the party. There's only so much that can actually fit in my car so they throw the kegs in the bed of Layne's truck, guess he's coming home with me.

The house is dark as we pull up. Quietly we begin to take everything inside. I open the pantry and am glad to see that someone cleared it out for me since that is where I was planning to store everything. Ben's bedroom door opens, I guess he's a light sleeper.

"Is there more outside, can I help?" he asks stepping out in sleep pants and no shirt. I guess he's quite comfortable around here now; I think to myself, admiring his physic. Layne takes him outside and they grab the kegs while I put all the bottles in the pantry.

"Alright, that was the last of it," Layne yawns, "I'm gonna take off and I'll be back in about six hours."

"Hey Man, why don't you just crash here. You have to be here early anyway and you look tired, we have the space," Ben offers patting Layne on the back. Wow, did I really just hear that? Layne looks relieved and makes his way to the couch and is out within minutes. I give Ben a big smile and tell him goodnight. On my way upstairs I grab a blanket from the cabinet next to the TV to cover Layne, not like he really needs it since it's mid-summer but James likes to keep the house cool.

The party company just arrived to set up the bounce houses, tables and chairs. The kids always have a blast here. Water balloon fights, Corn hole, Horseshoes, you name it we have it. Layne made a quick stop at his house to shower and change clothes. He returned, joining me in the kitchen to prepare the rum punch bowls. We will also be mixing drinks on demand but the bowls are always a hit. James is running around like a chicken with its head cut off, he wants to make sure everything looks great for Carmen's parents.

"Okay, all the grills have been dropped off and they are set up," Ben starts, "Can I help you guys with anything?"

"I think we are all set in here," I respond placing the last bowl in the fridge, "So how are Carmen's parents?"

"They are nice, her dad is very quiet but her mom is a chatterbox. Honestly I don't think they are here for a backyard barbeque, they seem like more of the charity dinner party kind of people. I think they are interested to see where Carmen will be living, "Ben explains with a bit of a chuckle. I can't help but grin, this ought to be interesting. No wonder James has been on pins and needles, but really what could happen? It's not like they can forbid her to marry him.

Ben, Layne and I walk out to the porch and we see a very nice black car pull up to the house, speak of the devil, it must be them. Ben goes back inside to grab James and I just watch as the driver gets out and opens the back car door.

Carmen's father is exactly how I picture and older Italian gentleman. Well dressed, a little pudgy, large bushy eyebrows and grey hair perfectly slicked to the back. His nose is his most prominent feature. Her mother carries herself very graceful, bronze skin, green eyes and curly hair just past her shoulders. It has the most unnatural shade of mahogany, obviously chemically achieved, but to my surprise she can pull it off.

Ben returns with James, Mason and Alex. "Mr. and Mrs. Moretti, what a pleasure it is to see you again, welcome to our home," James runs past me to shake their hands. Wow, James is a little more dressed up than usual wearing a grey and white striped polo shirt.

I feel underdressed in my faded blue jean shorts and cowboy boots but last I heard this was a barbeque. I glance over at Ben and Layne, they are just wearing t-shirts and jeans so I think I'm alright. After all the introductions are finished, James leads Carmen and her parents inside. They are very nice, but Ben was right, they seem a little out of place.

Betty and her family pull up and the five of us head to the truck to help carry the side dishes over to the table that is set up near the house. I tell Betty that Carmen and her parents are here and Betty being nosy as she asks for an introduction. Ben, Layne and I walk her inside and she takes over, "Oh my goodness I am so happy to meet ya'll," she walks over to shake everyone's hand, "Carmen is just such a blessing and I can see where she gets those good looks from," Betty says winking at Carmen's mother. She takes a seat on the sofa next to James and he looks relieved to have someone dominating the conversation.

Ben goes back outside to help with the grills and I grab Layne and lead him into the kitchen. People should be arriving any minute now and we need to get the punchbowls outside. We set up a table across the back door so everyone can just come up and order drinks; it's great because it keeps them out of our way.

The music is blaring outside, country of course. Layne and I decide to play our own in the kitchen, I love country music but a change once in a while is really nice. My Mp3 player has a mixture of Top40, Hip Hop, Dance, Folk and Country.

We've been pretty busy; it seems a little more crowded than in previous years. Layne takes a quick break to grab us a plate of food, in the meantime I mix us some drinks. Layne's favorite drink is whisky sour and mine is a mojito, we don't stop at one and I've hit the giggly stage.

It's been about forty-five minutes since anyone has come to the table to ask for a drink so we decide to shut it down, besides, there's plenty of beer and wine coolers on ice outside. Heading out, Layne joins Alex and Brittany on the steps.

The heat has most people hanging out near the house or under the trees. The kids are still full of energy, screaming and running around with water guns. I look around and Ben catches my eye. He's leaning against the open door of the shop with a beer in his hand talking to Shane. Since having a few mojitos in my system I feel a little brave. I grab one of the red plastic cups off the porch and head to the table with the orange beverage dispensers. After filling my cup with icy cold water I walk toward the shop. I stop right behind Ben, tug at the collar of his shirt and pour the freezing liquid down his back. He jumps, "What the fuck -" he turns around facing me, meanwhile Shane is laughing hysterically, I think he knew what was going down when he saw me coming.

"You know, you look so hot I just figured you needed a cool down," I giggle grabbing my hair and moving it to one side. I've only been outside for five minutes and the back of my neck is soaked with sweat.

"Oh yeah?" he chuckles handing his beer to Shane and removing his shirt with his free hand. His eyes take on a wild appearance I hadn't seen before, I start walking backwards.

"You better run Layla," emphasizing on the word better, "when I catch you, you're going wish you hadn't done that."

I take off running straight toward the wooded area, dodging trees, praying I don't fall and make an ass out of myself. Running in cowboy boots is not as easy as they make it look in the movies. I stop as I get to the end of the woods, the lake in front of me. Before I even get a chance to look back I feel his arms around my waist lifting me off the ground. I start to struggle but he just throws me right over his shoulder and starts walking.

"Sweet, you made it easy for me, thanks," he pants, throwing me directly into the water. I really didn't think this through at all; I can feel my make-up streaking down my face. Trying to wipe the black from under my eyes I can't stop laughing. He is still catching his breath as he holds his hand out. Grabbing it he pulls me out and I collapse on the grassy area.

He throws himself down next to me; we are shoulder to shoulder both amused. I turn my head over to the right to look at him and he's staring at me. His eyes take on a carnal appearance that is driving me wild. We're alone and I just want him to lean over and kiss me, maybe I should kiss him. My new found courage from earlier has left me entirely. Turning my head toward the sky I get up slowly and break the silence, "Well, I have to say you won, hands down."

He jumps to his feet, "That's right; you better remember this if you ever want to start something again. But seriously, thank you. I haven't had fun like this in years." Grinning I bump his side with my hip and we walk back to the party.

"Oh boy, he got you good didn't he?" I hear Shane yelling as he gives Ben a high five.

In that moment Layne comes up to us "Layla," he pauses, "What the hell happened to you?" he asks with a puzzled expression.

"Long story," I giggle.

"Well anyway, some of us are heading down to the creek for the bonfire, you wanna come?" Layne asks smiling at me.

"I would but we still have to clean this place up."

"Layla, you all go ahead and have fun, there are plenty of people to help clean up so we'll take care of it," Shane offers.

"Okay, sure why not," I decide, happy about the distraction. I run inside to change clothes, grab my phone and get into the car. Alex is driving since everyone else is buzzed.

Ben

We are just about done cleaning up, Shane and I are folding the last few tables as James, Carmen and her parents step outside, their driver is waiting holding the car door. Telling Shane to hang on a moment, I make my way over to them.

"Just wanted to say goodbye and that it has been a pleasure meeting you," I say shaking their hands.

"Pleasure's all ours," Carmen's father smiles, "Thank you for sharing your tradition with us, we had a wonderful time. We will be seeing everyone in about two weeks for the wedding."

"I can't wait to show you the French quarter. You're going to love New Orleans," Carmen adds.

"Alright, we better get going. James, thank you," Carmen's mother hugs him, "Our flight leaves in the evening, Carmen said something about the four of us having lunch tomorrow?"

"Yes, I'll drive up there and meet you at the hotel at around 11 am," James replies.
James gives Carmen a peck on the cheek and they get in the car and leave.

Before I can open my mouth James gives me a stare that pretty much says *'Don't ask'* and I respect that. I mean come on, a peck on the cheek? I've witnessed several make-out sessions the last time she was here. I suppose it wouldn't be appropriate to do that in front of her parents. I get back to Shane and we lean the tables against the house, the company will be picking them up Monday morning.

I'm too wound up to even think about sleep tonight. Why did she have to leave with Layne? Who the hell is he to her? I need to find out. I can't ask her about him, it would be too obvious, I know they work together but that's all. I can't stand the way he looks at her, that sly smirk almost like he's undressing her with his eyes.

I open my laptop and surf the web a bit. Nothing helps; she is going to be on mind all night. I couldn't believe that Layla poured water down my shirt, usually she's reserved and a little on the shy side. I freakin' love that about her. Almost like I just want to scoop her up and take care of her. Seeing her bold and taking charge just takes it to a whole other level. That was such a turn on. Lying next to her on the grass was almost more than I could handle, I wanted to kiss her so bad but couldn't. Heck I wanted to tear her clothes off but thank god I have a conscience. Man, if I was in my twenties I would totally make a move but I have seventeen years on her. I remember when she was born for god's sake.

I close my laptop and pull out my phone. It's 11 pm and I think she is still out. I want to text her but what do I say? I look for funny memes. Found a good one. I send her one with a guy pointing that just simply says **I got you**. Seconds later my phone buzzes. She already replied. I press the picture to enlarge it. It says **Bruh don't mess with me, you'll be sorry**. I can tell this is going to be a meme war. We go back and forth for a while, I guess the bonfire isn't that great. The last text she sends is a wink.

I wake up the next morning and I am hell-bent to get Layla on that bike, I'm sure if I sweet talk her enough she'll cave. I walk into the kitchen; looks like James already started the coffee.

"Hey Ben, I'm about to head out to Macon to see Carmen before she flies out," James says while pouring his coffee into a thermos.

"Alright, sounds good. Where's everyone else?" I ask wondering why it's so quiet at this time.

"Alex is at Brittany's, Mason and Layla are returning Layne's truck to his place. You need anything before I head out?" James asks while grabbing his keys off the counter.

"I'm good, thanks. See you later."

Wonder why Alex just doesn't move in with Brittany, he's rarely here. I go to the living room, sit on the couch and turn on the TV. A few minutes later I hear footsteps coming toward the door so I look up, Layla and Mason are back. Mason looks exhausted and walks upstairs, Layla comes to sit next to me on the couch.

"How was the bonfire?" I ask taking a sip of my coffee.

"It was fun, really crowded but fun. Those memes you sent last night were hilarious," she says with a sly grin.

"Well, I think your comebacks were better. There's some coffee left if you want some," I say pointing toward the kitchen. Her grin disappears a bit; she gets up and walks into the kitchen to grab a cup. For someone that says they love coffee she never seems to enjoy it much. When she returns I ask if she has any plans for today, shaking her head she says no.

After lunch I head outside to get the bike ready, grabbing two helmets from the shop. I send Layla a quick text telling her to come outside. It's a great day for a ride, not scorching hot like yesterday. She comes out, probably wondering why I texted her.

"You ready?" I ask smoothly.

"Ready for what?" she asks putting her phone in her pocket.

"You, me and the open road," I reply with a grin.

I knew this wasn't going to be an easy sell, she tries to come up with any possible excuse she can. Assuring her that I will be careful and promising to only ride on the property, she takes a deep breath and finally agrees. She is going love it. After putting on my helmet I climb on, I grab the other helmet and hand it to her. Reluctantly she puts it on and climbs on behind me.

"Wait, wait, wait! Do I hold on to that metal loop thing behind me?" she asks sounding terrified.

"Well, you can but it will probably be easier if you hold on to me," I explain. I go over a few basics with her like where to keep her feet, what to do when we turn and come to a stop. She places her hands lightly on my hips, I know once we get started that's going to change. Once she's ready, I kick up the stand and balance the bike, her grip gets a little tighter. As soon as I start the engine she jumps just a bit, I tell her everything is fine and to just hold on. After shifting into first gear I let the clutch out, apply throttle and we're off.

Layla's position has changed to clinging on to my body for dear life and must say I am really enjoying it. I turn my head to the side to ask if she is alright and she yells everything is okay. After a few laps I come to a stop and ask her if she is willing to venture further out. She gives me a thumbs up and my inner kid is jumping with excitement.

The roads around here are always quiet so it makes for a great ride. I can tell she's relaxed quite a bit but still clenched to me. Not one car passes us on the ride and after about thirty minutes we get back home, I figure that's probably long enough for the first time.

"So," I ask in anticipation, "what did you think?"

She removes her helmet, her hair is stuck to her face from sweating, "Well, I was scared to death at first but overall it was fun," she starts, which gives me the biggest smile, "but seriously I still don't know how you rode in that globe, you're crazy." I start to laugh, she is just so damn cute.

I'm a sweaty mess so I figure a shower is probably a good idea. After I get out I stand in front of the sink wiping the condensation off the mirror. I still have a big smile on my face, I haven't been this happy in a long time.

After James gets back I tell him about my success of taking Layla for a ride, he's impressed. Brittany and Alex join us for dinner and we are one big happy family.

"So Layla, did you have a nice ride?" James inquires while passing me the rolls.

"Umm, yeah it wasn't too bad. I'm pretty sure I cut off Ben's circulation there for a bit but he seems to have recovered," she answers playfully. *'Yep, you can cut off my circulation anytime'* is what's going through my mind. Being so close to her was exhilarating but also calming, hope we can do that again soon.

James grabs two beers and asks me to join him outside on the porch. "Man, I'm so happy you're here. You definitely bring something to this house. Mason looks up to you, he thinks you're amazing," James pauses, "and Layla. I mean I've never seen her smile so much; she really loves having you around. You two have become really close friends, huh?"

"Yeah man, she's really cool," I answer not really knowing what else to say in that moment. A minute ago I replayed the afternoon of having Layla's arms wrapped around me; James mentioning her makes me come back to reality.

He's right though, we are close friends, nothing wrong with that.

"James, are you and Carmen going on a honeymoon after the wedding?" I ask changing the subject but also because I'm curious.

"Yes, we will be spending three days in the Bahamas after the wedding. I just got my passport in the mail the other day. Carmen was freaking out because I kept putting it off but now everything is on track. I can't wait."

"That's awesome, you're going to love it," I reply not even thinking.

"Have you been to the Bahamas?" I knew that was coming. "Yeah, took a trip there with my Ex. It's beautiful, you need to check out the island with the pigs, they come right up to you."

"Your Ex?" he starts, "I know you said you were married before, tell me about it. How long were you married?" That's the last thing I want to talk about, damn it.

"Not much to say, just didn't work out. Six years." Before James can continue Layla steps out and asks if we want to watch a movie, I immediately jump up. She was my saving grace, couldn't have come at a better time.

Alex, Brittany and Mason are already sitting on the couch with a bowl of popcorn. We sit down and Layla is sitting between James and me. Looks like they picked a horror movie, nice, I love those. Layla and Brittany don't really seem to be fans of slasher movies. Brittany is almost sitting in Alex's lap and Layla has her eyes partially covered with her hand. I look over at James and he's knocked out cold. I can't believe him, this is a great movie. The ominous music starts and a figure appears on the screen, Layla grabs on to my arm and burrows her head between my shoulder and the couch. She really freaked.

"I can't watch this, "she mumbles still clenching my arm. I could totally get used to this; maybe we should do a horror night once a week. She looks down at my arm and releases her grip. "I'm so sorry," she starts apologizing, "After today you're going to end up with bruises all over from me holding on to you.".

Layla

God damn it, I hate scary movies. I'm always up for watching them but end up turning into a baby before they're halfway through.

I'm lying in bed wide awake trying to tell myself that there is nothing under my bed, I'm too freaked out to jump down and check. I decide distracting myself with social media on my phone is exactly what I need right now. After about twenty minutes I am feeling better and I may be able to sleep. I close my eyes and hear a loud boom. I jump up, heart beating like crazy. Great, a thunderstorm, fuck my life. Well I guess at least I'm not working tomorrow, that's a plus. My phone buzzes and I grab it from my nightstand. It's a text from Ben which reads **You alright? I remember you saying you hate storms**. Instant smile, wow he remembered. We end up texting back and forth for almost an hour.

It's morning and after waking up I notice I'm still holding my phone. I enter the passcode and the screen with the messages comes up. I must have fallen asleep while texting, Ben's last message reads ***I assume you've fallen asleep, sweet dreams***.

Looking at the time I know everyone else is already at work. I head outside and notice the party company just arrived to pick up their equipment. James is signing some paperwork for the pick-up and Ben has his head buried in the hood of a car next to the shop.

"Hey Layla," James stops me, "Betty called and said she left a few of her dishes here, I put them on the counter in the kitchen. Would you take them to her?"

"Yeah sure, I can go right now," I run inside grab the dishes and head to the diner.
When I get there I see Layne's truck parked outside. He should seriously consider working here, at least he would get free food.

When I step inside I find Layne sitting at the counter with his back turned to me. "Morning Layne," I say jabbing him with my elbow. "Layla! What are you doing here? Come on sit down," he replies wiping the side of his mouth with a napkin. I sit on the stool next to him and place the dishes in front of me. Betty comes out from the kitchen, grabs the dishes and hands me a menu.

"So how was the rest of your weekend?" Layne asks inquisitively.

"It was good. You won't believe this but I rode on a motorcycle," I broadcast proudly.

"What?" Layne almost chokes on his water," Are you serious? I just can't picture that. When did you learn to ride?

"Oh no, I rode on the back, Ben was in control," I clarify stealing a piece of his bacon.

"Oh alright, that pretty much explains it all," Layne rolls his eyes, "So what's going on there Layla? I know you told me you had the hots for him and judging by the way he looks at you I would say the feeling is mutual. So what's your next step?"

Layne asking that out loud makes me realize I don't have a next step, so I just shake my head. "Well, if you want my advice. To be honest, I think having a serious relationship is out of the question because of the age factor," he says and I must be making a face, "but wait, don't frown. There is nothing wrong with having a little fun, just get it over with and fuck him, you know, take what you can."

"Layne!" I cry appalled, I can't believe he just said that so casual with so many people in the diner. Betty comes back to take my order and we sit there a little while longer until Layne has to head into work. I end up staying about an extra ten minutes listening to Betty rave about Carmen's parents.

As I walk to my car I notice I have a flat tire, awesome. Grabbing my phone out of my purse I realize the battery is dead and I don't know anyone's phone number off hand. I walk back into the diner and ask Betty if she has James' cell number. She writes it down and hands me the phone on the counter. James says he'll be there in about fifteen minutes with a spare. I go outside, hop on the hood of my car and wait. I see James truck pulling into the parking lot but Ben is driving.

"Car trouble," Ben jokes as he gets out of the truck. He grabs the spare out of the bed and rolls it next to my car. Taking a good look at my flat he asks for the wheel lock key. I look at him like he's crazy, what does he want? He explains what it is and I tell him I have no clue where that would be.

Climbing into my car he searches every nook and cranny but comes up empty handed. "Damn, alright I'll take you home and we'll figure this out later," he decides, snapping a quick picture of the wheel lock.

I'm a little quiet on the ride home; I feel like I can't really look at him after what Layne suggested, it just feels wrong. But then again, imagining him and me together in that way is exhilarating. He's going on about some prank they pulled on Mason back at the shop and I'm thankful that he's doing all the talking.

When we get out of the truck I notice James running toward us, "Shit man I'm sorry I forgot to give you the wheel key, I keep it in the shop because I know Layla would lose it. I'll head there later this afternoon with you and get her car." Well now I feel better for not knowing what the hell it is, I've never seen this thing before.

Chapter Six

Ben

Only a few more minutes until I see Mom, I haven't been able to sit down since James left to pick them up at the airport. My nerves are getting the better of me and I'm afraid I won't be able utter a word. I'm really regretting being absent all those years, what was I thinking? I thought I did the right thing but I hurt so many people in the process including myself.

"Ben, everything is going to be fine, relax," Layla says trying to reassure me, "Here sit down, I'll get you some water." Layla really knows how to read me; she's so sweet and caring. Mason and Alex walk into the living room and sit down next to me. As Layla hands me the glass of water I hear the front door open. Mason and Alex jump up right away, running up to the door and Layla stays by my side.

"My boys, it's been too long since I've been here," Mom says hugging both of them. Her eyes move to my direction and tears roll down her cheeks. I walk toward her and feel myself getting a little emotional. She hugs me tight and I squeeze even tighter. She pulls back but grabs my hands.

"Ben," she sobs.

"I'm so sorry Mom, I shouldn't have disappeared like that. I really – "

"Don't apologize. It doesn't matter, you're here now, and that's what's important. I love you so much."

"I love you too, Mom," I reply as she squeezes my hands one last time.

"Layla," Mom smiles, reaching her arms out to her, "Sweetheart come here." I remember Layla telling me that they are close but seeing them interact really puts a smile on my face. Gerald comes up and introduces himself to me and after talking for a bit, he seems to be a really great guy. It's so surreal that she's here, everyone is so happy and it feels like the family is complete. After dinner mom asks me to join her for a walk at the lake. On the way she tells me about her life in Canada and how she met Gerald. I knew at some point the conversation would switch to me. I tell her about all the places I've lived, the jobs I've had, a quick recap of the last twenty years.

"Ben," she begins, "Why didn't you ever call or write. I knew you and your father wouldn't be able to work things out, but for years I prayed that you would reach out to me, but you never did. Not to me, not to James. It's like you vanished into thin air." I knew this was coming,

I've been dreading having to talk about this. James being the brother he is has never asked because he knows I'd rather not talk about it.

"When I left I was so furious, I figured if I removed myself from this place and everyone here, I could try to forget everything. I never planned to cut you or James out of my life but once I finally got settled time just passed by. There were many times I picked up the phone and almost dialed but I had no idea what to say, I felt as if I was a stranger. I thought about you all the time, wishing I could just man up and face things."

"Oh honey, it hurts me so much to hear you say that. I am sorry that you were cheated out of having the things you deserved in life. I am so happy you're back home, seeing you and your brothers together is something I thought would never happen again. We talk for a little while longer before heading back to the house. Layla is walking in our direction with a big smile on her face.

"She sure grew up into a gorgeous young woman didn't she? So sweet, loving and kind. She kept you alive while you were away. Always wanted to hear stories, see pictures. I loved sharing all of that with her," Mom says rubbing my arm.

"And I always said he would be back, I was right," Layla smiles, "Norma, Gerald is looking for you, something about his medicine."

Layla

Our flight leaves for New Orleans tomorrow and I'm packing up the last of my things. Watching Ben and Norma these last two days has left a permanent smile on my face, they are so happy. I can't wait for Carmen to meet Norma and Gerald, she is going to love them. Carmen's father took care of the airfare and emailed the ticket information. He is also paying for our hotel rooms. The reception will be held in the ballroom of the same hotel but the ceremony will take place at the Catholic Church that Carmen and her parents attend. Luckily James is catholic as well, but no one here ever goes to church, I wonder if that will change once Carmen moves here.

It's late but I decide to bring my suitcase downstairs anyway, we have to leave really early and I figure that's one less thing I have to do in the morning. Back upstairs I peek into the spare bedroom next to mine. It's been empty for years but Ben is staying in it while Norma and Gerald are visiting. Fortunately, we still had a foldaway bed in the basement, otherwise it would have been an air mattress on the ground.

At the airport, we still have about thirty minutes before boarding. I am super nervous, I've never flown before. Ben is picking up on my anxiety and puts his hand on my bouncing leg.

"Nervous?" he asks.

"Just a little, this is my first time flying. I don't know what to expect. It looks like none of our seats are together either," I reply a little anxious.

"Don't worry; it's not bad at all. I think you have a window seat, that's a good one," Ben tries to reassure me. My leg no longer bouncing I sit back in the chair and relax for a bit.

Oh boy, I've made it on the plane and found my seat. Now we are just waiting for everyone else to board. I look around and I see Alex and Brittany did get a seat together. Mason is already knocked out at a window seat on the opposite side and Ben is about three rows behind me. Carmen's father booked James, Norma and Gerald first-class tickets. An older woman sits down next to me and my nerves go haywire. If anything happens there is no way this lady could help me and I'm clueless. I look in Ben's direction again and he's not in his seat, the man that was seated next to him has disappeared as well.

"Hey Layla," I hear Ben's voice and turn to look in front of me, "this gentleman here said he'd be happy to switch seats with you so we can sit together." He doesn't have to tell me twice, I unbuckle my seatbelt and thank the man.

Ben

Poor thing was really freaking out. Luckily the guy was nice enough to switch seats; I would have hated to ask the old lady if she would move. Layla looks calm now but she may freak once we start taking off. She is following all the safety instructions in the book as they are being announced. I can't stop looking at her, it's cute.

Now that we are cleared for take-off, please fasten your seatbelts, secure your table and return your seats back in their upright position. We also ask that all electronic devices are powered down at this time. We thank you for your attention and wish you a pleasant flight to New Orleans.

As the plane starts to pick up speed I see Layla tensing up, I tell her everything is fine and she turns my way, giving me a little smile. As the wheels lift off the ground she grabs for my hand and I welcome it letting her fingers slip through mine. She closes her eyes, her head against the headrest and she's focusing on her breathing. I look down at our hands and she's got a tight grip, her knuckles are turning white. I reach across with my other hand and rub her arm, figuring that may help. It does, she starts to relax and her grip becomes looser.

Ladies and gentlemen, the captain has turned off the fasten seat belt sign and you may now move around the cabin. However, we always recommend keeping your seat belt fastened while you're seated.

Layla finally opens her eyes and sighs in relief, thank god because I really need to use the restroom, too much coffee.

"Hey, I'm just going get up and use the restroom, I'll be right back," I say and she releases her grip.

When I get back she's reading the inflight magazine, she looks like she's doing okay. The flight is only an hour and a half and when the announcement comes on that we are preparing to land, Layla looks at me and I grin, taking her hand.

After getting our luggage we wait for a taxi to take us to the hotel. James is relieved that not one piece of luggage is missing.

As we walk into the hotel lobby we are greeted by Carmen and who I presume is her son. James told me she has a son that is in college. You can tell he is Italian, black hair, green eyes and a deep tan.

"Norma, Gerald. I am so happy to finally meet you in person," Carmen announces leaning in for a hug.

"We are very happy to be here, this is my first time in Louisiana," Gerald says with a smile.

"Oh Carmen, you are even more beautiful in person," Mom smiles and Carmen blushes just a bit.

Carmen walks over to James planting kisses on his face, probably making up for the ones she didn't give him at the barbeque.

"I am so happy everyone made it, this is my son Gio, Gio this is everybody. Let me get you the room keys and show you where everyone is staying," Carmen explains walking toward the front counter.

I never thought about room divisions, wonder who I'll be staying with. After getting the keycards Carmen pulls out a piece of paper with names.

Gerald-Norma
Brittany -Alex
Mason - Gio
James - Ben
Carmen -Maria - Layla

Who the hell is Maria? I guess we'll find out soon enough. We head to our rooms to drop off our luggage. This hotel has got to be expensive; I don't think I've ever stayed anywhere this nice. It almost reminds me of one of the upscale hotels in Vegas.

"So James, you're not staying with Carmen?" I ask a little confused.

"Not until after the wedding. Her parents booked us the luxury suite after the wedding so you'll have the room for yourself, if you know what I mean," he says winking at me.

Is he seriously thinking I'm going to pick up someone at the wedding? No thanks.

We head out to the pool area and meet up with everyone again. The pool has a bar right in the middle of it so you can just swim up to get your drinks.

"Okay so here's what I was thinking, "Carmen starts," We have to be at the church in about an hour for a quick rehearsal. For dinner I want to take you to the best seafood place in the city. Tomorrow during the day, we can walk around the city a bit since the rehearsal dinner isn't until six. Once we're finished we can go out and check out the nightlife."

Wow, I don't think she took one breath while relaying her agenda. I look over at Layla and see that Gio has made his way to her, I don't like that smug look on his face.

Carmen continues, "You'll meet my sister Maria tomorrow after the rehearsal dinner. She is in Baton Rouge for business but will be here Saturday evening." Okay, so Maria is Carmen's sister, I remember her saying she had a sister but her name escaped me.

It seems as if we we've been at that church for hours, Layla and Brittany look as if they were amused watching us being moved around into different positions by Carmen's mother. The wedding party isn't as big as I expected, James' side has Alex, Mason, Gio and I. Carmen has four bridesmaids, Mom volunteered to stand in for Maria while Gerald and Carmen's dad struck up a conversation. Once finished Carmen's parents invite Mom and Gerald over to their house to get to know each other.

After returning to the hotel, Brittany suggests we hang out at the pool and make use of the bar. I'm really glad that James had extra swim trunks because I forgot mine. James and I meet up with Alex, Brittany, Mason and Gio since we are on the same floor and make our way to the pool. Carmen and Layla saved us some lounge chairs so we throw our towels on them. I take off my shirt and place it over the top of the chair and put on my shades. The planted palm trees give off just enough shade to make it comfortable. Carmen comes running with sunscreen screeching, "Everyone, sunscreen is mandatory. I don't want you burnt on our wedding day. Here pass it around." She's definitely prepared.

Layla is sitting about two chairs away from me, she stands up to remove her shorts and tank top and I damn near loose it. She's wearing a blue and white bikini that is sexy as hell. She looks amazing and this is the first time I've really noticed her curves, to me she's flawless.

"Layla, where did you get that bikini?" Brittany asks moving her sunglasses down her nose.

"I actually ordered it online. I was so worried it wouldn't fit but I got lucky," Layla smiles.

I find myself looking her way every so often, she seems to be having a great time with Brittany and Alex. Getting up I decide to take a dip in the pool, doesn't take long for the others to follow. I swim up to the bar and sit on one of the stone stools, asking the bartender how we pay. He explains we just give him our name and room number and we will get a bill. Sounds good to me so I order an Old Fashioned.

"I would so love to work here," Layla says as she swims up next to me taking the open seat.

"Yeah, I thought you'd like this, what can I get you?" I ask smiling and quite relieved she can't see my eyes right now since they're not directed at her face.

Stunned she turns to me, "Wow, I'm usually the one asking that," she pauses, "hmm I'm going to change it up a bit and have a Long Island Iced Tea." Oh boy, five different types of liquor, this ought to be fun.

"How much do you think our rooms cost," Layla asks, stirring her drink with the straw.

"It's got to be expensive, I'm guessing at least $300 a night." Her eyes widen as she takes a sip of her tea.

"How's your drink?" I ask, chuckling a bit.

"Stronger than the ones I make, that's for sure," she giggles.

Dinner was awesome, Carmen wasn't joking when she said the food was excellent. I notice Gio trying to engage in conversation with Layla whenever he can, I think he is trying to get lucky. Layla isn't having it though, she's polite and friendly but she couldn't act less interested if she tried. Gio is a really good-looking guy and close to her age, he almost reminds me a little bit of Layne.

Back in the room, James and I are relaxing on our beds flipping through channels. "Two more days Ben," James sighs, "Two more days and I'm married."

"Well, I'm sure you're excited for what happens after the reception," I snicker, "Not sure how you were able to hold out, Bro."

"God, don't remind me. It was so tough; there were a few nights where I seriously thought I was going to die in agony. Now I have performance anxiety, "he laughs.

"You should," I joke and he shakes his head laughing, "Nah Bro, you'll be fine. Probably won't last long but that's to be expected."

"Ben, you're such a smartass," James jokes, throwing the remote in my direction," but I wouldn't trade you for anything in the world."

I love these conversations with my brother. They remind me of when we were younger and always picking on each other. Sunday I get to stand next to him witnessing him marrying the woman he is crazy about.

Layla

My head is throbbing; I know it had to be that drink at the pool. Actually, it's probably from all of Gio's jibber jabber. I can tell he is trying to get in my pants, typical wedding cliché. I'm not the type for one night stands so he's barking up the wrong tree. Then again Layne and I started that way but we ended up dating. Now if it happened to be Ben, that would be a different story altogether.

"Hey Layla," Carmen taps me on the shoulder, "So what do you think of my son?" Shit what am I supposed to say, he acts like a douchebag and he's coming on way too strong probably wouldn't go over too well.

"He seems nice, what college does he go to again?" I ask, really not giving a shit.

"LSU in Baton Rouge, he has a full scholarship. I'm really proud of him, he's the only good thing that came out of my previous marriage," Carmen replies.

She never talks about her Ex-husband. James mentioned that he was ten years older than Carmen and died of a heart attack about five years ago. He was very wealthy and Carmen is pretty much set for life.

Carmen is on the phone talking to her sister, I can't wait to meet Maria. She's three years younger than Carmen and the two of them have always been close.

"Sorry Layla," Carmen apologizes for being on the phone, "Maria is so excited to meet all of you tomorrow. You're going to love her; she's a lot of fun."

"Is she going to make it to the rehearsal dinner?" I ask even though I won't be attending.

"Not sure yet, she'll definitely be going out with us after. Are you sure you don't want me to ask my dad to add you and Brittany?" Carmen asks feeling guilty.

"Nah, we're good, we'll go out to eat somewhere. This way the families can get to know each other a little better. We really don't mind," I answer, fibbing just a little bit.

Even though I would love to go I'm looking forward to spending some one on one time with Brittany. We've actually been getting along really well and it's nice to have another girl to talk to once in a while.

I look over and notice Carmen is already knocked out, you can tell she has been stressing all day. I'm tired but unable to fall asleep so I pick up my phone and play a game. Right in the middle I get a notification, a message from Ben. Excited I open it and it reads *What are you girls up to? James is out cold.* Suppose he can't sleep either so I tell him Carmen's asleep and I'm playing a game. I don't get a reply so I decide to continue playing.

About ten minutes later I get another message *Want to meet me by the pool in 10?* Reading that brings a smile to my face and I agree. I jump out of bed and head to the bathroom remove the bun from top of my head and slip into my shorts and tank from earlier.

Quietly shutting the door behind me I walk down the long hallway to the elevator, wondering why we aren't on the same floor as the others. As I walk through the door to the pool area I see Ben coming from the other direction. It's really dark outside but the area is lit up with strands of lights decorating the palms. For it being so late I'm surprised to find a good amount of people hanging around.

"You couldn't sleep either?" I ask as I sit on one of the lounge chairs.

He shakes his head as he sits down in the chair next to me. Before I can say anything else a waiter comes up to us and asks if he can get us something to drink. I'm tempted but with my headache almost gone I figure it's best not to. Ben ends up ordering two waters.

"So, what's the game plan tomorrow?" Ben asks with a hint of humor in his voice.

"Oh, since she's my roommate I'm supposed to know everything? I see how it is," I say sarcastically, "Just kidding. I think after breakfast she wants to do a little tour of the French quarter, then the rehearsal dinner and then clubbing."

"Clubbing? Seriously?" he asks baffled.

"Maybe more like barhopping, you know bachelor and bachelorette stuff," I reply rolling my eyes.

"We are all going out together, right?"

"I think so. At least that's what it sounded like when Carmen and Maria were on the phone. After the dinner you guys will come back to the hot-"

He interrupts, "Wait, what do you mean you guys? Where are you going to be?"

"Brittany and I aren't going to the rehearsal dinner, it's a family event so the two of us are getting dinner somewhere else," I respond. Ben leans back in his chair, "Well that totally blows," he pauses, "I'm glad I messaged you then."

I turn to him "What do you mean?"

"Well, we get to spend some time together now. You know the rest of the time it's going to be crazy, weddings are not enjoyable."

"Oh yeah? Was yours crazy?" I ask catching him off-guard. He's pretty closed up when it comes to anything personal from the past.

"They all are. Hey look," he says pointing up in the sky, "lots of stars, I bet we can find a constellation tonight." That was pretty smooth, totally avoiding my question but I decide to just let it go, I suppose it's touchy subject for him. Taking my phone out of my pocket I pull up the constellation map since it was really helpful last time. I'm stunned that I actually found one, Scorpius, I point it out to Ben.

"Wow, that's so cool," Ben pauses," You know, Scorpio is my zodiac sign."

"Really? When's your birthday?" I ask.

"November 4th. I know yours is in February but I don't remember the date."

"February 12th. Don't worry, my parents forgot it one year," I chuckle.

"You know, can't say I'm surprised," he says raising his eyebrows.

We lie around and talk for a while, the pool area has cleared out and we are the only ones left. I check the time and it's 1 am so we decide it may be a good idea to get some sleep. He walks me back to my room and we say goodnight.

Morning came way too quickly and Carmen is up bright eyed and bushytailed at 6 am. She's ready to conquer the day, dragging me downstairs to breakfast. Thank god my make-up still looks good from the night before.

After breakfast Carmen is ready to go, "Alright everyone, go shower and get ready and we'll meet in the lobby in an hour so I can show you my New Orleans."

She's dragged us from the Mardi Gras museum to the Lalaurie Mansion with various other stops in between. I'm really happy to have her as a guide though, she is like a book of knowledge, and you can tell she really loves this city. It's really easy to fall in love it's beautiful, I could spend all day just walking around. Norma, Gerald and Mason are walking together, it's really cute seeing Mason with his arm around Norma. Brittany and Alex are stopping every twenty feet to take selfies and Ben and James are following right behind Carmen, taking pictures with their phones. Gio hasn't left my side, acting as my personal tour guide. I just want to tell him that it's not going to happen and to just save his energy for someone else.

When we arrive back at the hotel Carmen is getting dressed for the dinner. There's a knock at the door and I answer. It's a tall skinny blonde woman with way too much eye make-up. I ask if I can help her and Carmen comes to the door, it's Maria. Wow, I did not picture her like this at all.

"Maria, this is Layla. Layla, Maria," Carmen introduces us.

"Carmen has told me so much about you, it's nice to finally meet you," Maria pauses and turns to Carmen, "My flight literally just got in and I just ran home to swap bags, I'm glad I'm going to make it to dinner. I know Mom and Dad were freaking out."

She comes in and plops her things on my bed. Her mouth is going a mile a minute and all I am thinking is where is she going to sleep? I know the three of us are sharing the room tonight and there are two queen sized beds. Minutes later Carmen tells Maria that the bed she threw her things on is mine and that they will be sharing the other bed. Kind of weird but okay, as long as it's not with me.

Carmen's phone rings, she answers and says it's James but he's asking for me. I wonder why he didn't just call my phone, quickly picking it up off the bed I notice it's on silent. I grab the phone from Carmen and sit down.

"James?" I answer curiously.

"Layla, quick question. Did you happen to bring your little sewing kit? The button on Ben's vest came off."

I always have a small sewing kit in my purse, something I learned from Norma. She made most of our costumes back when we performed and always had a kit with her in case of an emergency. Hers was much bigger, but I have all the necessities. I kind of wonder why they didn't call her, maybe they did and she doesn't have one with her. I tell James I will be right over.

Ben answers the door "Oh my god, you're a life saver. Thank you so much." I sit on the bed and sew the button back on, it takes me less than a minute.

"All right, all done," I say handing the vest back to Ben.

"I totally owe you," Ben grins placing the vest on a hanger.

"Hmm, I think saving me a dance at the wedding should suffice," I say with a hopeful smile.

"You know I don't dance, you don't give up do you?" he smirks.

"I know," I pause, "thought I'd try."

"Hey how about I take you to breakfast tomorrow?" Ben suggests.

James starts laughing "Good one, breakfast is included in our stay." Ben gives him an *'are you serious'* kind of look.

"Yeah, I know that. No, I'll take her out, there are a lot of cool café's near the hotel." Before James can say anything else I agree.

Brittany and I decide to eat at a Mexican restaurant right next to the hotel, the food is delicious. After finishing our dinner, we sit and talk for a while. Brittany asks what I thought of Maria since she only got a glimpse of her. I tell her that I think she's very talkative but something about her makes me think she could be quite a bitch.

"So, do you think you and Layne are ever going to get back together?" Brittany asks. Wow, that came out of nowhere.

"Umm, no. I don't think so Brit," I say giving her a look like she's lost her mind.

"You haven't dated anyone since Layne so I was just wondering if you two would maybe rekindle what you had."

"That's the thing, we didn't really have anything substantial, that's why it didn't work out," I explain.

"Well, you're young and you should have fun. What about Gio? He looks like he would love to get to know you better," she snickers. I just roll my eyes and shake my head, at least Gio gives us a good laugh.

Back in the room I'm finishing up getting ready for tonight. I'm wearing black skinny jeans with heels and a dark blue sheer flowy top with a black camisole underneath. I decide to add a few loose waves to my hair for a different look.

A few minutes later Carmen and Maria come in the door and Maria gives me a look over. "Oh, Layla, you look nice," she says not sounding very genuine. I can already tell we aren't going to be friends. As they finish getting ready I get a text from Ben saying they are down in the lobby. Carmen is dressed in a white lacey short dress wearing a sash with *BRIDE* written across. Maria is wearing a white pencil skirt with a black crop top, her breasts practically hanging out. You can tell they have been surgically enhanced, she should have maybe considered going down a cup size or two.

As soon as we make it to the lobby Maria runs over to James draping a *GROOM* sash over him and winking at Ben. I just brush it off, Ben would never go for someone like that anyway. Bourbon Street is only about two blocks away so we go on foot. Everything seems to be in walking distance, you really don't need a car here. We start out at a Jazz club which is totally not my thing, that type of music puts me to sleep. Thank god it's too crowded so we don't stay long. We stop at some really cool looking bars along the way and have a few drinks. Some random people keep paying for Carmen and James' drinks; I guess the sashes were a good idea. I notice every time Ben either sits near me or talks to me Maria finagles her way in, the more alcohol I consume the more annoyed I get.

At one point Brittany comes up to Ben and me, "Looks like someone is looking for a hook up, Ben," Brittany says discreetly pointing in Maria's direction, "she's practically throwing herself at you."

Oh my god I feel like I am going to be sick.

"Hell no, not interested," he replies laughing and my heart is happy again.

Our last stop is a nightclub; the music is more upbeat and hip. As soon as you walk in you can see the massive dancefloor which is packed, this must be the place to be. Carmen gets us a spot in the VIP area and orders a round of shots. A few minutes later Carmen grabs James' arm and is ready to dance. This ought to be interesting; I've never seen him dance to hip-hop before. Brittany begs Alex to take her out on the dancefloor, but everyone knows he doesn't do fast songs. Instead Gio volunteers and Brittany takes him up on it.

"Ben! Come dance with me," Maria jumps up and playfully tries to grab Ben's hand. He declines just as I figured he would, pulling his hand back. Mason takes the opportunity to offer himself to dance with her, she's hesitant but agrees. Alex heads to the bar to get us some more drinks; probably wants to check on Brittany on the way there. Ben looks over at me, "Do you think Maria is high?" he asks shaking his head and I start laughing.

"You look really nice tonight," Ben says leaning in. I wasn't sure about my outfit when I put it on, especially after seeing Carmen and Maria in their dresses. I do feel pretty though, it's very different from my usual look.

"Thank you, Ben. You're looking quite handsome yourself."

"I do what I can!" he jokes. I guess we are both out of our comfort zone when it comes to our clothes.

"How do you like New Orleans?" He asks getting a little closer since it's so loud.

"I've fallen in love; the European influence, street musicians, the art, it's just amazing. I've always wanted to come here but when we traveled around we never stopped here. Then life happens and you forget. When I heard Carmen was from here I was stoked."

"This was actually my first stop after leaving home," Ben explains, "I lived here for a bit with a friend. His parents used to work for a carnival that we paired up with once in a while. I was really lucky to have him and his family."

Another small tidbit from his past, little by little I will get everything out of him. He seems quite relaxed leaning against the back of the sofa. We joke about James dance moves for a bit until we are interrupted by everyone coming back to our area. Alex supplies us with a round of Jell-O shots. Gio asks me to dance and I politely decline.

"Layla, you love to dance," Mason turns to Gio, "Gio, Layla and I used to dance together in our show. I'm really surprised she's not jumping at the opportunity." Leave it to Mason to always throw me under the bus.

"You know Mason," I start, "I think after all these shots I'm lacking coordination." He rolls his eyes, throwing his head back.

"Well, Mason is an excellent dancer. I had a great time. Save me a dance at the reception," Maria declares flirtatiously playing with her hair. Hell, maybe she wants Mason, he'll go for it. We end up staying out until 3 am, James has had one too many, leaning on Ben and Gio while walking back to the hotel.

In the lobby, James and Carmen exchange a very long, passionate kiss and tell each other goodnight. She says the next time he will see her will be at the altar.

Ben walks over to me, "Hey so how about I pick you up at 9 am, sound good?" I tell him I will be ready, before he can say anything else, James hugs him blabbing something about brotherhood.

As soon as Carmen, Maria and I get to our room the interrogation begins. "So, what's going on tomorrow morning? Are you and Ben going somewhere?" Carmen asks.

"Yeah, we are going to breakfast."

Maria butts in "Oh how about we all join you, it will be fun." I can't believe she just suggested that, so rude.

"I can't," Carmen sighs, "I really didn't want to see James before the wedding." They babble a little more back and forth until I interrupt. "We aren't having breakfast at the hotel, it's just Ben and I and we are going out." They both look at me like I have three heads but I just leave it at that, it's none of their business anyway.

As I was getting ready I can feel Maria's eyes on me but it doesn't bother me one bit. At 9 am Ben knocks at the door. "Good Morning, you ready?" he asks. I nod and quickly shut the door behind me. I tell him we need to get out of here quick before Maria tries to tag along. He smiles, shaking his head and picks up the pace.

We walk a few blocks before we get to a cute little café situated right on Decatur Street. There is a little breeze so we can actually sit outside. The waiter comes up and asks what we would like to drink. Ben orders a cappuccino and I decide on an orange juice.

"Really? No coffee? We're at an authentic French café and you order orange juice?" Ben asks surprised. I bite my lip looking at him and I figure right now may be a good time for me to confess.

"I need to tell you something," I hesitate for a moment, knowing I will look like a dumbass, "I hate coffee. You're going to think I'm crazy but remember the day after you got home and I was in the pantry?" He nods, with a cool grin.

"Well when your bedroom door opened I was startled and just grabbed the first thing I could find, which to my demise was coffee. Not wanting to look like an idiot I decided to make it look like I was getting it for myself. Basically looking like an idiot now." There, I said it, I'm embarrassed but also relieved.

"Ha, I totally knew it," Ben chuckles and I give him a confused look, "I knew you weren't a coffee drinker, it was so obvious. I just wanted to see when you'd actually own up to it."

"Well, that's great. So, you were playing a game with me while I was in agony. That's alright, I'll get you back for that," I laugh.

"I doubt it, remember being thrown into the lake?" he says grinning with one raised eyebrow. God yes I do, that moment hasn't left my mind, I've had dreams about it. Only thing is in my dreams things usually went a bit further.

After breakfast, we walk a bit further and find a beautiful park in front of a large church, I noticed it yesterday but it wasn't one of Carmen's stops.

"This is Jackson square and that church there is the St. Louis cathedral," Ben says pointing at the church. It's breathtaking, there are merchants everywhere selling a variety of things, dogs running around and people on blankets enjoying the beautiful weather.

"Hey Ben, let's take a picture with the cathedral in the background." I position my phone so we are both in the shot. A young woman comes up to us with her dog and asks if we would like for her to take our picture to get the whole background. For a moment I ponder not wanting to hand my phone to a total stranger but end up agreeing. We stand together and he puts his arm around me, cocking his head to the side touching mine. My arm automatically finds his waist and I smile for the camera. I get a little excited since this is our first picture together; I thank the woman while Ben plays with her dog. After she leaves we peek at the picture, it came out great!

"Layla, you'll have to send it to me." His phone chimes and I tell him I already did.

Walking out of the square a man approaches us about taking a mule drawn carriage ride. "Hey, I have two spots left. Come on what do you say, you'll learn all about the city."

I look at Ben and he's a bit hesitant but agrees. There are two vacant seats left in the back of the carriage. Our guide is so funny and entertaining. Even though Carmen showed us great places yesterday, there were so many things that she just passed by.

After the tour ends we figure it may be time to go back to the hotel. There is a small shop that catches my eye and Ben looks over at it. "Oh, a voodoo shop," he says in a spooky voice.

"Can we go in?" I ask, curiosity written all over my face. He gives me a *'you can't be serious'* expression but opens the door for me to go in. I have never seen anything like this, it's amazing, all these little trinkets and potions. A woman comes up to us with that typical Caribbean accent and offers us different potions. I end up buying us matching keychains with the symbol of Damballa on it; the woman said he was one of the most important spirits also known as the sky father and creator of life. Not knowing anything about it I take her word for it.

Chapter Seven

Layla

In the room the stress level has reached an all-time high. Carmen says her parents should be arriving within thirty minutes and the make-up and hair crew are on their way as well. Figuring this may be a good time to get cleaned up I jump in the shower. Carmen offers that I have my hair and make-up done professionally and I take her up on it. It's really nice of her to include me even though I'm just a guest.

Carmen's mother is having her hair put up and her father is on the phone. The make-up artist asks me to sit in the chair so she can start. The next time I look into the mirror I don't recognize myself, the makeup is perfect. The gold really brings out my blue eyes, I tell myself I need to buy gold eyeshadow when I get back home. For my hair, they just end up curling and braiding it in a loose braid down my right side, few strands pulled out on the left to balance it out. I change into my dress and take a look at myself. Overall, I'm happy but I've already decided that the braid may have to go after the ceremony.

Carmen is slipping into her dress; she is gorgeous, wearing a classic ball gown with a corset waist. James is going to be at a loss for words. The bridesmaid's dresses are grey to match the groomsmen's shirts. Our room is filled with so many people that it's become a challenge to move around. Getting word that James is at the church, Carmen's father leads with an Italian prayer before we head out.

I walk into the church and the pews on both sides are packed. I stand there and take it all in for a moment before making my way down the aisle staring at Ben, he looks smooth in that tux. Carmen's idea of the groomsmen not wearing the jackets is actually great, it makes the groom stand out. James is looking very nervous; Ben seems to be talking him through it though. They haven't noticed me come in and I quickly slip into one of the rows. I have no clue who I am sitting next to, it's an older couple with friendly smiles on their faces. The music starts to play and the bridesmaids are walking down the aisle, one by one until Carmen appears with her father. The music changes and they make their way to James. I glance over at him and his eyes are tearing up. The ceremony was absolutely beautiful. When their shared their 'First Kiss' everyone cheered and applauded. I find Norma and Gerald, they are sitting next to Carmen's parents in the front row. Both mothers are drying their eyes with handkerchiefs. I decide to head back to the hotel for the reception, knowing the wedding party and family are planning on taking pictures it will be a while before I see them. I find Brittany and we get into one of the limousines provided to take guests to the hotel.

On the way to the grand ballroom we pass a beautiful courtyard with a fountain in the middle. "Heck, I would have chosen to get married here," I whisper to Brittany.

"Me too, this is gorgeous with all the trees. I hope we are sitting at the same table Layla, it's weird that everyone we know will be at the head table," Brittany remarks.

As we walk through the French doors we find a completely transformed ballroom. The lighting is dim and the tables are lined with white table cloths and grey runners. The centerpieces are different sized candles with shimmering stones and pink rose petals around them. Enlarged pictures of James and Carmen are displayed on tall metal easels perfectly placed around the room. The dancefloor is a nice size right in the middle of the room. The head table is a typical long table with the same centerpieces scattered around. One thing you can't overlook are the massive chairs designed for the Bride and Groom at the head table, they look like thrones. Looking over to the right I spot the DJ, he's a younger guy so I'm guessing the music should be good.

We take a look at the board with the seating arrangements, Brittany and I are sitting together.

Within an hour, the room is packed. Most people have found their seats, others are still mingling and having cocktails. The doors open and I see Ben, Mason, Alex, Norma and Gerald walking in. Brittany jumps up to greet Alex and I walk over with her. I've never seen Brittany this crazy about Alex, it's really sweet to watch. As we walk toward them, Ben focuses in on me with that gorgeous smile.

"Layla, you look beautiful," Ben claims and I start to blush, "Were you at the church? I didn't see you."

"I was sitting pretty far back that's probably why you didn't notice," I say, my cheeks still burning. Norma gives us a little smile, her eyes moving back and forth between Ben and me. For a moment I feel a little uncomfortable. Norma is a smart woman, she can probably tell I'm totally crushing on her son.

"This place is gorgeous," Norma starts and I'm relieved she's changed the subject, "Gerald and I peeked in here yesterday and I would have never recognized it."

Suddenly we hear tapping on the microphone else, DJ comes on and asks everyone to go to their seats. "And now if I could please direct your attention to the entrance way. Being introduced for the first time as husband and wife, please give them a nice standing ovation and make some noise for the new Mr. and Mrs. James Parker!"

James and Carmen come walking through the door, the crowd is going nuts. The DJ announces that they will now share their first dance. Watching them makes me tear up a bit and Ben glances my way bumping my shoulder. Even though James and Carmen are surrounded by 200 people they seem as if they are in their own little world. When the music changes Carmen's father cuts in for the traditional father/daughter dance and James dances with his mom

Once everyone returns to their seats it's time for introductions and toasts. This has always been my least favorite part of weddings. Maria's toast was very, very long and in typical Maria fashion, she ends up mainly talking about herself.

Brittany and I get to know the guests at our table a little better over dinner. Two of the men are husbands of the bridesmaids and the others are Carmen's cousins. Everyone is making use of the open bar; I would say a quarter of the guests are drunk by the time dinner was over. Next the cake is wheeled out to the middle of the dancefloor to be cut and served. Like everything else, it's stunning, white, four tiers with grey trim and pink roses on top.

Once the servers clear all the dishes from the tables the DJ starts the music and people gravitate to the dancefloor. Knowing I won't see Ben there I look over at his table and am met by his glance. Our connection is interrupted by none other than Maria planting herself next to him. I decide to mingle with some of the other guests for a distraction. James walks up and asks me to dance, I don't think I've ever danced with him before. While dancing, he blabs on about how thankful he is to have me and how good I am to them; clearly, he's had a few.

Once the song ends I walk back over to my table and see Maria is still in action, she's positioned herself very close to Ben, her arm draped over the back of his chair. His eyes find mine again and he looks really uncomfortable. I decide to walk over, "Excuse me, I'm sorry to interrupt but can I borrow Ben for just a few moments, thank you." I don't even give her a chance to reply, I grab his hand and he follows me out to the courtyard.

"Oh my god, thank you so much. I didn't know how to get out of that one," he says laughing.

"No problem, you looked like you were in pain," I pause, opening my braid and releasing my hair, "Are you having a good time?"

"Yeah, I am. How about you?" he asks leaning against a tree.

"I'm having fun. I think it turned out just the way Carmen wanted. Sure is a lot to take in, luxury everywhere. Not really what I would want but still it's beautiful."

"Really? So how do you envision your wedding?" Ben asks curiously. I wasn't expecting that question but it's an easy answer.

"Okay, my dream wedding would be outdoors with just me, the man I'm marrying and close friends and family, so basically your family since mine sucks."

He smiles, "You're kidding right? So you're telling me you don't want all the frills, just something simple?"

"Yep. I mean this wedding is really nice and all but I think a wedding is something intimate between two people who are in love. They are making a decision to essentially become one and walk their path together. You don't need two hundred people to witness that," I continue.

"Wow, you're like every guys dream," Ben pauses and gets down on one knee, "Layla, will you marry me?" We crack up laughing and he gets up, he must have had a few shots of something to get this silly.

"I saw you getting a bit emotional while they had their first dance, noticed a tear or two," Ben says.

"People cry at weddings," I remark, "I was caught up in the moment, they looked so in love, it was beautiful."

"Yeah, I agree. They are a great match. You want to head back inside to check out the scene?" Ben asks.

"Sure, maybe Maria has found a new victim," I joke.

After grabbing some water, we head to a table where Alex and Brittany are sitting. There are a few seats open so we decide to join them. Mason comes walking up from out of nowhere,

"Layla, come on dance with me, for old times' sake." I shake my head but he keeps insisting.

Alex butts in, "Oh come on Layla, just do it." I cave and let Mason lead me to the floor. It's a slow song so I'm relaxed, Mason can get pretty animated when dancing and I want no part of that. On the dancefloor, I see Gio's attention has turned to a girl that's quite smitten with him.

It's getting late, Carmen and James decide it's time to turn in and on their way out they do the bouquet and garter toss. Some guests start to leave but the DJ is still pumping music while others are dancing. Norma and Gerald stop by our table to tell us goodnight. A little while later Brittany says she's getting tired so Alex gets up and they head out leaving me and Ben at the table. I have no idea where Mason has disappeared to. I realized I also haven't seen Maria around for a while; maybe the two of them are having their own party somewhere. As the next song starts to play, Ben gets up and grabs my hand, I guess he wants to leave too.

"Dance with me Layla," he says, I can't believe what I'm hearing.

"What? Are you serious?" I ask, on the verge of dying of excitement. He doesn't respond and just leads me to the floor. Taking my hand in his and placing the other on my lower back I feel a tingle run down my spine. Draping my other hand around the back of his neck I notice his eyes smiling back at me.

"I love this song," I sigh, playing with the collar of his shirt.

"Oh yeah?" he pauses, "I know I've heard it before but I don't remember what it's called."

"It's *'MAKE YOU FEEL MY LOVE'*. I used to have this on repeat in my car for months," I giggle.

I look deep into his eyes and see everything I have ever wanted; my world will never be the same again. For these three and a half minutes I feel as if it's just the two of us and he belongs to me. The song ends and I don't want to let go but it would be awkward not to.

"Thank you so much," I smile, "You just made my night."

"Anytime," Ben grins.

The DJ announces last call for drinks and Ben and I decide that one more can't hurt so we decide on a shot of tequila.

The party has come to an end, most people are already gone. We walk out through the French doors, back into the courtyard. I thought it was gorgeous before but seeing it at night leaves me speechless. The fountain looks like it's glowing in the moonlight and the trees are decorated with lights. Ben sits on the rim of the fountain and signals me to come over. I sit down and lean against him laying my head on his shoulder. He lets out a snort and I start to giggle.

"My god Layla, look at what you do to me. Taking rides in horse drawn carriages, voodoo shop, dancing, I don't recognize myself."

I sit up, my speech may be just a bit slurred, "Whoa, whoa, whoa. Just wait one minute there buddy. First of all, they're not horses, they're mules. Also, I recall you asking me to dance I didn't force you. Not sure why you don't dance because you're amazing." I pause, "By the way, you totally owe me for saving you from Carmen's crazy sister. I'm surprised she didn't tear off your clothes and throw you on the table."

"Do I sense a little jealousy?" he asks with a surprised expression and my cheeks start to burn, "I'm just kidding. You're an awesome wingman. That was much appreciated, I needed the save." He gives me that eyes sideways glace with the right side of his mouth curled up.

"Hey Ben, let's take a picture together, I love this fountain." Taking my phone out of my bag I hold it in position and he presses his head against mine. I decide to go with the famous kissy face and I think that's how I got that big smile out of him. He shakes his head, "You're something else. Come on, I'll walk you to your room."

We have about fifteen more feet to go. Wow that last shot really did me in. I brace myself on him so I don't stumble all over. I get to the door and turn to him, "I'm so happy you're here. I've had the best time. Seriously, thank you."

I throw my arms around him and give him a big squeeze; I can't get over how good he smells. He holds me tight and I feel his breath on the back of my neck. Pulling away and taking one last look at him, I recognize that glare he is giving me.

"Layla," he whispers. Before I can say a word his hands grab my wrists, pins me against the wall and his lips are pressed to mine. His kiss is hungry, dominant but unsure at the same time. He frees me and his hands start to explore my body. I feel the slightest touch of his tongue and I welcome it. I grip the back of his neck, fingers entangled in his hair. Moving his tongue down to my neck we are suddenly interrupted by the elevator ding. Ben releases me and jumps back with panic written all over his face. Before I can say anything he starts apologizing, he looks very worried. The high I am feeling is rapidly dropping, I'm devastated. Did he really not mean to kiss me? He looks apprehensive so I try to ease his conscience, "Hey, don't worry about it. We both had a lot to drink tonight. It's not a big deal at all." He takes a deep breath and looks as if a weight has been lifted.

Ben

Swiping the key card, I rush inside and slam the door behind me. I am so relieved that I have this room to myself tonight. There's no way I could face anyone right now. Standing with my back against the door I can feel my heart pounding, still trying to comprehend what just happened. We've gotten to be so close and now I fucked it up. This would have never happened if she hadn't hugged me; it drove me over the edge. Who am I kidding? I've wanted to kiss her for a while and it was hot. She encouraged it, even started taking control. The way her fingers were grasping my hair, I could have exploded right there. The elevator interrupting us was a godsend. Brought me back to my senses really quick, I know exactly what would have happened if we got past that door. Then I remember that she's sharing the room with Maria. Oh my god if anyone had seen us, what the hell would we have done?

I get up, leaving a trail of clothes on the floor as I walk to the shower. This is exactly what I need right now. I just stand there, water rolling down my back, hands stretched out, palms facing the wall supporting my weight. Goddamn it, I can't get her out of my head. That dress accentuated every single curve on her body, the lacey part above her breasts was such a tease but classy at the same time. My grin suddenly fades, maybe she didn't intend for any of this to happen. She did mention that we had too much to drink and just played it off like it was nothing. Hell, she may be sitting in her room right now regretting it. I just hope things won't be awkward.

My alarm goes off and I'm exhausted. Our cab will be here in about an hour to take us to the airport. Deciding to skip breakfast I just lie on my bed staring at the ceiling for a while, thoughts running through my head. My phone starts to ring and I search for it finally finding it in my pants on the floor. It's James and he's said he just wanted to go over a few things for the time he won't be at the shop. He also asks me to keep an eye on everyone. I get up, get dressed and quickly throw everything into my bag. A few minutes later there is a knock at my door. I answer and find a cheery Layla standing in front of me.

Layla

It took everything I had to get up this morning. It was a rough night and I woke up with a splitting headache. I think I stood in the shower for thirty minutes last night crying and now my eyes are puffy. Putting on make-up, I successfully disguise the redness under my eyes. Maria notices that I'm not in great shape this morning and asks if I need an aspirin. Deciding to take her up on her offer I feel like an ass for thinking so negative of her. After getting dressed I grab my things and tell Maria goodbye. Everyone except for Ben is ready to go sitting in the lobby.

"Where's Ben? I thought he'd be with you," Alex asks. Oh my god, did he see us last night? His room was on a different floor so there's no reason he would have been on mine.

I decide to act cool, "Don't know. I don't keep tabs on him."

"Well, you guys just hang out a lot so I figured you may have had breakfast together."

I look at my phone; the taxi will be here any minute. I decide to be brave, put a smile on my face and go check on him. I get to his room and take a deep breath before knocking on the door. I'd rather face him alone after what happened last night. Ben opens the door and looks surprised.

He turns around and grabs his bag and I do my best to be upbeat and happy as we walk toward the lobby. On the way to the airport Norma is doing most of the talking which is a huge relief to me. Right now I feel as though I can't get two words together.

I fall asleep on the plane. The flight is short but lack of sleep finally caught up with me. Of course, this time around our seats are together with the exception of Norma and Gerald's seats being in first class again. I recall our flight to New Orleans and Ben getting me through it. As soon as we make it to the runway my anxiety returns but I don't dare grab Ben's hand. I'm not sure where we stand and there's no way I could handle rejection right now.

Back home, Brittany decides to spend the night and calls the local pizza place to have dinner delivered. She ordered way too much food. We lounge in the living room, pizza and wing boxes all over the table. James would kill us if he knew this was going on since he's very particular about this couch. The conversation is very light, filled with memories of the weekend. I am pleasantly surprised how easy the interaction is between Ben and me, as if nothing ever happened. He even jokes about being out on the dancefloor with me. I start to wonder if maybe I made it up. No, it happened. I know I was tipsy but the kiss was real.

Mason pulls me out of my thoughts, "Hey I actually have a pic of that." He hands me the phone and Ben leans in to take a peek, I remember that moment so clear.

"That's a pretty damn good picture," Ben jokes looking at me, "I mean for someone that doesn't dance, I think we made a great team." He never fails to make me smile so I decide to put that night behind me and appreciate what I do have with him.

James and Carmen won't be back until later in the week so we get to spend the next few days with Norma and Gerald. It's so much fun having them here, Norma has taken over the cooking and makes the guy's favorite childhood meals. Everything Norma cooks is delicious, Gerald acts as her sous chef and it's so sweet to watch. Before Paul died she was always very quiet, stayed out of things and was unhappy. With Gerald she's completely come out of her shell, is funny and carefree, I am so happy she found him, just wish they lived closer.

"Layla, would you like to take a walk with us?" Norma asks as Gerald grabs a bottle of water.

"Sure, sounds good," I say and we walk out of the door. Mason and Ben are outside working on a car sweating profusely.

"Hey, where are you guys going?" Mason asks wiping his forehead.

"Just taking a walk, you guys want to join us?" I ask with a grin.

"Hell no," Ben chuckles, "Don't want to be outside in this heat any longer than I have to."

We don't take the usual path to the lake, instead we walk down the long bumpy driveway and turn at the end of the road.

"Layla, I just want to thank you for everything you do around here. I know it's not easy living with these guys," Norma laughs.

"You say that every time," I smile, "They really are not that difficult to live with. Yeah Mason and I pick on each other once in a while but it goes both ways. I am very lucky to have them."

"Ben seems to have adjusted very well," Gerald mentions.

"Yes, I'm sure that thanks to Layla as well," Norma turns toward me, "I know things have been rough for him in the past. He's hardened a bit, much quieter than I remember. He used to talk so much I would tell him his tongue would fall out. He seems to be really comfortable around you though, I talked to him when we first got here and he had nothing but wonderful things to say about you. I'm so glad you two became friends."

All I can do is try to smile while the image of him pinning me to the door flashes through my head. Screw what James would think, what the heck would Norma think, it's her son.

Chapter Eight

Layla

James and Carmen arrive back home on Thursday. Great timing, the moving truck filled with her things just pulled up to the house. Honestly, I wonder where everything is going to go. I literally only have time to say hello and I'm out the door heading to work. Norma and Gerald's flight leaves early in the morning so I already said my goodbyes, there's no way I'll be up at 430 am.

I haven't seen Layne, he was supposed to be at work on Tuesday but he ended up switching shifts. We've texted a little here and there but I haven't told him much about my weekend.

When I wake up the next day, I hear furniture being moved around. After getting myself together I go downstairs and see we no longer have a sectional and Carmen's furniture is in place. There's a ton of new artwork on the walls as well. Carmen is standing in the middle of the room directing James and Ben on where to place the sofa. Her phone rings and she steps out to take the call.

"Fuck, I'm getting too old for this, oh hey morning Layla" Ben says wiping his forehead.

"Good morning," I pause, "James, where did your couch go?"

"It's upstairs in pieces, I'm going to sell it but I had to get it out of the way for now," James replies sighing as if he lost his best friend. I remember when he bought it, he loves that thing.

"This furniture doesn't look comfortable at all," Ben points out taking a seat on the sofa. James just shakes his head laughing, saying it will be fine.

"Man she has you whipped," Ben jokes, "Probably her plan all along. Withholding until you're married and then get rid of your shit, good strategy. Smart woman, Layla you may want to take notes." I start to laugh, he's probably not that far off. Carmen comes back in and I ask about their honeymoon.

"It was like paradise," Carmen pauses for a minute, "so beautiful and peaceful. We went horseback riding on the beach, did a couples massage, dinner on a private boat, the perfect getaway."

"Did you see the pigs?" Ben asks and I give him a confused look. He explains, "There's an island where you can swim with wild pigs, it's really neat."

"No, we didn't make it there, we will next time though," James says.

The rest of the day is spent moving things from one room to another to find the perfect place. Carmen is a little more high-strung than I thought. Ben has seen enough and decides to go work in the shop. It's time for me to go to work and as I get into my car Ben walks up.

"I can't believe you're seriously going to leave me here with these two crazies. It's like an *'I LOVE LUCY'* episode," he chuckles.

"Well, I've never seen that show so I'm not sure what you're talking about," I reply shrugging my shoulders.

"Really Layla? You've never seen *LUCY*? Oh, that's right, I forgot that you're like ten," he jokes.

"Really? That's just so wrong," I laugh closing my car door, smiling he waves goodbye.

"I've been having Layla withdrawals, come here, give me a hug," Layne grabs me as soon as I get behind the bar, "It's been so boring without you. So how was New Orleans?"

"It was amazing," I start, "you'd love it there, the people, the music and my god the hotel was like a resort. They had one of those swim up bars at the pool."

"Did you take pictures?" he asks while filling a glass with ice.

"I did, give me a minute and I'll show you," I say opening two beer bottles. Once the bar area clears out a bit I take my phone out of my bag under the bar and start showing off the pictures.

"Oh wow, now I want to go there. Must be a dream working that bar, I mean all the women you're serving are barely dressed, "Layne laughs, of course that would be the first thing on his mind. I haven't looked at these pictures since I got back so it's nice to scroll through them.

"Looks like you and Ben spent a little time together," he grabs my phone and keeps looking through them. "Whoa, looks like he lost his inhibition in this one." I yank the phone out of his hand to see which picture he's talking about, it's the one at the fountain after the reception. So far I've done really well putting what happened that night behind me, this just brings it all back. Debating if I should just delete it I end up just throwing my phone back in my bag, I'm not ready to get rid of it.

Layne catches me up on what I've missed while being away but I'm only hearing about half of it, my thoughts are somewhere else.

"Earth to Layla! Are you still with me?" Layne asks waving his hand in front of my face.

"Yeah of course, you were talking about a girl you met here on Monday," I reply, at least that's the last thing I remember hearing.

"Nope," he smirks shaking his head, "I just asked you if you wanted to sneak into Randy's office to have sex on his desk and you just smiled and nodded. That's how I know you weren't listening. What's on your mind?"

Oh my god, how embarrassing. I tell him I don't want to talk about it and he keeps pushing me. Eventually he gives up and says if I change my mind he's there anytime. Deciding I need a distraction I volunteer for karaoke, one of us usually acts as the icebreaker to get people to find their courage to go up.

It only takes Carmen about two days to transform the house. The sectional has been sold and the extra bedroom is set up as another guest room. Carmen's old bed has a padded frame and headboard, grey in color. The walls are covered with art work from New Orleans. I love what she did to the room and figure I may ask for help to spruce mine up at some point. She's also taken over the kitchen but the cleaning is something she left to me.

At dinner James informs us that he and Carmen are planning a trip to Atlanta next weekend to see a Broadway show. Ben can't keep the smirk off his face so he uses his napkin to cover his mouth. I know exactly what he's thinking, James and Broadway? That goes together like nails on a chalkboard, must have been Carmen's idea. They invite all of us to come along but the only one interested is Alex, mentioning he will have to check with Brittany.

Friday comes around fast and Randy originally planned on line dance lessons but invited a band to play instead. He also informed us that from 8 pm to 10 pm it will be *'Dollar Drink Night'* so he asks Josh to come in and help us with the crowd. I'm really glad that he is here because it's been nonstop and we've got about ten more minutes to go before the cutoff.

"Hey Layla, busy night," Mason yells over the crowd.

"Mason? When did you get here?" I ask opening three more beer bottles.

"Just now," he says and I notice Ben squeezing his way through the crowd to get to the bar.

"It's just the two of you tonight?" I ask looking around for James and Carmen.

"Yep," Ben starts, "I guess everyone else wanted to get some sleep since they are getting up early for Atlanta tomorrow. The show isn't until 2pm but they wanted to have lunch before. Oh, Alex and Brittany decided to go too."

"Well is there anything you guys want to do tomorrow since it's just the three of us?" I ask, hoping someone has an idea.

"Just you two," Mason corrects me, "I made plans with some friends, sorry."

I just stand there not knowing what to say, I'm not ready to spend the day alone with Ben. If this was before New Orleans I would have been crazy about the idea but my emotions are getting the better of me right now. I look at Ben and he's staring at me, almost as if he's trying to gage my reaction.

"Hey guys! What's up?" Layne comes up just at the right time, "So I heard New Orleans was a blast, saw some pictures. I think I need to take a trip there sometime." Mason and Layne usually don't have much to say to each other but tonight they are talking like old pals.

"You doing okay?" Ben asks, studying my every move.

"Me? Yeah of course, I'm great. How are you?" I reply lying right through my teeth.

"I'm alright. Been a long week and I'm kind of happy to have a Carmen break tomorrow," he smiles.

"I know what you mean, she's been a little overwhelming since moving here. Probably just adjusting," I assure him.

James, Carmen, Alex and Brittany weren't kidding when they said they wanted to get an early start. I got up at 8 am and they were already gone. Atlanta is only an hour away so I figure they must have come up with something else to do before the show. As I walk into the kitchen Mason passes me with a piece of toast in hand saying he'll be back in the afternoon. Ben is looking through the classified ads in the newspaper spread over the counter.

"Good morning Ben, sleep good?" I ask as I open the fridge to grab a yogurt.

"Yeah thanks. Any idea what we can do today?" I shrug my shoulders and tell him I don't have a clue.

"Alright, how about we go on a ride then, no destination," he suggests waiting on my answer.

Inside I'm screaming 'YES' but at the same time I'm wondering if I really want to be that close to him again. I end up agreeing and we decide to leave in about an hour.

I look out my window and see Ben getting the bike ready. After changing into more appropriate clothing and tying my hair back into a ponytail I make my way outside. Seeing the bike up close, knowing I will be on the back in a few minutes makes my blood pressure rise.

"You ready to go?" he asks with a big grin and I nod. I climb on behind him and wrap my arms around his waist, resting the bottom of my helmet on his shoulder. All of my fear just instantly disappeared just holding him close. Once we get to Macon and we are stopped at a traffic light Ben turns to ask if I'm comfortable enough to go on the highway. Thinking I will do whatever keeps me on this bike I tell him yes. We ride south on I-16 for about an hour until we hit Rockledge and stop for an early lunch.

"I'm so proud of you, this is a long ride and you're a champ," he complements me.

"Thank you," I smile, "I can see why you love to ride, it's like being free."

"Exactly! It's hard to explain so it's best to just experience it. Maybe next I can teach you and you can give me a ride."

My eyes widen in fear, "Oh no, I don't think I can do that. Just watching you with the clutch and gears confuses the hell out of me. Remember, my car is an automatic," I respond and he bursts out laughing.

We stop at a gas station to fill up before making the trip back home. On the way so many things run through my head; the lake, lying in his truck looking at the stars, him holding my hand on the plane, the dance that I never dreamed would have happened and then finally that kiss. Unintentionally I squeeze him a bit tighter and I feel his head turn just a bit.

Pulling up to the house we come to a stop, I climb off the bike holding on to Ben's shoulders. In a way, I am really happy I went but also a little dispirited. Flashbacks running through my mind while holding him. It's almost as if having something dangled in front of you but you just can't reach it.

"So, if you ever want me to take you out again, just let me know. I'd be happy to," Ben smirks taking off his helmet. Yep, everything is back to normal for him. I seriously need to talk to someone, keeping it bottled up is driving me crazy.

"Sure will, thank you. I had fun," I reply handing over my helmet. Right at that time Mason pulls up in his car.

"Hey Ben, you busy?" Mason asks getting out of the car.

"Nah man, just go back, what's up?" Ben replies climbing off his bike.

"One of my friends has been having some issues with his bike. I looked at it at it but couldn't figure it out, was wondering if you could check it out."

"Sure, when?"

"He's on his way right now, it's loaded in the back of his truck." Mason continues, "Should be here in about five minutes."

His timing couldn't be better. I pull out my phone and text Layne to ask if he's home. With Layne's record of not responding to texts I start to wonder why I even bother. I start walking toward the house as my phone buzzes in my hand, it's Layne saying to come over. Must be my lucky day.

"So Layla, what's bothering you," Layne asks with a concerned look.

"Ok, so you need to promise me to keep this to yourself, okay? " I ask and he nods. I lean back into the couch. "I don't know where to start. It's like things have been building up and in New Orleans it finally came to a head." I tell him about the entire weekend, everything from the pool to the dance, and finally our encounter in front of my room.

"Really? Just a kiss has you so frazzled? I suppose I figured you were going to tell me something different. Anyway, so you're saying he's acting like nothing ever happened?" Layne asks.

"Yes, it's like he hit a reset button. It's not like he's ignoring me, heck he took me on a bike ride today."

Layne smirks, "Don't you turn into one of those biker chicks now."

"Really Layne? Don't get sidetracked," I say rolling my eyes.

"So, what is it you want? You want my advice or do you want me to go over there and kick his ass?" Layne asks with a grin on his face.

"Well I definitely don't want you to kick anyone's ass, just so we're clear," I pause and sigh, "I guess I just wanted to tell someone, you know, get it off my chest. It's been eating at me."

"Awe, come here," he pulls me toward him and gives me a hug, "I'm not used to seeing you like this Layla. Even though you didn't ask for my advice you're gonna get it anyway. I think you need to be a little patient and if it's for you it will happen. I know it's not what you want to hear but what's your other option? Trust me, I'm a guy, if he wants you he'll make sure you'll know." Hearing Layne say that makes me smile, he's right, I shouldn't drive myself nuts.

Layne's little pep talk did wonders, I feel like I'm me again. My heart still pounds like a hammer whenever Ben is close but I've got it under control. Things are back to the way they were before New Orleans.

Saturday has now become movie night in our house, thank god they haven't been horror movies. I know the guys love them but come to find out Carmen is a bigger baby than I am.

Ben

It's amazing how one simple kiss can throw your life off track. Hell, it was anything but simple, who am I kidding? Those first few days after we got back from Louisiana were really awkward. I contemplated about backing off a bit and throwing myself into work but I love being around her. Her smile is contagious and we always have great conversations. I've taken her out on the bike a few times and she seems to love it but refuses to learn to ride on her own. Every time I hint at it she just rolls her eyes and says she's not a biker chick. Her facial expression just kills me; I think I keep bringing it up just to see it.

It's the middle of August and it is humid as hell. James, Mason and I have been in the shop all day even though it's Saturday. Business has been booming and we are just trying to play catch up from the week before. Unfortunately, we lost Rick and Carol about a week ago. Rick has had back problems all his life and it's just gotten to the point that lifting anything over ten pounds was causing him excruciating pain. Just as I had assumed Carol and Rick are an item, just kept it private. They decided to move to Florida, Rick's sister lives there and invited them to move in with her.

"Holy crap, it's already 6 pm," James starts wiping his forehead, "they probably already have dinner on the table. Come on, we can finish tomorrow."

I'm not going to argue with that, I'm starving. As I walk in the door I smell pizza and I'm happy. I love pizza, especially if it's homemade. I head into my bathroom to clean up before going to the dining room.

There are three different types of pizza on the table, cheese, peperoni and one really odd looking one with shrimp.

"Layla had the idea to make pizza, I've never made my own dough before so I learned something new," Carmen states while grabbing a piece of the one with shrimp on it. I go with the peperoni and it is delicious.

"I'm starving, "Mason grunts while grabbing a third slice.

"You know, I never thought Rick did all that much when they worked here but now that he and Carol are gone it's been nonstop work. Thank god Shane is still here, I'm wondering if I need to hire another mechanic so we don't kill ourselves," James says exhausted.

"Nah, I think we can handle it James. It's just going to take some getting used to but we'll be fine. You know since Layla's been hanging out in the shop I bet she's picked up some things so we'll just put her to work if need be," I say winking at her. She looks over at me and jabs me right in the ribs with her elbow, I knew that was coming.

"Oh no, I hope things die down just a bit. I got a call from Maria today saying she wants to come for a visit. She was thinking the last weekend in August. She mentioned that she's looking forward seeing you again, you must have left quite an impression," Carmen grins looking straight at me. Great, just what I wanted to hear, shoot me now.

James winks at me, "Well that will be fun; maybe you can take her out one night. What do you say?" Goddamn it, what am I supposed to say? "Uhm," I pause coughing into my napkin.

"Yeah sure, I can do that." Right at that moment I hear Layla choke on her water which sends her into a coughing fit.

"Are you okay Layla?" Carmen asks concerned.

"Yeah, I'm good," she gets up from the table, still coughing, "just swallowed wrong, I'll be right back." She disappears into the kitchen and I want to jump up to follow her but Carmen beats me to it. About two minutes later they both return, Carmen with a pie in hand. Layla sits back down next to me and just smiles, it's the fakest smile I've ever seen.

After dinner Mason picks a movie for us to watch, finally an action movie. With Carmen here we've been watching a few too many romantic comedies lately. The new living room furniture is so uncomfortable. James and Carmen usually end up lying on the sofa and I sit in one of the armchairs. Layla and Mason make themselves comfortable on the floor with pillows, god I miss that sectional. The movie is pretty good but I can't really focus. I glance over at Layla a few times and she's busy with her phone. I am really dreading Maria's visit, I guess she didn't get the hint that I wasn't interested. I must have been too subtle about it, didn't want to be a jerk.

When the credits roll I get up and decide to call it a night. Lying on my bed I'm wide awake just thinking about everything, the reason I came here, the shop being so busy, Maria's upcoming visit and Layla. I pick up my phone and think about texting Layla, I really miss all those funny messages we used to send each other. It doesn't happen very often anymore. Thinking about what to say I look through all of the messages she sent me since I got here. I stop at a picture message, it's the one we took at the fountain after the reception, I didn't realize she sent that one to me. Don't know why I'm surprised, she sent all the others right after taking them too. I just stare at the picture and you can just tell looking at our eyes that we were drunk. In a way, I'd give everything relive that evening.

I send her a meme of a cat lying on the floor *I didn't choose the rug life, the rug life chose me*. That's the best I could find, I thought it would work since she was camped on the floor during the movie. Instantly I get a response and it makes me smirk *Too funny!! Quite accurate though. Damn fancy furniture*. This is exactly what I needed to be able to go to sleep. I know it wasn't just a coincidence that she happened to choke right when the Maria topic came up. I think Carmen mentioned she's only going to be here for about two days so how bad can it really be.

Shane came in on Sunday to help us out in the shop. It must be really weird not having Rick and Carol around, he's still living in the same house and is looking for room-mates for the other bedrooms. I know the three of them have always been together so I was curious why he didn't move to Florida with them. He said he really liked living here and met a woman that he's really into. Guess it makes sense, Rick and Carol have each other, at some point Shane needs to find his own way.

It's Wednesday night and I'm exhausted but can't sleep, I go outside to sit on the swing. It's a really nice night, clear sky, full moon, crickets chirping.

Those damn crickets are so loud, I hadn't really noticed them before. I pull out my phone and decide to search for cricket season. Just as I figured I got a bazillion different answers and it's not like it really matters anyway. I notice a flash of light shining toward the house and look up, it's Layla's car. Wow, it's already after 1 am, I've been sitting out here a long time. As she makes her way up the steps I say hello and she jumps back dropping her bag.

"I'm sorry, I guess I scared you sitting in the dark," I reply feeling bad.

"What are you doing out here?" she asks as she sits down next to me.

"I couldn't sleep, was just thinking about some things. It's so nice out and we've been cooped up in the shop for the last week," I pause, "So, Maria huh?"

She sighs, "Gosh, please don't remind me. I get this feeling that she doesn't particularly like me very much, but then again, she was really nice when I left. She even gave me an aspirin for my headache." I smile; I know exactly what she means. The looks she was giving Layla that weekend were anything but nice.

"So, how was work?"

"I actually did very well for a Wednesday. There was a group of about ten guys there I hadn't seen before and they tipped really well."

"Oh, I'm sure they did," I say sarcastically.

We stayed out until about 3 am just talking and joking around. She was reminiscing about New Orleans but steered clear of anything that could have made our conversation awkward. Every time I look at her I just want to hold her close, not going to happen though. Still that kiss was freakin' amazing, it may have only lasted twenty seconds but those were the hottest twenty seconds of my life. I've had my share of women but none have messed with my head this way before, it's like she's a drug that I've become addicted to. Thank god thoughts are private.

Chapter Nine

Layla

I hear the front door open and recognize the voice in an instant. "Wow, I love this place. It's so rustic. Carmen, your things fit in so well, it's like urban country chic." Great! Maria is here. I have been dreading this moment all day. Who knows? Maybe I'm just exaggerating a bit.

"So, is Ben around? I can't wait to see him." Maria says, "I really think we hit it off at the wedding." Nope, no exaggeration. This is going to be a terrible weekend, I can feel it. I'm standing in the kitchen and I really should walk out and say hello but I can't bring myself to face her right now. I have to go to work in a few hours and the thought of not knowing what will be happening here is giving me an uneasy feeling. I toyed around with the idea of calling in sick, but I can't do that to Layne. It's going to be a really busy night.

"Yes," Carmen answers "he's here. He's still outside in the shop with the guys. They should be done in about an hour or so." Maria says she wants to freshen up so Carmen takes her upstairs to show her where she will be staying. I figured she would be staying in the room Carmen fixed up, unfortunately it's right next to mine. I move to the living room with a glass of water and sit on the couch grabbing a magazine from the side table. After about thirty minutes I hear them coming down the stairs. Okay, one deep breath, exhale and be nice.

"Oh, hi Layla. Nice to see you again," her voice is screaming sarcasm.

"Hey Maria, it's so great to have you here. I hope you will enjoy your stay. I love your shirt." I really don't have to be that nice, especially after she was being a bitch, but I tell myself I'm the bigger person.

"Thank you so much." The look she is giving me is just plain mean. She asks Carmen if they can go out to see Ben. She tells her to go on ahead and she'll be right out.

Carmen's eyes are fixated on me. "Layla, can we talk for a few minutes?" Okay this is really weird. I agree and she sits down next to me. "I just wanted to ask you for a favor."

"Sure, anything," I reply a little more at ease.

She starts, "I know you and Ben are really close and I think that's great," she pauses, taking a deep breath, "I don't want this to sound weird but I wanted to ask you if you could maybe back off him just a bit while my sister is here. You know, give them a chance to really get to know each other. I'm not saying lock yourself in your room or anything like that, just give him a little space."

I cannot believe the bullshit coming out of her mouth. Is she really serious about this? Maybe Ben mentioned something to James about me hanging around too much and she's bringing it up. Now I'm baffled. I tell her that it won't be a problem at all and she hugs me. She walks out the front door to catch up with Maria. I can't describe what emotion I am feeling right now, I just want to get out of here. I decide to go to work early, at least it will keep me busy. I grab my keys, phone and bag and head out the door. As I walk to my car I look over in the direction of the shop. Everyone is outside and I see Maria is in full on flirt mode.

Ben looks over at me, "Layla, where you going?" He knows my shifts and it does look a bit odd that I'm leaving over an hour early when it's only a ten-minute drive.

"Randy texted me that he needs reinforcement. I guess it's already picking up." I say with a smile on my face and get into my car. It's a typical Friday night, or so I thought. Layne can tell I'm a little uneasy so he asks what's going on.

"Well, Carmen's sister got here today so I feel like I'm in hell. The worst part was that Carmen decided she needed to have a sit down with me. She said she knew Ben and I were great friends but asked me to take a backseat so he and Maria can get to know each other a little better. So long story short I'm livid. I came to work early and told Randy I'm just volunteering my time and asked him to keep it to himself."

"Damn, she laid down the law didn't she? I mean I guess I can see why, you can be totally domineering," he chuckles, sarcasm written all over his face. He pauses for a second with his eyes on the door, "So not to get you going or anything but it looks like they just walked through the door." What? I turn around to find Ben, Maria, James and Carmen walking over to one of the free high-top tables. Carmen waves and signals for me to come over.

"Layla, the Mrs. is calling, you better go before she cracks that whip again," Layne chuckles with a tad too much enthusiasm.

Fucking fantastic. I wipe my hands with a towel and head over. "Hey guys! So cool of you all to come in, can I get you anything?" I notice Maria has changed shirts. Well I wouldn't call what she is wearing a shirt; the front has a slit that stops a little above her navel.

"Yes, yes, yes!" Carmen says. "Can you bring whisky on the rocks for the guys and two Pina coladas for us? You know, just like the one you made for me the last time I was here. Maria, it is delicious." I have never seen Carmen so hyper. Maybe I should make hers a virgin or she may be bouncing off the walls.

Maria speaks, "That sounds great. Oh Layla I wanted to ask, are there any special events planned for tonight? I was told Fridays are the best." What I really want to say is *'Oh why yes we do, on the left we have the whore convention and on the right you'll find the I'm trying too hard meet-up, you should enjoy either one'*, but I contain myself.

"We will be doing Karaoke tonight, you should totally do it. Randy is always looking for more people to go up." Her eyes widen, "OH. MY. GOD. I have always wanted to try that. Benji, lets sign up, please, please, please." What did she just call him? What really got my blood boiling was how nonchalant she said it as if they'd been dating for years.

"Nah, I'm good, thanks," he replies politely.

"Oh don't feel bad Maria," I say looking directly into Ben's eyes "I don't think karaoke is Benji's thing. I'll go get started on your drinks and be right back." I feel his glare on me, he looks heated so I turn and walk back to my safe place.

"So how did that go?' Layne is so nosy. I can't blame him, I've already involved him too much, this is like reality TV and today is just a new episode.

I start pouring the rum into the blender "Layne, can you do me a big favor?"

"You know I'd do anything for you," he replies.

"Can you please bring them their drinks?"

Karaoke is in full swing, some people are great while others think they are. While working I have already witnessed Maria and Carmen on Diablo getting their picture taken by Ben. I must be crazy for counting but I've seen that bitch touch his arm at least a dozen times but the worst thing is he doesn't seem to mind. I see them all laughing together, taking selfies, just acting like they've been friends forever. I think my drinks are getting stronger as the night goes on, I'm enraged.

"Layla, if you press any harder that glass is gonna shatter." Randy pulls me out of my trance. I ruined that mojito. He continues "Just wanted to check if any of ya'll wanna go up there and sing". I shake my head.

"Think about it I'm gonna go set up the next song for James and his friend." James? Is he seriously going up there with Maria? He hates karaoke. I can't wait to see this.

The music starts and I recognize the song right away, *'TIME OF MY LIFE'*, good choice. As I watch their performance unfold I am pleasantly surprised, they actually did a decent job. I noticed Maria sending flirtatious looks in Ben's direction, just great. This whole *'I've never done karaoke before'* was a crock of bull.

Layne bumps me with his shoulder, "Ooooh Layla! You gonna let her show you up?"

Hell no I'm not, it's on! I grab Layne's hand and yell across the bar, "Randy! Number Five." The crowd cheers as we make our way up to the stage. The regulars have seen us sing this song many times. *'JUST A KISS'*, one of my favorite songs.

The music starts and I get lost. It's more of a show with us since we don't need the lyrics anymore. I have managed to ignore Ben the entire time. As the song comes to an end I let my eyes peer in his direction and he's staring at me. Even with fifteen feet between us, it's a look I recognize immediately and it takes me back to New Orleans. Not until the end I realize that this song is an accurate portrayal of my current emotional state, as more time goes by I do believe that he may be the one I've been waiting for my whole life.

I got in late last night and actually slept really well for a change. The work week is over and all I want to do is relax but I figure that will probably not happen until Maria leaves. I keep telling myself one more day. One more day and her ass will be back on that plane to New Orleans and things can go back to the way they were. I just hope she doesn't come back. I'm quite surprised to find the house very quiet. I see Mason at the dining table eating his cereal.

"Where is everyone?" I ask taking a quick glance around.

"They went to Atlanta for the day. They'll be back at around dinner time."

"Where's Alex?"

"Alex and Brittany went with them. I guess they're doing a triple date thing." Triple date, really? I am so heated but I bite my tongue. I take a deep breath, grab an apple and head toward the front porch. Mason passes me and says he is going to visit his friend Steven for a while. I sit down in the swing and feel a bit relieved that I'm by myself. My hair is up in a messy bun and I'm wearing a tank with yoga pants. I don't have anywhere to go so I'm just going to be a slob all day, well at least until they get home. The day actually flies by. After cleaning the shop, house and the inside of my car I decide it's time to shower and make myself look presentable.

I still have a little time to kill so after putting on my makeup I curl my hair. I'm really proud of myself, it came out just like I wanted it, nice loose waves and the best part, I didn't burn myself this time. I get a text from James **Will be there in 30 min** so I go into the kitchen and start cooking. I decide on spaghetti, it's quick and easy and everyone loves it. I hear the front door open, Mason and Steven come walking into the kitchen.

"Hey Layla, wow you look nice," Steven declares. I don't take it as a compliment though. For years, he's been trying to get me to go out with him but I'd rather have a root canal. He's not ugly but not attractive either and has no personality, just blah. When I started dating Layne last year, his advances stopped. At least one good thing came out of our fiasco of a relationship. I thank him anyway and Mason asks if Steven can stay for dinner. I think to myself, sure why not, the more the merrier.

I hear a car pull up right as I finish cooking. Within minutes voices fill the house and things feel normal again. Mason already set the table and I bring out two big dishes, one filled with the pasta and the other with meat sauce. I pause for a second and look at the table. A smile comes over my face because it reminds me of how things used to be, three more people and the table would be full. It is very short-lived and fades when I hear a screechy voice, Maria.

James steps into the dining room, "Layla, did you do something different with your hair? Looks nice. Alright everybody it's time to eat."

Looking around the table everyone is engaged in conversations about their day. It's a little depressing, since I spent mine alone, cleaning. For a moment I think to myself, I feel like the damn maid right now. Maybe instead of eating I should be waiting on them hand and foot. I'm sure Maria would love that, Carmen too. I mean they grew up rich so I'm sure they had hired help. Okay, enough of that, I'm in serious bitch mode. Ben is sitting at opposite end of the table. Every so often our eyes meet but one of us ends up breaking contact. I've managed to block out most of the chitter chatter but then I hear hysterical laughing.

"I really thought I was going to die, I'm so happy Benji was there. I wouldn't have done it without him. You are a true gentleman." Maria says giving him a sideways hug while he smirks. She thought '*She*' was going to die? I am dying right now listening to this crap. I don't know what she is talking about but I need to remove myself before I explode. I clear the table and start the cleanup and to my surprise Brittany tells me that she will take care of the rest. That is not like her at all, I think she can feel that I am in a weird mood. Unnoticed I walk past everyone and go up to my room. I throw myself on my bed and stare at the ceiling fan. About five minutes later there is a knock on my door. Why can't they just leave me alone for like thirty minutes?

"Come in," I say reluctantly, eyes focused on the fan.

"Hey Layla, can we talk?" I look at the door and find a very anxious Ben.

"Yes, of course!" I sit up and move to the side of my bed. He comes in, closes the door behind him and sits down next to me. All I can think of is how much I want him to pin me down and continue where we left off.

"I know this is probably not the right time but I think we need to talk about it." I recall Carmen's conversation from yesterday. Great, it was him that wanted me to back off.

"Listen, don't worry. Carmen already talked to me," I assure him, taking a deep breath.

"What are you talking about? What did Carmen say?" he asks his voice sounding concerned.

"She just asked me to pretty much stay away from you while Maria is here so you two can get acquainted."

"What?" he looks mad, "I'm sorry she said that Layla, I didn't know anything about that. It's not why I'm here though." Thank god! So it wasn't him, what a relief. He starts again. "I'm talking about what happened at the hotel. Obliviously I can't take it back or I would." He really just said that, I'm shattered.

"Damn, it's not coming out right. What I'm trying to say is," he pauses and takes a deep breath, "Okay, I can't get you out of my head and I feel like I'm losing my mind. I'm so attracted to you Layla, in ways I can't even understand. When I'm close to you I want you so bad that I have a hard time controlling myself." My heart skips a few beats, he wants me, he just said it and I'm blown away.

"Ben I –" he doesn't let me finish.

"I also realize I am twenty years older than you."

"Seventeen!" I correct him, not like it makes a big difference.

"Okay, seventeen. But not just that, I've known you since you were a little girl." I roll my eyes, he knew me until I was four. It's not like he watched me grow up.

"I mean what am I supposed to do, just say ok let's do this? That would be so selfish of me and irresponsible on top of that. Do you have any idea what people would say, what James would say? I know for a fact that he wouldn't be asking us to join him and Carmen on double dates. It's just wrong on so many levels." I focus on my breathing. I manage to stand up and tears start to stream down my cheeks, I can't take this. He immediately gets up, grabs me and hugs me tight.

"Geez, Layla. I didn't mean to make you cry, please don't cry." We stand there for a moment, our heads on each other's shoulders. He just broke my heart but I don't want to let him go. Slowly he pulls away and I look into his eyes, all I see is pain. He places both hands on the sides of my face, resting his forehead to mine. I grab on to his arms and close my eyes, wishing time would just stop and we could stay like this forever. With my eyes still shut I suddenly feel his lip graze mine ever so slightly. I press my lips to his and he pulls away abruptly.

"Fuck! That's exactly what I'm talking about." He stands there, his hands on top of his head. "Okay seriously, this will never happen again. I don't want this. I'm done!" The door slams and he is gone. Still trying to comprehend what he just said, I freeze. I have never been this confused in my life and feel like now I am really going to fall apart. Needing to get out of this house I get myself together, grab my bag and go downstairs.

"Layla, where are you going?" James asks.

"Out! Don't wait up for me," I reply heading out the door, passing Ben avoiding eye contact. I drive around for a while before deciding to call Layne. Luckily he's just getting off work so he tells me to head on over to his place. He answers the door and asks what happened. I can't get a word out and start to cry. Immediately he grabs me and walks me inside.

"Layne, I just don't get it. He told me he wanted me. This actually makes it worse, before I just kept wondering but now that I know, how am I going to go back there and pretend everything is fine?"

"You're going to hate me but I get his point. Come on Layla, the two of you are on completely different levels. You know my stance on the age thing so I'm not gonna harp on that. I honestly think you don't need to put yourself through this madness. If you keep pursuing him you're gonna end up burned," he pauses, "I remember you mentioning that he's not very open about his past, maybe he's screwed up and doesn't want to pull you down with him. Either way, you're beautiful and a sweetheart, you can have anyone you want." Great, I don't want just anyone, I want Ben. I sit and think for a while and being a typical woman I'm still trying to find the fault in myself.

"You look so tense. Relax! Do you want me to get you a drink?" he asks heading into the kitchen.

"I don't know what I want," I sigh leaning into the side of the couch. He looks over at me, running his hand through his hair. Taking a deep breath, he walks toward me reaching for my hand.

"I know exactly what you need, come on." I grab his hand wondering what the hell he's talking about. He leads me into his bedroom and starts removing his shirt.

"Err, Layne? What are you doing?" I ask with raised eyebrows.

"I'm giving you a release, don't worry Layla, no strings attached and I have condoms," he smiles. What? He can't be serious? From one moment to the next I feel him grab my waist and pull me in. Grabbing my hair and pushing it to one side he kisses my neck. I am surprised I'm not stopping him, but then again I've never been able to resist him in these situations. Maybe he's right, this may be exactly what I need right now. Very gently his lips make their way to mine, he's careful, wanting to make sure I'm not going to freak out. It's so easy to get lost with him in this moment. I start to unbuckle his belt and I feel him grin against my lips. His pants fall to the floor and just like I assumed, no boxers, he always goes commando. As I try to touch his face he pushes me onto his bed, climbing on top of me removing my shirt and bra. His tongue finds all of my sensitive areas. While planting kisses around my hips he slowly removes the rest of my clothing. I hear the tear of a wrapper and before I know it I feel his tongue make its way from my navel back to my mouth. He starts out slow but then turns into the Layne I know. He knows exactly what to do, how to move and what to say. Barely touching him I slowly move my fingertips from his lower back up toward his shoulders, knowing it drives him mad. The sensation makes him groan and his movements become wilder. I let go, for a moment I forget everything that happened the entire weekend.

Layne collapses on me nuzzling into my neck, "Layla," still catching his breath, "We should really consider becoming friends with benefits." I huff and slap his butt as I push him off me. "Hey, why don't you just stay here tonight? You never know, it may make Ben think a little. Also if you go home with that hair, he's gonna know exactly what happened and if he finds out it was with me, boy he will never touch you." I give him a puzzled expression.

"Come on Layla, you know nobody can compete with this." There's a little part of me that feels like I've just made the biggest mistake of my life but lying on his chest is the most comfortable place in the world right now.

I wake up from the beams of sunshine gleaming through the shades. Layne is still asleep so I get up, grab his T-shirt from the floor and put it on. I walk into the living room looking for my phone. Finding it between the couch cushions I press the home button to check what time it is and notice a slew of text messages. They are all from Ben. He's apologizing in the first two messages and the next few sound as if he's worried. The last one makes my eyes widen *Layla where the fuck are you?????* Layne steps out of the bedroom, sweatpants hanging low on his hips exposing that perfect V right below his abs.

"Morning babe. Why the frown? Come here, I'll put a smile on your face." He really is a sight for sore eyes, for a moment I consider maybe giving us another shot but then I realize nothing has changed.

"Good morning. So I have a few texts I missed last night," I answer biting my lip.

"See I told you, boom! Made him think, didn't it? I love being right." Layne boasts doing a little victory dance.

"I'm actually not concerned with that at the moment. What am I going to say if they ask where I was last night? I don't usually go out and not come home."

"Honestly Layla, you don't owe anyone anything. If you feel that you have to explain yourself, just tell them we met up last night, went to a party with some friends and you crashed at my house because you were drunk." Luckily Layne always has a story on hand. I gather the rest of my clothes and get dressed. The walk of shame I think to myself, I did the same thing last year. Layne walks me to my car and gives me a big hug.

"Thank you for everything. I don't know what I'd do without you," I say squeezing him tighter.

"Awe, Love ya Layla," he pauses with a sly grin, "Also, I just want to remind you, if you're ever interested in what I mentioned earlier, I'm your man."

Ben

Damn it. I was awake all night waiting to hear from Layla. I was way too harsh on her, just didn't know how to get my point across. Why do I keep fucking things up? I got up a few times to check if she ever made it back home but she never did. I'm really starting to get worried about her. She always texts back immediately. No wonder she isn't replying, I deserve this. I turn around and Maria is coming downstairs.

"Good morning Benji. Did you sleep well?" This Benji shit is really getting on my nerves.

"Great, thanks. Hey by the way, it's just Ben, don't really go by Benji," I am so irritable right now but manage to smile.

"Oh sorry. Hey let's get some coffee, come on," Maria suggests walking to the kitchen. I can definitely use some right about now. As we wait for the coffee to brew she tries to get a little closer to me. "You know I had such a great time with you. I really like you, hope we will keep in touch." That's the last thing on my mind.

"Yeah sure, "I lie and she frowns a little before turning toward the coffee maker. Hey, maybe she's getting it. Even if Maria wasn't crazy I don't think I'd want to get involved. I'm definitely not ready to jump into a serious relationship. She sure tries really hard and Carmen is her accomplice. Right at that moment James and Carmen come through the door. The two sisters hug and tell each other how much they are going to miss one another.

It's almost 9 am and Layla still hasn't come home. No one else here seems to be worried whatsoever, maybe they haven't noticed that she isn't here. Maria heads upstairs to get her things together; she brought a lot of luggage for a two-day visit. Mason volunteers to carry her bags downstairs and sets them down at the door; I think he may have the hots for her.

"Hey Mason, have you heard from Layla?" I figure it's safe to ask him.

"Nah, she said she was going out last night I think. Probably crashed somewhere," he answers as if it were something that happens all the time.

"Okay, I think I got everything. Thank you guys so much for having me," Maria says leaning in to hug James.

"You're welcome here anytime. It's been really great having you," James replies and Maria's eyes are fixed on me.

"Ben, thank you so much. I had so much fun. Remember keep in touch. Come here give me a hug." She grabs me and right at that time I hear the door opening, it's Layla. Finally! She looks straight at me but then turns away.

"Layla, great you're here just in time, Carmen is about to take Maria to the airport," James says.

"Maria, it has been so nice seeing you again. I'm sorry I got a little tied up this weekend but I'm sure you had a great time," Layla smiles and I don't think she could sound any less sincere.

"Oh, I sure did," Maria replies winking at me, "Oh, Layla sweetie, you may want to take a peek in the mirror, your make-up is really smudged. You must have had a rough night." Wow, she is ruthless; it's pretty obvious that she despises Layla. As Carmen and Maria walk out the door Layla gives her a quick wave and closes the door.

"Don't let the door hit you on the way out bitch," Layla mumbles.

"Layla, that was uncalled for. She could have heard you. What's wrong with you?" James snaps at her.

"Hello? Did you not just see the attitude she had with me? I don't like her," Layla responds looking upset.

"Not sure where you woke up this morning but it definitely was the wrong side of the bed," James says while walking upstairs. I'm a little nervous approaching her in the state she's in, but I have to.

"Hey, I was worried about you," I whisper trying to read her, "Listen, I know I have no right to ask where you were but I -" she interrupts me.

"I was at Layne's and yes, you're correct. You don't have a right to ask that." Damn, she is mad. Her eyes went from agitated to furious in a matter of seconds. Why the fuck did she have to run to him? There's silence between us, it's so uncomfortable but I can't take my eyes off of her.

"I didn't see the messages until this morning, otherwise I would have texted back," she adds and now her whole demeanor has changed, carrying a softer tone, "Well, I'm going to run upstairs and take a shower, so I'll see you later." I can only manage to give her a half smile. I should have never gone to her room last night. If I had just kept my mouth shut things wouldn't have escalated, I really thought I was doing the right thing.

I spend most of the day in the shop to avoid Layla, desperately needing a distraction I throw myself into work. Mason comes in to help and I haven't listened to one word he's said. I just can't concentrate; the thought of her with Layne is infuriating me. I'm not an idiot, I know something happened. He doesn't look like the type of guy who will just sit and listen to her sorrows.

James stops in, "Hey Ben, let's go to Betty's to pick up dinner. Give the girls a break from cooking." On the way he talks about Maria nonstop.

"She sure is something special isn't she? She's spunky, fun and beautiful too. I think she's a good match for you."

"I'm not interested in dating anyone," I reply.

"Oh come on Ben. You guys had a great time. That trip to Atlanta was so much fun. Maria really likes you. She would have never gone on that Ferris Wheel, but you put her at ease."

"Yeah we all had a good time, but that doesn't mean I want to marry her," I reply sounding annoyed.

"Gosh, no one is talking marriage, I'm just saying give her a chance. See where things go." I just keep my mouth shut. Obviously there's no reasoning with him right now. Finally we get to the diner, those ten minutes felt like two hours.

"Hey boys. Here ya go." Betty says handing us menus. She is such a sweetheart, always has a smile on her face. James places our order and we wait at the counter.

"Oh my lord. Layne Tuner. Where have you been? I feel like I haven't seen your gorgeous face in weeks," an overly excited Betty screeches.

"I'm so sorry. I swear I haven't been cheating on you. Just been kinda busy," he replies and turns to us, "Oh hey guys, how's it going?" Layne smirks, plopping himself in the empty chair next to James.

"Layne, it's good to see you. You really need to visit sometime. How about you come for dinner? Just arrange it with Layla," James says in a very welcoming tone and Layne agrees. This shit can't get any worse.

"Hey Ben, everything good?" Layne asks with a smile like he's got one up on me. Well hell, he probably does.

"Yup, things are great." That's all I can manage to say. Layne and James carry on their conversation. I just listen and watch his every move. Our food is finally ready and I'm dreading the car ride. I swear if there's any more talk about Maria I may lose it.

"I hope Layne does make it to dinner sometime. He used to come over a lot," James starts and suddenly my interest peaks, maybe I'll learn something about the Layne and Layla dynamic.

"Alex met him years ago and they became friends, he practically lived at our house. God he must have thought that we were a crazy bunch with all of the people with us. After a while Layla and Layne became close. I wasn't surprised when they started dating; I knew it was just a matter of time."

"Oh, they did? When was that?" I ask nonchalantly.

"Last year. It didn't last very long. They said they were better off as friends." In the back of my mind I figured as much. I see it in the way he touches her, looks at her, talks to her. When they were up on stage singing that song they were so familiar with each other, however, when it ended she looked into my eyes and I knew it was meant for me. Doesn't matter now, I said my piece and god help me I will stick to my guns.

Layla

I don't want to be here. At dinner Carmen just went on and on about Maria this and Maria that. It's really hard to sit there with a smile on my face. I feel James watching me, probably waiting for me to make a smart comment. For a moment I think about leaving and going to Layne's. I know he would be happy to have me there but I'm going to be tough. It's pretty much a given that we would just end up in bed again and even though I don't regret it, it doesn't need to become a regular thing. I've always been the type of person that deals with issues instead of running, so I'm not going to start at the age of twenty-four.

I need a few minutes to myself so I go up to my room. I think about a lot of things. Realizing I don't like the Layla I have become I decide I just have to stop. Ben said he doesn't want this and I am just going to accept that. It will be hard but what else can I really do? I refuse to be humiliated. The rest of the evening really isn't so bad. Everyone is in the living room watching a movie, Mason and I are lying on the floor with our pillows. About thirty minutes in Mason is already passed out.

"Hey Layla, is Mason asleep?" Alex asks.

"Yep, he barely made it past the opening scene." Ben and Alex crack a few jokes. Amazing how a few hours can change everything. This morning I was furious and hurt and now I'm okay. Carmen asks me to go shopping with her in Macon tomorrow and I agree.

The next day I get up and continue with my routine of primping before going downstairs, it's become a habit now. I've gotten really good and it only takes me about ten minutes total. I walk into the kitchen to find Ben leaning against the counter reading a newspaper.

"Good morning," I say cheerfully. He looks at me, his eyes uncertain.

"Good morning Layla." Geez, there's something about how my name rolls off his tongue that drives me…nope, I'm not going there. I take a deep breath. I need to keep the conversation light.

"So, I have a big day planned. Going shopping with Carmen, it's going to be exciting," I joke, he starts to chuckle and I see a sparkle in his eye.

"Well, you guys have a good time, we're just working. James said that someone's dropping off some riding lawnmowers to repair." He has a hard time keeping a straight face.

"You guys should totally do mower races. I mean, if you can fix them," I suggest, why did I just say that? Am I five?

"Oh really?" he steps a little closer, "You don't think I can fix a mower?" I just start laughing which in turn makes him chuckle. Carmen comes in and says she's ready to go so I grab a pastry on the way out.

"Real healthy Layla, next time how about I just make you some real breakfast," Ben offers.

"Sure, I won't turn that down," I reply taking a bite. Alright, this is going way better than I thought, maybe that night with Layne was a cure-all.

On the way to Macon, Carmen starts talking about her sister again. I take a deep breath and don't let it get to me; she's gone and that's all that counts. When we get to Macon we stop at Ryan's, a discount department store. Knowing Carmen shops forever I split off and browse the aisles for some new outfits. She finds me about forty-five minutes later and we head to the dressing room. I actually grabbed a few dresses and skirts as well, even though I never wear them. I completely fall in love with a black hi-lo skirt. I think it will look great with my cowboy boots, a tank top and maybe a short jean jacket, all of which I have in my closet. I try on a dress that I actually like. It's lilac in color and comes just above my knees with a sweetheart neckline. It has a lace overlay that stops right below my neck, kind of reminds of the dress I wore to the wedding. The bottom flares out a little and the back has a beautiful cutout in the shape of a diamond. It's gorgeous but the color makes me uncertain so I want Carmen's opinion.

"Hey, what do you think of this? Does it look okay?"

"Oh Layla, it is stunning. I love the color on you. You have great legs and you should show them off in something other than shorts," she says. I think about it for a moment. I'm not sure where or if I will ever wear it but for $12.99 I can't pass it up. It's close to lunch time so we just grab a quick bite to eat before heading to the grocery store.

We come home and find a line of mowers parked outside the shop, I count eight total.

"Wow James, "Carmen says as we step into the shop, "When you said a few I was thinking less than five. Looks like you're going to have a busy day."

"Nah, sweetie. The ones outside are already done, just have these two left in here. Most of them just needed small adjustments. Easy stuff," James replies.

"So Layla, Ben said something about mower races, you in?" Shane asks having a hard time keeping a straight face.

"Oh my god, that was just a stupid joke. Ben I can't believe you told them that," I say covering one side of my face in embarrassment.

"It's ok, they all thought it was funny. For a minute we were actually considering it," he laughs wiping his hands with a towel.

As the days go on I find myself not being able to keep away from Ben, him living here doesn't make it any easier. Being at work is a godsend; there I don't have to pretend, unless it's a day where he decides to come in. Ben and Mason have become frequent visitors at the Bull, usually on Friday nights. Once in a while James and Carmen tag along but I think they really enjoy their time at home when everyone's gone. Tonight is one of those nights where it's just Ben and Mason.

"Hey guys, how's it going?" I ask as they come to sit at the bar.

"Pretty good," Mason answers, "You totally missed something when you left earlier."

"Oh boy, what did I miss?" I ask jokingly.

"Alex is moving in with Brittany, I think she's pregnant," Mason assumes.

"No, man I don't think so, he probably just realized that he spends most of his time there anyway and wants to take it to the next level," Ben says looking over at me.

"Yeah, I agree with Ben, there's no way that would happen, you know Brittany," I mention.

"Well, I guess we will find out, time will tell," Mason says convinced that his assumption is true. Brittany and I have had that conversation before; she told me she had a rod put in her arm about a year ago that prevents pregnancy for up to four years. I looked it up online and after watching a video I decided I will stick to condoms.

"Hey guys what's happening?" Layne jumps in, he was in the back helping Randy with a few things,

"Layla hasn't offered you anything to drink, man you're slacking girl." After sitting around talking for a bit Mason asks if I will sing a song with him. I am totally shocked, I have never heard him being interested in karaoke, must be the alcohol. Figuring I can't miss this opportunity I go up him. He chooses *'HEY SOUL SISTER'* which is another surprise to me since it's a bit older. It's not a duet so I suppose the both of us will be singing at the same time. After the first few lines I notice that Mason is a damn good singer. Deciding to let him shine I stop singing and he gives me a look of disagreement but continues on. I chime in every so often and we have successfully turned the song into a harmonious duet. When the music stops everyone applauds and Mason gives me a hug before we walk back to the bar.

"Wow," Layne comments, "I didn't know you could sing like that. Here's another beer, my treat."

"Thanks man," Mason replies wiping his forehead. After Mason finishes his beer he gets up and says he'll be back in a little while. I watch him make his way across the room, stopping at a table to talk to a blonde girl. I've seen her around town but have no idea who she is.

"Look at my little brother, I was starting to think girls weren't his thing," Ben laughs.

"Well, he definitely likes girls. He just doesn't know how to approach them. Alcohol removes inhibitions and makes you brave," I smile but quickly remember the last time we were drunk and what happened then.

"Amen to that," he chuckles raising his soda and I laugh.

"You have a really beautiful voice Layla," Ben remarks and I can feel the tingling in my cheeks, "I'd love to hear you solo sometime."

"Hell yeah," Layne interrupts," She totally rocks it." I can only manage to smile, trying to avoid sending my emotions on another crazy roller coaster ride. About fifteen minutes later Mason comes back with a huge grin on his face.

"So," I begin, "Did you get her number?"

"Wouldn't you like to know," Mason replies sarcastically. About a half hour before closing time Ben and Mason leave.

"So Layla, you still have it bad for him don't you?" Layne asks as he's closing out the register.

"Is it really that obvious? I thought I was doing well keeping that locked away somewhere," I frown.

"It's probably just because I know you. When you look at him your eyes light up, it's cute," Layne says grinning at me.

"Well, doesn't really matter, can't change things anyway. Maybe in another lifetime," I sigh.

Layne walks over to me and gives me a hug, "Oh I almost forgot, I ran into James the other day and he told me to come by the house for dinner sometime. Randy gave me a day off on Monday and I figured since you're not working that may be a good time." Telling him it should be fine I say goodnight and walk out to my car and head home.

Carmen has a great idea to spend Saturday afternoon at the lake, she ordered a few Adirondack chairs online and they got here yesterday. We load up two trucks, one with the boxed up chairs and the other with our grill. It's the middle of September so the weather is still great for a cook out, Brittany and Alex are joining us as well.

At the lake I grab one of the boxes, open it and spread the pieces of wood on the ground.

"You're going to put that together?" Ben asks sounding surprised.

"Yes I am, I love building things. Do you have an extra screwdriver?" Grabbing the tool box out of the truck, he digs around and hands one over to me. There are six chairs total which works out great since Mason is hanging out at Steven's house.

The guys are at the grill while Brittany, Carmen and I lounge in the new chairs.

"God it's so beautiful here," Carmen sighs.

"It really is," Brittany adds, "I don't think I'll be jumping in that water though. Not really a fan of the creatures that may live in there. Hey I was going to ask, what's up with Mason? He kept giving me this weird look before Steven came to pick him up."

"He thinks you're pregnant," I blurt out.

"What? I have an implant in my arm. Do I look fat or something?" she jumps up, looking herself over.

"No Brit, he thinks that's the reason Alex is moving in with you. I told him he's wrong, but he's convinced." I explain.

"You know, I think he's just a little jealous," Carmen starts, "I wouldn't worry about him." After lunch James tries to entice us girls to jump in the water, after debating a little Carmen gets up and walks in.

"Hey Layla, Brittany come in, the water is great," Carmen says while floating on her back. Brittany says there's no way in hell she's getting in. I sit up a little and see the guys are having a great time splashing each other.

"No thanks, I'll keep Brittany company," I say putting on my sunglasses, leaning back into the chair to soak up some sun. All of sudden I feel someone grab my wrists and throw me over their shoulder.

"Alex goddamn it, no. Put me down right now," I scream punching his back.

"Nope, you're coming in," he laughs.

"Alex stop," I say as he gets close to the water, "Alex! I have my phone in my pocket, unless you want to buy me a new one I suggest you stop." I can't believe he is patting my ass to find my phone and once he realizes that I was a lying he throws me into the lake. Ben and James just think it's hilarious and can't stop laughing, I notice Alex is sitting in my chair making himself comfortable.

"You like to find yourself in these situations don't you Layla," Ben continues laughing. I jump on his back to push him underwater and we both end up going down. Once back at the surface James is laughing and Carmen has a weird look on her face.

"Layla," James gets out between laughs, "You have green stuff all over your hair."

"Oh my god, get it out, get it out!" I scream.

"Hold still, I'll get it," Ben says starting to pick pieces of algae out of my hair, "Okay, that's the best I could do but you may need a shower." Deciding that now is a good time to get out I grab a handful of mud, hide it behind my back and walk toward Alex and Brittany.

"See Layla, that was fun wasn't it?" Alex asks snickering and I waste no time smearing the mud all over his chest up to his neck.

"Are you serious? That is disgusting," Alex whines, debating if he should wipe it off with his hands.

"Oh you're welcome," I say, wiping my hand on my shorts looking at Brittany who is laughing hysterically. Alex gets up and I assume he's about to come after me but to my surprise he turns the other way and gives Brittany a big hug. She's kicking and screaming for him to get off and once he does her shirt is a total mess. Everyone else gets out of the water and I remember yesterday's conversation with Layne.

"Hey James, Layne said something about you inviting him to dinner, he asked if Monday would be okay."

"Yeah, Ben and I ran into him at the diner last week. Carmen, is Monday alright?" James asks.

"Of course, that will be great" she says, I knew she wouldn't have a problem with it.

Chapter Ten

Ben

Just great, Layne should be here in a few minutes and I'll have to endure dinner with him. I really wish I could just sit this one out. The doorbell rings and I suppose I should answer since I'm less than ten feet away.

"Hey Ben, what's up man?" Layne greets me with that sly grin on his face, holding a bottle of wine.

"Not much, come on in. Good to see you again," I lie.

"Thanks, where's Layla?" he asks and my irritation start to build.

Layla comes walking in from the kitchen, "Hey Layne, I'm surprised you're not late. Oh wow, and you brought wine, fancy."

He walks toward her giving her a hug and kiss on the cheek. "You say that like I'm never on time to anything. You know what, never mind, don't reply to that," Layne jokes.

At dinner, Layne is sitting directly across from me and I'm avoiding eye contact. Seeing him at the

Bull is one thing, he's usually distracted talking to countless women.

"Carmen, I love how you transformed the house, it looks amazing," Layne mentions with a smile.

"Oh thank you so much. I still find myself rearranging here and there but it's coming along. So nice of you to notice," Carmen says happy as can be. He is really smooth, I give him that.

"I saw a few pictures of New Orleans and the wedding," Layne remarks, winking at Layla, "What a great time. That venue was absolutely stunning."

"It was beautiful, even better than I could have imagined. If you've never been to New Orleans you really need to go sometime," Carmen turns to Layla, "Layla, you could have just brought Layne as your date." Layla rolls her eyes and shakes her head.

"Unfortunately that train has already left the station," Layne says laughing.

We spend the rest of the evening on the porch and I've realized that Layne is really not that bad and I'm actually having a good time talking to him. It's already after ten and everyone heads inside leaving me, Layla and Layne on the front steps.

"So Layla tells me you guys lost some workers at the shop, I knew it was a matter of time with Rick. I don't know how he was able to hold on that long," Layne says leaning back on his elbows.

"Yeah, he tried to be tough but it was killing him. I'm glad Shane's still around. We finally got caught up a little over a week ago. James was thinking about hiring another mechanic but think we can manage between the four of us," I reply.

"Hell, at least you'll be making more money," Layne grins.

"Good point," I reply.

"Well I still can't believe Rick and Carol have been dating all these years. I would have never guessed," Layla says, still surprised. To the outside it looked like Carol was swinging for the other team.

"I told you, but no one wanted to believe me," I reply laughing.

"Gosh these mosquitos are eating me alive, I think I'm going to head in and go to bed," Layla says, swatting at her arm.

"Alright, I'm about to leave too, just gonna finish my tea and I'll be on my way. Love ya Layla," Layne waves.

"Good night guys." She walks in the house and shuts the door.

"So Ben," Layne starts, looking straight at me, "I know Layla would kill me for bringing this up but I have to. What's going on with the two of you right now?"

"I don't know what you're talking about," I reply, breaking eye contact and just staring out straight ahead.

"Come on man, I know what happened in New Orleans. She was so distraught and confused; she needed to talk to someone. Believe me, I'm not here to judge or anything." Not able to get out a single word I just sit there in silence. What the hell am I supposed to say?

"Look, sorry if I bombarded you with this. Honestly, I really wasn't looking for an answer. I just want to let you in on something in case it's not obvious. Layla is crazy about you, the way she looks at you, the way she talks about you, I've never seen her this way with anyone. Sure she's had boyfriends but this is different. Heck, I wish she had half of that fire when she was with me. You should consider yourself lucky," he pauses for a moment, "I also want you to know that there is no way in hell she'll make a move, she's afraid of rejection. So I guess what I'm trying to say is the ball's in your court, you can choose to shoot or walk away."

I take a deep breath, "You know, it's not that easy Layne. There are a lot of things I have to take into account."

"Man who cares that you're older, it's not that big of a deal. James will be fine, I know you're probably worried about him being your brother and Layla living here. I know it's a very unconventional situation but don't let anyone stand in the way of your happiness."

"You don't even know," I pause, "I'm not this great guy she's imagining, I come with issues. She's so young, she needs to live life and enjoy it."

"Man, we all have issues. Some worse than others but still we all come with baggage of some kind. Who's to say she couldn't enjoy life with you? I just really think that you could make her very happy. I don't want to sound sappy and talk about soulmates since I don't believe that shit but there is a connection there that is undeniable. If you want her, I'm telling you, she's yours."

If I want her, she's mine. The thought of it makes my heart race and I don't know what to say.

"So what are your issues Layne?" I ask, trying to redirect the conversation.

"My issues? Man, I can't keep a relationship to save my life. I had the longest run with Layla which doesn't say much since it was barely six months. I push people away that get too close because there could always be someone better out there. Layla is the only one I ever let in but that didn't even work out."

"You're still young though, you have plenty of time work on that," I say with encouragement.

"Exactly, and you're getting up there in age so I suggest you jump on it before it's too late," Layne chuckles, "I'm kidding man but seriously, think about it."

Never have I pictured myself having a one on one conversation with Layne about Layla, I'm glad I did though. He brought up a good point, either shoot or walk away. I can't keep living in this limbo of emotions, I need to come to a decision and the smartest one for both of us is to just let go. Maybe getting involved with someone else will make me just enough of an asshole for Layla to move on. God I know it would tear her apart but it's not like she's really happy now, she puts on a great act though. Heck, Maria has been texting me quite a bit since her visit, that would be really easy. What the fuck am I thinking? Have I lost my mind completely? What I really need to do is let Maria know that I'm not interested.

The next day Carmen comes into the shop, "Guess what? My sister will be in Atlanta for a conference at the end of the week. She wants to drive down here to visit us for the weekend, she should be here Friday." Speak of the devil.

"That's wonderful Carmen. We'll have to plan something," James says looking at me. I just nod and continue working, great just my luck.

Carmen made Shrimp Etouffee for dinner and I've come to the realization that shrimp must be her favorite food, she puts it in everything. When Layla is working, our dinners are a little less lively, the way her and Mason mess around is hilarious. Alex moved out a little over a week ago but still stops by quite a bit.

It's only 11 pm and the house is quiet. I'm not tired so I turn on the TV and flip through the channels. I hear the front door open and it's Layla.

"Hey. Got off early?" I ask

"Yeah, not much going on so Josh and I flipped a coin to see who would get to go home," she says sitting down in the Armchair, "What did you guys have for dinner? It still smells really good."

"Shrimp Etouffee, it actually was pretty good," I reply smiling.

"I knew it was going to be shrimp, Carmen really loves her seafood. That pizza we made a few weeks ago was really weird, did you try it?" Layla asks scrunching her forehead.

"No way, it didn't look right. Who puts shrimp on a pizza," I chuckle, "Carmen is a good cook but I really miss your cooking."

"Awe, that's sweet of you, thank you," she smiles blushing just a tiny bit.

"Well, right after you went to work Carmen came in the shop and said Maria will be here this weekend. I guess she's attending a conference in Atlanta this week."

She rolls her eyes sinking back in the chair and lets out a sigh, "Well I better be on my best behavior since James didn't approve of my comment when she was here last."

Layla

When I get to my room I flop myself onto my bed. The thought of seeing Maria again is pissing me off, she really brings out the worst in me. I can't let her get to me this time; we're not in a competition anymore.

Friday rolls around and I'm already at work wondering what time Maria will be arriving at the house. There's not too much going on here, Randy doesn't have anything special planned for tonight. I do notice that same group of guys from a few weeks ago; Layne said he's seen some of them at his gym in Macon. One of them keeps eyeing me but I've been ignoring him. He's really hot though, over six feet tall, longer medium blonde hair, really blue eyes, hell maybe I should flirt around a bit.

"Layla, you didn't tell me she was visiting again," Layne nudges me and rips me out of my thoughts.

A few moments later I hear that voice I detest, "Hi Layla, nice to see you again. I told Carmen we had to come back here; we had such a great time when I was here last month. And look at that, we can actually sit at the bar this time," Maria says just trying to get a reaction out of me. Carmen, James, Ben and Mason take the rest of the seats at the bar.

"Yes, I heard you were in Atlanta for a conference, how did that go?" I ask trying to sound like I care.

"Great. It's mainly networking, tips on reaching more clients, you know, things that probably wouldn't interest you."

Man what a bitch, think before you respond Layla. "Yeah you're probably right. Hey, but can I interest you in a drink?" I ask with a smile.

Layne gives me a look like he can't believe what just came out of her mouth. After making their drinks I step outside for just a minute, figuring fresh air will do me some good. The door opens and I pray to god it isn't Ben, the last thing I need is for him to check on me. It's Maria, even worse.

"You know Layla, I'm not letting you get in my way," Maria starts giving me a glare as if I'd wronged her.

"I don't know what you're talking about Maria," I answer and she laughs.

"You know, that little act may work on everyone else but you're not fooling me. I see how you look at Ben with those *'I'm so sweet and innocent'* eyes of yours. Carmen told me that the two of you are really close but I'm just going to let you in on something sweetie, you and him would never happen. Keep fantasizing. That man in there is more than you could ever handle. He's looking for someone with experience and I'm sorry to break it to you but you're not on that level."

Wow, what an attack. "Well, I'm sorry to disappoint you but you're wrong. Ben and I are friends, nothing more. I'm not standing in your way whatsoever. If Ben is who you want then you need to work it out with him and stop wasting your time on me," I say as if I have it together, inside I'm shaking.

The door opens, Ben and James walk out staring at us. "Is everything okay?" James asks looking a bit worried.

Maria smiles and nods and I take it to the next level, "Oh yeah, I was telling her about this sushi place in Atlanta that Layne and I have been to a few times, turns out she was there two days ago. Isn't that a coincidence?" Ben looks at me like I've lost my mind, James just looks relieved.

Back inside, Carmen takes James hand and leads him to the dancefloor for a slow dance. Maria is trying to convince Ben to dance but he refuses.

"Hey Maria," Layne starts, "I'd be happy to take you out there."

"Ben, will you really not come out there with me?" Maria asks while touching his arm.

"No, sorry," he replies, taking a drink.

"Alright, I don't really need to dance anyway, we'll just sit here," she smiles and I can tell she doesn't trust one thing I told her.

"Wow Layla, I think this is the first time I've been turned down by a beautiful woman, that shit hurts," Layne frowns looking at Maria, covering his heart.

"Oh I'm sure you can find a gorgeous girl here that will be happy to dance with you," Maria responds, damn Layne's charm isn't working.

"Oh, I know I can," Layne says in a cocky tone, "I wasn't looking for a girl though." Wow, that actually made her blush just a little but she still doesn't budge, she's got her eye on the prize.

After they leave I can't wait to hear what Layne has to say. "Man, that woman is a cold bitch. I saw her walk outside after you, did she say anything?" Layne asks curiously. I relay everything word for word and Layne's expression is pure shock.

"What the hell did you ever do to her? Well I wouldn't worry, she's her own worst enemy and

Ben is not interested whatsoever," Layne assures me.

"Oh well, I don't care anymore," I say wiping the counter.

"What? Where is this coming from? The other day you were daydreaming about him and today you're cool as a cucumber, I'm not buying it Layla."

"Layne, I've thought long and hard about this and it's useless. What am I supposed to do, get on my knees and –"

"Now Layla," Layne interrupts, "That may get the ball rolling." Even though that comment was completely inappropriate it's typical Layne and it makes me laugh.

When I get up the next morning I find Mason on the couch watching TV. "Where is everyone?" I ask, thinking they must have planned an outing for today.

"Carmen and Maria went to Macon for a little bit. I think Ben and James are in the shop working on stuff. I go into the kitchen and stand in front of the pantry debating on what to eat as the back door opens.

"Hey can I talk to you a minute," Ben asks in a serious tone. Great the last time he said that my whole world fell apart.

"What did Maria say to you yesterday?" he demands.

"Nothing, she was talking about her stay in Atlanta," I start.

"Layla, please don't lie to me."

Great, with the way he is looking at me I'm having a hard time lying. What am I going to say? "She said that she's really into you and won't let anyone stand in her way. Honestly I'm a little uncomfortable talking about this Ben," I say looking away and the next thing I know he's out the door.

Ben

I know she had to have said more than that; Layla's face gave it away. How do I tell Maria I have no interest in pursuing anything with her without ruining the rest of the weekend? Maybe I'll wait until tonight or tomorrow right before she leaves.

"Hey Ben, I think we'll finish up next week. The girls will be here in a little while, let's get cleaned up so we can spend some time with them," James says putting the wrenches away.

"James can I talk to you?" I ask and right at that moment I hear Carmen right outside announcing they are back and picked up lunch on the way.

After lunch James breaks out pictures of the old days when we used to perform together. In a way it is really nice to look through them, seeing all the people, wondering where they are right now. It also brings up painful memories, things I've put behind me and would rather not revisit.

It's evening, Layla and Mason come walking down the stairs.

"Hey what's going on guys," James begins," I'm about to go outside to set up the fire pit. Do you want to join us?"

"We were just about to head out," I explain grabbing my keys off the side table.

"Going anywhere good?" Maria asks, just trying to make conversation.

"Just some nightclubs in Macon, we're meeting Alex and Brittany. Did you guys want to come?" Mason asks.

"No thank you, maybe next time," Maria answers for all of us and they head out the door.

We've been sitting outside at the fire pit for about an hour. Carmen and Maria tell stories about when they were younger. Come to find out Maria has been married twice already, can't say I'm surprised. Sounds like she's lived a pretty wild life, you wouldn't think that the two of them were sisters.

"There was this one time we nearly died in the globe while we were trying something new, remember Ben?" James asks looking at me.

"Yeah, timing was just off by about two seconds. We both ended up with really bad cuts. You're lucky the bike didn't hit you in the head," I say shaking my head. I still remember that day, thank god it was while we were practicing and not in the middle of a show. Mom was terrified. Dad was just freaking out saying we were idiots;

he was scared we would be out of commission for a while. As soon as I was able to get up I walked straight to Sarah's trailer and asked her to marry me. I was a bloody mess but having that near death experience made me want to settle down. Sometimes I wonder how life would have been if I had forgiven her and stayed, would I be happy today?

"I think we are going to head inside, I'm a little tired," Carmen yawns, "But you two stay out here as long as you want, have a good time." She winks at Maria, James gets up and pats me on the shoulder before he and Carmen make their way up the steps and into the house.

"Wow, this weekend flew by so fast. I'm happy I got to see you again, maybe next time you can come visit me in New Orleans. We'll have so much fun together, just the two of us," Maria suggests throwing me a flirtatious look.

I was going to wait until tomorrow but this is my opportunity and I better take it. "Hey listen, I'm sorry I don't really know how to say this. I'm not looking for a relationship right now. I just need to be on my own and I'm sorry if I gave you the wrong impression. You're really nice but I just can't get involved." There I said it, I think I did pretty good.

"No one said anything about a relationship," she says, glaring at me, "I think you and I could have a lot of fun if you know what I mean. I can show you a good time, let's not worry about the future, just live in the moment. I'm telling you, you won't regret it."

Wow, I can't believe she just said that. A younger version of me probably would have jumped right on that, sex with no commitment, hell yeah. "I'm sorry I can't. Believe me I feel flattered but I'm just not interested."

She stares at me like she's never been turned down before. "Can I ask you a serious question?" she asks and I nod, "Are you involved with her?"

I know exactly who she's talking about. "Who are you talking about?" I say in a cool tone.

"Layla!"

I chuckle, "That's a joke right? Layla? Come on, I can't believe you'd think that." She stares at me in silence, I'm not sure if she's thinking about what to say or if she's trying to figure out if I'm lying. Technically I'm not lying; Layla and I aren't together.

"Okay, I'm sorry. I just...well never mind, it was stupid of me to ask that. Well I guess I'll have to respect that, I'm glad that you were honest with me. Don't lose my number though, if you change your mind, call me, I mean it."

Layla

I'm glad to be away from the house right now but a nightclub wasn't my first choice. I used to love to come out and dance but I'm just not into it right now. After a few drinks I loosen up just a little bit and walk around the club. I notice Mason talking to someone across the room and realize it's the same girl from the Bull. A dark haired guy comes up to me and asks me to dance, politely I decline but he's not taking no for an answer. He's getting a little closer and I tell him to back off.

"You heard her, back off," I hear a voice that I know all too well, Layne. What is he doing here? He should be at work right now.

"Who the hell are you?" the guy asks, getting in Layne's face.

"Her boyfriend. I suggest you back the fuck off me before I beat your ass," Layne says getting louder, towering over him. The guy throws his hands up and disappears.

"Oh my god, thank you so much. What are you doing here? Aren't you supposed to be at work?" I ask.

"Took a vacation day," he grins, "I texted Alex to see if he wanted to grab a drink and he said you guys were here."

"Well your timing couldn't have been better, he wasn't getting it," I laugh. Layne throws his arms around me and squeezes me tight before we go to find Alex and Brittany. Eventually Mason joins us bringing his new friend along. Her name is Amy and apparently the two of them have known each other for a few weeks already. She's really cute, petite with long blonde hair, exactly Mason's type.

James got up early to make a big breakfast for everyone this morning. As I go to find a seat at the table I notice Maria sitting in my chair next to Ben. I predicted that one; it's turned into her spot whenever she's here. James outdid himself, eggs, bacon, sausage, pancakes, hash browns and grits.

"Did you guys have a good time last night?" James asks looking at Mason.

"Yeah it was fun, Layne came out too and he totally saved Layla from this guy that was hitting on her," Mason chuckles.

"Not funny Mason, that guy wasn't giving up," I remark grabbing a piece of bacon.

"Well I guess you can thank Alex for inviting Layne, otherwise you would have been screwed," Mason adds.

Maria hasn't been her aggressive self which is surprising to me. I was ready for another attack but it never came. When it was finally time for her to leave she gave Ben a quick hug, not a longwinded goodbye like last time.

Later that evening I find Ben sitting outside on the swing playing around on his phone. "Hey, what are you doing?" I say walking toward him.

"Nothing much, just looking through my pictures," he answers with a smile.

"So Maria wasn't the chatterbox she normally is, did something happen?" I regret asking as soon as it comes out of my mouth. The two of them could have hooked up last night and this could have been the awkward morning after, I don't want to know.

"I told her I wasn't interested. She didn't believe me at first but eventually she gave up," he says putting his phone in his pocket.

"Well good that you told her that you're not interested," I pause, "I mean that it worked out the way you wanted it to." *'Oh my god shut up Layla'*. Ben turns toward me and just starts laughing. I'm so happy the Maria issue is done but it still doesn't change anything, Maria was never the obstacle.

The next morning I wake up early and can't get back to sleep. Eventually I make my way downstairs to the kitchen and grab an apple. As I'm cutting it, the knife slips and I slice my finger instead. Letting out a bloodcurdling scream I grab a towel off the counter and sit on the floor covering my finger. It must be a deep cut judging from the blood seeping through the towel.

I hear Ben's door open. Within seconds he finds me and kneels down. "Oh my god, what happened?" he yells freaking out a bit.

"I was cutting an apple and got my finger instead, I don't even want to look at it," I reply with my eyes shut and turn my head in the other direction.

At that moment I hear James and Carmen asking what's going on. "She cut herself, it's bleeding through the towel. Layla, can I please look at it?" Ben asks and I nod, my eyes still closed. Slowly he uncovers my finger and immediately covers it back up holding pressure on the area. Oh boy, that's not a good sign.

"What do you think?" James asks concerned.

"I think we need to go to the Emergency Room, it's really- "

"No. I'm not going. I'll just keep pressure on it and superglue it once it stops bleeding," I protest in fear.

"Layla, it could get infected. You need to see a doctor," Carmen cries.

"Look at me Layla," Ben pleads and after taking a deep breath I look into his eyes, "I'm going to take you to the ER and I'll be with you the whole time if you want. I won't leave you I swear, but we need to go." I haven't actually seen the cut so I'm just going to have to trust him. Carmen grabs a clean towel and rewraps my finger.

The downside about living in a small town is that it's a twenty-minute ride to the nearest hospital. Once we walk into the lobby I'm relieved that only one other person is waiting. Within minutes we're taken back to a room and the doctor comes in to check my finger. The bleeding finally stopped and he determines that it's best to place sutures. He explains that he will need to give me a quick injection to numb the area and terror must be written all over my face.

"Layla, it's fine. I've had so many stiches it's really no big deal. Just don't look and it will be over before you know it," Ben says trying to reassure me.

I'm sitting in the chair not at all convinced by what he just said. Reluctant I stretch my left arm out over the little table and I start to shake, I absolutely hate needles. Ben catches me by surprise when he leans in close to me, placing his right hand over my cheek to keep me from looking at what's about to happen. I grab his free hand and squeeze it tight closing my eyes. I feel him stroking my cheek with his thumb to distract me and it's totally working. Once the doctor finishes Ben steps back and I let go of his hand.

"You did great. You'll need to come back in about a week to have the sutures removed. In the meantime, don't remove the bandage until tomorrow, keep the area clean and no soaking in water. You want to make sure not to overexert your finger. What do you do for work?" the doctor asks.

"She's a bartender," Ben answers for me.

"It may be best to at least take a few days off, I'll write you a note for work."

Back in the car I look over at Ben and he grins back at me. "Thank you Ben. I really appreciate you taking and staying with me," I pause for a second, "and talking me through it."

"Of course, I'm glad you let me," he replies with a grin.

"Now I feel like an idiot, it wasn't as bad as I imagined."

Ben

What a day. Why do I keep finding myself in these close situations with Layla? Makes the thought of backing off much harder. For being terrified of needles she did great, she could totally handle getting a tattoo. Layla said she doesn't have to go back to work until next Tuesday but Randy wants her to come in Friday night for Karaoke. Sitting on the porch I hear the door opening, it's Carmen.

"Hey Ben," she says as she sits down next to me. Great, I'm sure this is going to be about Maria.

"Hey," is all I can manage to say, Carmen and I don't have a lot of one on one conversations.

"I'm glad you took Layla to the hospital, that was really nice of you," she smiles.

"Of course, I'm just surprised we convinced her, sometimes she can be really hardheaded," I laugh, relieved that Maria hasn't come up yet.

"You're right," she adds, "You know, sometimes I look at Layla and I see myself."

"How so?" I ask curiously

"I was always a little on the quiet side, didn't have a lot of friends. Before I met my late husband I spent most of my time with my family. I wouldn't go back and change anything but I think Layla should get out more, meet people. How is she ever going to meet anyone in a small place like this?"

"Well, she's traveled most of her life and been around a lot of people, believe me, sometimes it's nice to be a bit secluded. "

"That's right, I always forget about the circus. I would have loved to know you guys in those days. I know you enjoy the quiet but it must have been an exciting life," Carmen sighs.

"That lifestyle had its moments, made us who we are. It was a lot of hard work too, a lot of uncertainty. I would never want to do it again," I reply.

The workload at the shop has been steady all week, since Rick and Carol left we definitely are making more money. I've been able to save up quite a bit and I'm thinking that maybe I should look into getting my own place sometime soon. James always says he's happy to have everyone around but he and Carmen are newlyweds and I'm sure they would love to have more alone time.

"Hey Shane, hand me that wrench over there," I say reaching out my hand.

"So, do you have any plans tonight?" Shane asks.

"Nah man, not really. Mason and I usually hang out at the Bull Friday nights but he's busy so I think I'm just going to be around here."

"Well if you want to go, I'll join you. I haven't been there in almost a year," he chuckles. Come to think of it Shane and I haven't done anything outside of the shop so I take him up on his offer.

It's quite crowded when we get there and there's a group of girls onstage singing. I do a quick scan to find Layla but I don't see her anywhere. Making our way to the bar, Layne greets us with a smile.

After getting our drinks Shane finds an open table in the back and we sit down. "So did you ever find roommates? I know you mentioned something a while back," I ask taking a sip of my whiskey.

"Yeah, I actually did. It's called having a live-in girlfriend," he laughs, "she moved in about a month ago and we're splitting the bills and everything seems to be covered. I was so relieved because the thought of having strangers in my place made me really uneasy."

I hear Randy on the mic, "Alright, if ya'll don't wanna hear a sappy song next, I suggest for ya'll to march up here and sign up. Seriously, it ain't no country song either," he pauses, "no one? Okay well I warned ya'll."

Shane jokes that maybe he should volunteer to sing and we both have a laugh. I look toward the stage and spot Layla. I'm glad I came in, she's actually going to sing this one on her own. The music starts and I recognize the melody in an instant, it's the same song we danced to at the reception. I notice her eyes are closed, as if she is feeling every word she's singing. For a moment I wonder if she chose this particular song because of me but then again I'm sure she hasn't even noticed us sitting here. When we danced to it I didn't pay attention to the lyrics because I was lost in conversation with her, but sitting here, focusing on every single word I know that she is everything I ever wanted.

Chapter Eleven

Layla

I was so happy that Ben didn't come in tonight. It was really stupid of me to choose that song but I really love it and from the look of all the couples slow dancing, they did as well. I decide to leave a little after eleven and head home, I thought about staying around to hang out with Layne for a little while but he's been so busy at the bar he barely had time to say hi.

The next day my phone rings and it's Brittany. She's asking if I'm interested in having a girl's night with her and some friends and I figure why not. I've never been too keen on a bunch of girls hanging out and painting nails but since I've been home all week I figure what the hell.

At lunch Carmen mentions that she and James will be going to a movie tonight and a part of me wants to cancel my plans since it will just be Ben and Mason. What am I thinking? What good would that do? I suppose I like to torture myself.

"Well I got invited to Brittany's tonight," I start.

"Wow, you and Brittany are friends, who would have thought," Mason comments.

"Well, we got closer in New Orleans, believe me I would have never predicted for that to happen either," I laugh.

Upstairs I throw a few things in an overnight bag and make my way downstairs. I notice Alex sitting on the couch and for a moment I forgot that he lives with Brittany.

"So I guess we're trading places tonight Layla," Alex says grinning, "don't go sneaking in my bed."

"Alex, I like Brittany," I pause, "but not that much, I'm 100% into guys."

"Then why don't you ever date one?" I hear Mason yelling from the kitchen. I decide to ignore him and walk out the door.

It's really strange, it just dawned on me that I've never seen Brittany's apartment. She's invited me over in the past but I always had an excuse not to go, I'm really interested to see what it looks like.

"Layla, I'm so happy you came," Brittany hugs me and tells me to come in. Wow, her apartment is super modern. A lot of white and orange and abstract art all over the walls. She introduces me to two of her friends, Paige and Kat. I've seen them around but have never talked to them, I always thought they seemed a little stuck up.

Brittany ordered Chinese food and we sit on the living room floor talking and drinking wine. I'm already on my third glass when the Layne subject comes up.

"So, you know Layne pretty well don't you?" Paige begins, "Is he seeing anyone right now?"

I take a big sip of my wine, "Nope, he's not seeing anyone as far as I know."

Kat sighs, "God he is so hot, I seriously got a gym membership at his gym just so I can stare at him working out. Layla, you guys used to go out right?"

I stand up and walk to the kitchen counter to refill my glass, "Um yeah, we used to date for a little while."

"Why did you break up?" Paige asks.

"Guys, seriously, stop bombarding her with questions," Brittany interjects and it surprises me a bit. Brittany has definitely calmed down quite a bit. She used to be just like these girls.

"Oh come on Brit, this may be the closest we ever get to Layne," Paige frowns.

"Okay well I'm just going to get to it, how was he, you know, intimately? He just looks like he knows what he's doing," Kat says winking at me. Oh my god these girls are crazy, on the other hand I really need to remember to tell Layne about them, they are some easy conquests and it seems as if that's all they are looking for.

"Sorry girls, I don't kiss and tell. You'll have to find out for yourselves. Just go up and talk to him, he's a really nice guy," I suggest. My phone buzzes and I turn it over, it's a text from Ben which reads *How's girl's night going?* I smile and since Paige and Kat are distracted still discussing Layne I take a picture of my wine glass and reply *Fourth glass lol*.

"Was that Layne?" Paige asks, I guess they weren't that distracted. I shake my head and Brittany decides to change the subject and breaks out some board games. Ben and I exchange a few messages back and forth; he mentioned that Mason, Alex, Layne and he are sitting outside having a bonfire. Seeing Layne's name puzzles me for a moment, I figure Alex must have invited him over. It's Saturday night, why isn't he working again? My phone buzzes and it's a selfie of the four of them, the fire in the background. I smile and figure maybe it may be fun to add some fuel to the fire. "Oh hey girls, want to get your Layne fix?" I ask turning the phone toward them revealing the picture.

"Look at Alex grinning like a little kid," Brittany remarks.

"Let's go over there right now," Kat starts, "seriously, four guys, four girls, it couldn't be more perfect."

"I think we've all had just a little too much to drink for that," I comment laughing.

"Hey can I see that picture again?" Paige asks and I hand over my phone, "I mean Layne's a total babe but what about that cutie next to him with the goatee, I'll take him." She is talking about Ben and I can feel my blood pressure rising.

"Oh, that's Ben. He's Alex's older brother, when I say older I'm mean way older Paige," Brittany says with raised eyebrows.

"Well I didn't say I wanted to marry him. I can just be his little Lolita, that's every man's fantasy isn't it?" Paige giggles. That totally backfired, guess I added the fuel to my own fire.

A knock at the door rips me out of my sleep. I press the home button on my phone and notice it's already 11 am. Before Brittany can get up the door opens and Alex comes walking in.

"Why did you knock?" Brittany asks rubbing her eyes.

"Well, I wanted to give you a little warning before just barging in," he laughs, "well you all look like you had a long night."

He's probably talking about the messy buns and makeup smudges on our faces, we stayed up way too late but overall I must admit I had a great time. I get up, fold the blanket I used and place it on the sofa along with the pillow. I thank Brittany for inviting me over; the other two are still fast asleep so I grab my things and head out the door.

Once back home I go straight upstairs to jump in the shower. I've become a pro at washing my hair using just one hand, thank god these stiches are coming out tomorrow. After getting dressed I go downstairs and join Carmen in the living room.

"Hey Layla, did you have a good time?" Carmen asks turning down the volume on the TV.

"Yeah, I did actually. We watched a movie, played some games, gossiped a bit. I had no idea how clueless I was about people in this town until last night. I may never be able to look at them the same way again," I say jokingly.

"I guess that's what happens in small towns. James, Ben and Mason are fishing at the lake.

Hey I wanted to ask you, Halloween is coming up in a few weeks. Does anyone host any parties around here?" Carmen asks.

"Well Randy does at the Bull, nothing fancy but people get dressed up and have a good time. Last year I was working and he had a pretty good turnout," I recall.

"Well, Halloween is on a Saturday this year so you should be off right?" Carmen asks and I wonder where this is going.

"Yeah, I won't be working. Why?"

"Back in New Orleans we always had Halloween parties, I love dressing up. What do you think about all of us going there to celebrate? Could be a good time, don't you think?"

"Well, good luck getting James to go. He detests anything Halloween," I chuckle.

Ben

Luckily the shop is pretty dead today, I have a few things I really need to take care of in Macon. "Hey James, do you mind if I run a few errands here in a little while?" I ask while we eat our lunch.

"No problem. If you're planning to head to Macon you know Layla has her appointment there in about an hour, you could ride together and save gas," James suggests.

"Um, it's not going to be really quick so I'm sure she'd be bored. Have to print some documents, fill them out and send them back to St. Louis. Also want to pick up a new socket wrench set while I'm out," I respond eager to get on the road.

I knew it wouldn't' be a quick trip but I never thought it was going to take over two hours. It was such an overwhelming feeling going through pages and pages of documents, at least I had everything I needed with me. My mind being so preoccupied I completely forgot to stop by the hardware store on the way back. As I pull up to the house I see Layla getting out of her car.

"Got the stiches out?" I ask as I get out of the car.

"Yeah finally. I had to wait over an hour even though I had an appointment. I ended up playing on my phone until it died. Can't picture a life without technology anymore, kind of sad," Layla sighs.

At dinner Carmen brings up the idea of all of us dressing up for Halloween and celebrating at the bull. I think the last time I dressed in a Halloween costume was when I was a teenager but I think it could be fun. I hear James sighing and making a face, even as a child he wasn't really into Halloween. Eventually he gives in and agrees to go.

Later that night, realizing I left my phone in the shop I go outside to grab it. On the way I notice Layla lying on the picnic table, it's quite dark outside but there's just enough light coming from the moon to see her long dark blonde hair hanging off the sides of the table.

"Stargazing?" I ask with a smile.

"Haven't seen one star, it's just me and the lonely old moon tonight," she sighs turning her head to face me.

"That's too bad," I pause, "I forgot my phone on the workbench in there so I'm just going to grab it an-" she interrupts me.

"You're welcome to stay if you'd like, no pressure though," she says smiling. How the hell can I say no to that? I recall all the times we used to lay out at night and the great conversations we had, seems like such a long time ago now.

"Sure," I say and she gets up and walks toward my truck. Lying shoulder to shoulder she brings up some interesting facts about the moon that I didn't know. The conversation seems really odd and impersonal right now so I ask her about the sleepover at Brittany's. She starts to chuckle and shares all the gossip. Some of the things are just way over the top, but I'm sure they could be true.

"How many glasses of wine did you end up having?" I ask looking up at the moon.

"Oh god, I don't even remember. The other two girls kept asking questions about Layne, swooning over him. I'm telling you, he's like the town's own celebrity, the effect he has on most women is just mind-blowing."

"Is that what got you?" I ask wondering what her response will be. She turns to look at me with a puzzled expression.

"James told me you two dated for a bit, I figured it must have been his charm," I smile.

"I've known Layne for years, his charm wasn't what brought us together," she pauses, "One night we were both drunk and we hooked up.

The next day when I woke up I was horrified that I let myself get so wasted. Honestly, he was kind of shocked with what happened as well, I really think the only reason we started dating was because neither of us wanted it to just be a stupid mistake. Realizing we were better off as friends we called it quits and here we are now, best friends for life."

"Shit happens when people get drunk," I comment with a grin.

"As we know," she chuckles and surprises me just a bit.

"Yep, as we know," I say, eyes back on the night sky.

I'm not very forthcoming about my past but decide to tell her a story about when I lived in St. Louis, after about ten minutes I notice she hasn't said very much so I look over and notice her eyes are closed. This is the first time I've seen her sleep and I could stare at her the rest of the night. She looks so calm, beautiful and peaceful. I am so tempted to brush the strand of hair away from her face but I don't want to wake her.

"If you only knew," I whisper, "I can tell myself whatever I want, still doesn't change the fact that I'm falling more in love with you every day." She moves just a tiny bit and I pray to god she didn't hear what I just said. After about twenty minutes I decide to wake her, we can't camp out here all night. Sitting up I gently tap her shoulder, she twitches and slowly opens her eyes.

"Oh my god did I fall asleep? I'm so sorry," she apologizes.

"That's alright, my story must have bored you," I say jokingly.

"No, no, not at all, I didn't realize I was so tired."

We hop out of the truck, I shut the tailgate and we make our way inside. Layla starts walking up the steps while I lock the front door. As I turn to walk to my room I notice Layla stopped in the middle of the staircase looking at me.

"Ben," she begins and a shudder runs through my body, did she hear what I said? "Just wanted to say goodnight, sleep good," she smiles and I feel relieved.

The next day Carmen is already in full organization mode planning a trip to Atlanta to shop for Halloween costumes. It's still about a month away but you can tell she's excited. One of Shane's friends just brought a car for us to work on, an old timer with a carburetor issue. Can't wait to get my hands on that one, but we still have a few others that we need to finish up.

"So James, I was thinking about looking at apartments. Do you know of any in town or do I need to look in Macon?" I ask as James is pouring oil through a funnel.

"An apartment? You want to move out?" he asks puzzled.

"Well, I love living here but I need to start getting on my feet again and besides I bet you and Carmen will appreciate more alone time," I say winking at him.

"I understand. Well it's going to be hard to find something in town, there are a few places. I can check with one of my buddies, he has a few properties he rents out. You'll have more choices in Macon, it'll be a twenty-minute ride to work though," James pauses, "Wait, you're still planning on working here right?"

"Not really, I think I'm going to apply for a suit and tie kind of job," I joke, "I'm kidding man, of course I'm going to stay here."

Chapter Twelve

Layla

It's my first day back at work after my fiasco with the kitchen knife. Having a week off was really nice but I was eager to get back to work. It takes me just a bit to get back in the swing of things because I'm still babying my finger a little.

"It's so awesome to have you back Layla," Layne says bumping me with his shoulder.

"Well if you missed me that much you could have come by the house," I joke.

"Totally impossible, had to pick up some of your shifts while you had a quick impromptu vacation. I was there on Saturday but you decided to hang out with your new BFF."
I roll my eyes, impromptu vacation? Hell maybe I should have taken the time and actually gone somewhere.

"Oh yeah, by the way, why weren't you working Saturday?" I ask.

"Your absence jacked all the schedules around so Saturday was my day off," he smiles, "How was girl's night, any girl on girl action?"

"You wish. Oh, there were two girls that were very interested in everything they could find out about Layne Turner though. Paige and Kat, do those names ring a bell?"

"Paige, brunette, kind of a bitchy look on her face?" Layne asks and I nod chuckling.

"Oh and Kat, she's the one with the short blonde hair, I think she goes to my gym."

"Bingo. I seriously think these two girls will do anything to get close to you." Layne smiles but doesn't say a word which strikes me as odd. I was ready for one of his smart comments; he almost looks as if he's hiding something. As the night comes to a close I've noticed Layne hasn't been his flirtatious self with the ladies tonight so I decide to ask if everything is ok.

"Well Layla, I think I met someone," he answers and I'm surprised, I've never heard him say that.

"Really? Who is she?" I ask dying out of curiosity.

"Her name is Ella. Not sure if you've ever really noticed her, she's the redhead that comes in from time to time."

I think for a moment and I recall him talking to a redhead about two weeks ago. "Oh, I know who you're talking about, she seems really nice and fairly quiet. How did you get her to come out of her shell?"

"If you're asking if I've hooked up with her the answer is no," Layne confesses and I'm shocked, "I really want to attempt to do this the right way, you know, go out on dates and actually get to know her before taking it further. Obviously the other way doesn't seem to work out for me."

"I think that's a great idea Layne, I'm really happy for you and I hope it works out," I smile and give him a hug.

After getting home I go to bed but have a hard time falling asleep. I'm truly happy for Layne but a little piece of my heart feels shattered right now. It's not like I want to be with him, I've had every opportunity. Maybe it's because I know our friendship is going to change. It's quite possible it has nothing to do with what Layne said at all, I may just feel discouraged because I can't have Ben. Either way, I need to start making some changes, need to open myself up to meet someone and stop wasting time. I don't want to look back when I'm thirty and say I've been pining over someone that doesn't want me.

Ben

It's Friday and I'm anxious to see if the documents have been delivered. I log into my email account to see if I received any notification, no new messages. The woman at the post office did tell me that with the type of certified mail I chose it's possible that it could take up to ten days. Pulling up the post office's website I decide to double check with the tracking number they provided me with. After entering the twenty-digit code I click submit, still nothing. I guess I'll just have to be patient and wait until next week to check again. There's a knock at my door and it's James.

"Hey Ben, we're planning to go to O'Malley's for dinner tonight, did you want to come with us?"

"Is Mason coming?" I ask.

"No, Mason has a date with that girl he's been talking about, so it will just be the three of us," James says.

"Nah, man. You and Carmen have a nice evening together, I don't want to intrude," I say leaning back in my chair.

"Ben, you're not intruding, and anyway, Carmen told me to ask you," he chuckles and I agree to join them.

As I walk into the living room I notice Carmen sitting on the couch painting her toenails. "Damn it," she curses under her breath and looks up at me, "hey Ben, would you be so kind and run upstairs to grab the nail polish remover? That's the one thing I forgot to bring downstairs, it should be in our bathroom under the sink."

"Sure, no problem," I say, heading upstairs. After rummaging through the most of the cabinets in the master bath I am unable to find it. I walk out into the hallway to check the other bathroom. I stop at the doorway as I see Layla standing in front of the mirror fully concentrating on curling her hair. For a moment I stand there just staring. That black shirt she is wearing looks like it was molded to her body, so sexy and I've learned that those ripped blue jeans must be her favorite.

"Hey Ben, what's up?" she says pulling me out of my daydream.

"Um," I pause, completely forgetting my words, "Not much. Carmen sent me up here to grab nail polish remover but I couldn't find any so I thought I would check in here."

"Oh sure," Layla says while she places the curling iron on the sink. She opens the medicine cabinet to the right, grabs the polish remover and hands it to me. For a moment her hand touches mine and she gives me a coy little smile. That smile has caused me many sleepless nights in the past, feeling myself getting weak I thank her and hurry downstairs.

After handing Carmen the nail polish remover I sit in the Armchair and grab a magazine. About five minutes later Layla comes downstairs, goes into the kitchen and returns to the living room with a soda in hand.

"Alright guys, I have to go," Layla says while opening her soda, "Enjoy dinner and I'll see you in the morning."

When we get to O'Malley's I'm surprised that it's not very crowded for a Friday night and we are seated right away.

"Oh I almost forgot," James begins, "I talked to by buddy the other day, he said he doesn't have any rentals coming available anytime soon. One of his tenants mentioned something about possibly moving out in January but it's not a sure thing yet. He said he will keep me informed."

"Hey thanks, I've looked online a little and noticed a few in Macon that seemed really nice with some amenities," I mention as the waiter sets our food on the table.

"How about Brittany's complex?" Carmen asks looking at James.

"I forgot about those, they are really nice. I believe they have a pool and a gym there as well, that's another place to check out," James smiles. Sounds really good to me, I'm just not sure I want to live so close to Alex and Brittany. It can't hurt to check it out though.

"Hey, let's stop by the Bull on the way back, we haven't been there in a while," Carmen says getting up from the table after finishing our meal. The last time James and Carmen went there was while Maria was visiting. God I don't even want to think about that, I'm just happy I put an end to that.

On the car ride over, Mason's new girlfriend is the topic of conversation. James mentions that Mason invited her over for dinner tomorrow night so we can meet her. I remember seeing her at the Bull that one time but honestly can't even remember her hair color.

After arriving, we step inside and Carmen makes her way toward the bar, waving at Layla. It's fairly quiet and the three of us find a seat at the bar.

"Hey, nice to see you guys. What can I get you?" Layla asks with a big smile. Her hair is up in a ponytail and I wonder why she even bothered curling it in the first place.

"I'll just have a water, "I look over at James and Carmen, "You guys go ahead, I'll drive us back." Carmen orders a Pina Colada, no surprise there and James goes with a beer.

"Hey, where's Layne at?" I ask looking around. I see Josh at the bar with Layla which is unusual for a Friday night.

"Oh Layne has a date, so he and Josh switched shifts," Layla responds handing a glass to Josh.

"A date?" Carmen interrupts, "Do you know her?"

"Not really, I've seen her before. She's pretty but doesn't seem like his usual type, she's really quiet."

I notice Randy has switched up the music just a little, normally he only plays country music but he's added a variety of top hits from the last few decades. Carmen and James take the opportunity to have some alone time and head to the dancefloor. Josh starts telling Layla and I about the pranks he and Layne pull on each other and in no time we are cracking up laughing. I look to the side because I can feel someone standing next to me and it's a really tall guy with longer blonde hair.

"Hey, can I get you anything?" Layla asks still smiling.

"No thanks, still have my drink at the table over there. My friends and I have been coming in for a few weeks and I just wanted to come over to introduce myself. My name is Weston," he says reaching his hand out to Layla.

Looking a little unsure, she shakes his hand, "Hi, nice to meet you. I'm Layla," she pauses, "And this is Ben and Josh." He gives us a quick nod but then his eyes return to Layla.

"So I just wanted to ask, would there be a chance you'd let me take you out to dinner sometime? I'd really love to get to know you," Weston asks with a smirk. I grab my water to take a sip, biting on the straw I can feel myself getting heated, this guy really just asked her out on a date.

"Um," Layla starts, "I don't know what to say. I'm pretty busy most ni-" Weston interrupts her.

"God I'm sorry, I didn't mean to put you on the spot here in front of your friends. Think about it," he winks at her before making his way back to his friends.

"Well Layla, just in case it's unclear to you, that guy totally wants you," Josh points out, chuckling just a bit. Layla looks over at me and our eyes lock, I'm feeling a crazy indescribable connection right now and I would love to know what's going through her mind.

Layla

It's 3 am and I'm finally leaving work, boy has it been an interesting night. Why did Weston have to come up and ask me out right in front of Ben? I was so overwhelmed and honestly I can't even remember what I said, at least he didn't demand a yes or no answer. Part of me would really love to get to know him, in the past he's caught my eye once or twice. He must be over six feet tall and he has hair that any woman would kill for. I really do believe if Ben hadn't been sitting there I would have totally taken him up on his offer, next time I guess. As I drive up to the house I notice light coming from inside the shop but the house is pitch-black. I'm guessing someone forgot to hit the switch before leaving. When I get out of the car I walk toward the shop and grab the door handle, of course it's unlocked. I walk in and I see Ben sitting on the ground, his back against the wheel of a car, he looks like a wreck.

"Ben, is everything alright?" I ask walking toward him.

"Fuck!" he mumbles and I freeze for a moment. "I'm sorry Layla, you weren't supposed to hear that," he says as he gets up. He's looking directly at me and it seems as if he's had a rough night. I just saw him a few hours ago and he seemed fine, what could have happened?

"Are you ok? What's wrong?" I ask, I've never seen him like this and it's worrying me.

"I'm fine, I was just thin-," he stops and takes a deep breath, "Fuck it, you know what? I'm not fine, who am I kidding?" He walks toward the workbench leaning against it, both palms on his forehead with fingers spread. "I just can't do it anymore, I can't," he says to himself.

"Ben, what is it, tell me. Did something happen? Tell me," I demand walking toward him, touching his arm. He lowers his arms and holds on to bench behind him taking a deep breath just staring at me.

"Layla, I can't go on like this. I go around pretending that everything is fine while I'm falling apart inside," he pauses, "I've tried telling myself that this is wrong but the more I fight it, the more I want you. I don't want to stay away from you anymore." My heart is pounding; I can't believe he's standing in front of me saying this. For a second I wait for something else to follow but he's silent.

"Then don't," is all I can manage to say and I touch his hand. He turns his head away just a little.

"Layla, you have no idea. I have unresolved shit that I need to deal with, and James what is-"

"I don't care Ben, there's nothing you can tell me that would change the way I feel about you. As for James, we don't have to tell anyone, I'm serious," I respond hoping to ease his mind. He turns to me, giving me a little smirk.

I take that as an invitation and drape my hand around the back of his neck and pull him towards me. He removes his hands from the bench finding my waist, barely touching me. All I feel is the warmth of his breath on my lip and if I don't kiss him now I feel as if I will go insane. Carefully I press my lips to his, studying his reaction at the same time. He kisses me back with the same uncertainty; it's beautiful, slow and steady. His grip starts to tighten and I feel his tongue graze my lip. I slip my other hand under the back of his shirt, touching his back and his kiss livens.

Abruptly he stops and switches positions leaning me against the bench, holding my hands down with his and my heart skips a beat. Very gently he plants kisses down my neck, he releases one of my hands and I feel his fingers attempting to peel my shirt down my shoulder. His tongue finds my lips again and his kiss sends a jolt through my body. Releasing my other hand he starts unbuttoning my shirt. Within five seconds it falls to the floor exposing my bra. All I can think is thank god I chose to wear a cute one today.

Finding the seam of his shirt I start lifting it, grinning he quickly pulls it over his head and throws it to the side. Pressing his body to mine, the feeling of his bare skin is sending a sensation through me I can't even begin to describe. He plants kisses down my shoulder as I feel his hands unclasping my bra. When he gets to the last clasp he stops and steps back. Oh my god he's having regrets, I can't believe this.

"Layla," he begins and I stare at him catching my breath, "You have no idea how bad I want you right now, how often I've fantasized about this. It's seriously taking me a lot of self-control to stop." I'm speechless, just standing there staring at him in utter confusion.

"Listen, I don't want to screw things up. I want us to take our time, there's no rush. We already took a huge step tonight. I'm serious about you and it just doesn't feel right doing this in the shop," he pauses and smirks, "at least not the first time."
"Oh my god," I pause, "I seriously thought you were going to say you were making a mistake."

"No way," he grins, "I'm past all that, there's no going back for me now."

"I'm totally fine with taking our time," I say as I grab my shirt off the floor and he flashes me a big smile while putting his shirt back on.

Walking toward the house it's hard for me to grasp what just happened. If someone had told me this was on my agenda when I woke up yesterday, I would have said they were delusional. I go to the kitchen to grab a bottle of water out of the fridge and see Ben leaning against the door frame of his room gazing in my direction. The only light is coming from the small lamp on his dresser so it's hard to make out his expression. Walking toward him he meets me halfway, draping his arms around me and all I can think is I'm so happy everyone else is asleep. Telling him goodnight he gives me one more earth shaking kiss that instantly makes me weak. Reluctantly I pull away, letting go of his hand and turn to walk out of the room. Not even a second later I feel his hand grip mine.

"Fuck waiting," he groans, pulling me into his room and locking the door behind him. Leading me over to his bed he sits down and pulls me toward him so I'm standing between his legs. He removes his shirt and I slowly start to unbutton mine. He scoots further back and lies down and I climb on top of him. Straddling him I can feel that he is aroused. I reach behind, I undo the last clasp on my bra, I didn't bother to fix it before putting my shirt back on at the shop. He slowly pulls it off me and bites his lip. Running his hands over my breasts he tells me how beautiful I am which in turn makes me blush. He flips me over on my back so he's on top of me, kissing me gently as if he's savoring every moment. When he gets to my navel I feel him undoing the button on my jeans, pulling down the zipper and slowly removing them along with my underwear. He's pretty slick, I have no idea when his pants came off. Making his way back up to my lips my hands run down his back until I reach the waistband of his boxers. Playfully I tug at them and start pulling them off with his help. Resting his forehead to mine, he looks into my eyes.

"Layla, I don't think I can wait much longer, are you ready?" he asks, wow, this is new to me; no one has ever asked me that.

"Oh yeah, like two months ago," I joke and he chuckles a bit.

He slowly sinks his hips into me which immediately makes me cry out in pleasure. I cover my mouth, afraid that someone may hear me; he moves my hand replacing it with his lips. His movements are gentle but steady; I can tell he is holding back. His hands are entwined with mine, feeling him is driving me over the edge. I move my lips to his shoulder, my tongue exploring a trail from his collarbone to a sensitive spot right under his earlobe. Moving his hands to my sides he invades my mouth and his kiss becomes untamed and his thrusts faster, deeper. My fingernails dig into his back and I feel myself clench around him. Moments later he lets out a loud groan and I feel his body quiver as his pace slows. After catching our breath he kisses me delicately, holding me tight in his arms and I feel as if I could lie here forever entangled with him.

"Don't go," he whispers in my ear. Laying my head on his chest I run my fingers over the dragon covering the side of his body. This really just happened, I tell myself unable to keep a smile off my face. I decide to stay until he drifts off, if we intend to keep this a secret then there's no way I can let myself fall asleep next to him.
Back up in my room I know there is no way I am going to sleep. I'm still feeling a rush running through my body and all of a sudden it finally hit me, Ben is mine. I've spent countless hours, days, nights dreaming and hoping that this would happen, but honestly I just figured it would remain a fantasy. The way he kisses me is just breathtaking and last night topped anything I had ever imagined.

Chapter Thirteen

Ben

As I wake up I realize Layla is gone, I'm sure she left as soon as I fell asleep. I'm still having a hard time fathoming what happened. I had such good intentions, really wanted us to take our time but that last kiss in the kitchen did me in. Now we're together, just the thought of it brings a big smile to my face.

It's already 10 am so I get up and quickly jump into the shower. After wiping the condensation off the mirror I turn to check my back and notice a few scratches that Layla left on me, just seeing that is a total turn on. Walking into the dining area I find Layla and Carmen sitting at the table. "Good morning Ben, sleep well?" Carmen asks.

"Excellent, thanks," I smirk and notice Layla smiling back. It's like I just woke up to a whole new life and in a way this is a whole new chapter.

"Carmen, are you ready?" James comes in grabbing his keys off the counter, "We're just running to the store really fast, do you guys need anything?" Layla and I both shake our heads and they leave.

As soon as I hear that door close I walk up to Layla and she has the most mischievous grin on her face. I grab her waist and pull her close, "Morning beautiful. I woke up and you were gone, nearly broke my heart," I say with a frown.

"Believe me, I didn't want to go but you know I had to," she responds draping her hands around the back of my neck. I smile and her lips move closer to mine but she doesn't kiss me. She twirls my hair with her finger and feeling the warmth of her breath on my lower lip is torturous. She's teasing and it's really sexy, I kiss her hard, as if my life depends on it. All kinds of ideas are running through my head until I hear a cough in the distance. Layla instantly pulls away, adjusting her shirt. Mason walks through the doorway rubbing his eyes.

"Hey, good morning guys," he says sitting down at the table, a second ago I was imagining Layla on it, that fantasy died pretty quick.

"Morning," Layla responds, "How was your date?"

"It was great, we went to this cool new restaurant in Macon, a Japanese place. Then we took a walk at the River park, it is so beautiful at night."

After about twenty minutes Layla disappears, heading up to her room. Mason's phone starts to ring, he answers and by the smile on his face it must be Amy. He says he's going to step out for a while and his timing couldn't have been better.

Once Mason is out the door I take the opportunity to see Layla. Her bedroom door is open and she's standing in front of the window pulling her hair up into a ponytail. I walk in, shut the door behind me and immediately she turns in my direction.

"Hey stranger," she says in a very playful tone, "How can I help you?"

I chuckle, she's being really damn cute right now, "Oh I think you know exactly how to help me."

"Possibly," she responds with a wild look in her eye, walking towards me. She kisses me and we continue where we left off downstairs. In no time our clothes are covering the floor and I'm lying on the bed. Layla climbs on top, straddling me with her legs on either side of my hips. She leans forward running her tongue down my neck and chest. Moving my fingers through her hair I slowly remove the elastic band holding her ponytail in place. The sensation of her hair falling on my skin is electrifying. At this point I am completely turned on pulsating with the need to feel her. Her hovering right above me is driving me crazy and I start to groan. Suddenly she grabs me and very slowly lowers herself onto me. I feel as if I'm about to lose it, she's completely taking control. She starts rocking back and forth and I grab her hips, guiding her. Her breathing has picked up and I can tell she is trying her hardest to suppress a moan. Grabbing my hands, she moves them up to her breasts and there is no way I am going to last much longer. Never breaking contact, I move my hands to her back and flip her over so she's underneath me, exactly where I want her. That little grin of hers reveals more than words ever could. Kissing my lips, her hands make their way from the middle of my back up to my shoulder blades. Playfully tugging at my lower lip with her teeth I feel the pressure building and my thrusts increase in speed. Suddenly she pulls me tight and I feel her muffled moans on my shoulder, nails digging into my back I can tell she's reached her climax. Unable to hold back any longer I feel a rush shooting through me and fight the urge to groan.

I could lie here with her all day, just taking in her sweet scent and looking into those beautiful blue eyes. It really feels as if my life is complete.

Layla

It's already Sunday and I am way behind on my chores. After grabbing my clothes out of the dryer I go up to my room to fold them. While putting things away a smile comes over my face, I still can't believe Ben and I are together, it seems so surreal. In a way I am really surprised how comfortable we are with each other. Usually there's a little awkward phase when you start sleeping with someone but we seemed to have bypassed it. The only thing that sucks is keeping it a secret from everyone, but in a way it's also very exciting.

As I go to sit on my bed my purse falls to the floor, everything spilling out, I guess it's a good time to go through it and throw out old receipts. Reaching for my wallet I notice a package of condoms to the right of it. Fear sets in immediately, I never asked Ben to use a condom. What was I thinking? Obviously I wasn't thinking or I wouldn't be in this predicament right now. I feel like a total hypocrite, I always preach about safe sex and here I am doing the total opposite. Chills run down my spine just thinking of the possibility of pregnancy. What the hell am I going to do? I grab my phone, pull up the web and search for the morning after pill. After reading everything on the official site I'm relieved to find out that I can take it up to seventy-two hours after unprotected sex and I'm still in the window. I need to get to the pharmacy as soon as possible.

As I pull up to the town's only pharmacy I can't get myself to go inside. There's so much talk in this town and me buying the morning after pill will get around pretty fast I'm sure. I decide to drive to Macon and pray to god I don't run into anyone I know.

I head to the family planning section of the pharmacy and search for the product, finally I find the spot where the package is supposed to be stocked but there's just a card in place that says *Please see Pharmacist for details.* I walk in the direction of the counter and stand in line, suddenly someone says my name and I turn around. Oh my god, it's Weston.
"Hey Layla, cool to run into you here," he says with a smile. This is just great, this guy asked me out the other night and now I'm going to buy the morning after pill. Actually this could work out in my favor, because he'll know I'm with someone.

"Weston, how are you?"

"I'm great, just picking up a prescription. So did you have time to think about me taking you to dinner?" he asks, smiling.

"Listen, I'm sorry, I may have sent some mixed signals the other night, I'm actually seeing someone right now. I should have just come out and said so," I say.

"Oh," he pauses, "Damn, bad timing on my part. If for some reason that doesn't work out, please let me know," Weston grins.

I hear the pharmacist call the next customer and that's me. I tell Weston to go ahead because I have a bazillion questions and it may take a while. After he leaves I walk up and ask the pharmacist about the pill to see if they have it in stock. Luckily they do, I guess they just keep it behind the counter. She asks if I ever used it before and I shake my head and she starts going over all the instructions right there, she has one of those voices that carries and I feel as if the entire place is going to know my business. She kept reiterating to make sure the pills are taken exactly twelve hours apart. As soon as I get into my car I open the package and take the first pill. I set the alarm on my phone to remind me of the last dose. Suddenly I feel a sense of relief until I realize that I have to figure out a way to tell Ben that we need to use condoms in the future. Well I guess that will be our awkward moment.

I make it home just in time for dinner and as I walk in I'm greeted by Brittany in the living room.

"Hey, long time no see. Carmen said she was just about to call you," Brittany says as she gets up from the couch.

"Oh Layla, there you are. I went upstairs to look for you earlier and couldn't find you," Carmen mentions as she takes off her apron.

"Sorry, I had to run a quick errand. Didn't see anyone around when I left, it took a little longer than I thought."

"What did you make, it smells delicious," I say diverting the conversation.

"It's ratatouille with a fresh baked olive loaf," Carmen responds.

At dinner we have a pretty full table, Mason invited Amy along and come to find out she is a vegetarian. I'm sure that's why Carmen made that dish. I'm sitting in my usual spot next to Ben and there are a few different conversations going at the same time.

"Hey Layla, Paige and I are going to check out this new coffee shop in town after work tomorrow, did you want to come along?" Brittany asks. I'm having a hard time concentrating on what she is said, Ben has been running his fingers over my thigh and it's making me forget my name.

"Um, sure sounds like a plan," I answer smiling.

Once dinner is over everyone moves in to the living room, most of us are sitting on the floor because of the lack of seating.

"James, I really regret selling that sectional now, there's no room for people to sit," Carmen points out, placing little strips of paper on the coffee table, "Okay guys, let's play a game, it's called the song game. We'll split into two teams. Only one team plays at a time. I printed out little slips of paper with popular song titles. So when you pick a title you have to hum the song and the others on your team have 10 seconds to guess it."

"Oh boy, count me out," Ben laughs.

"No, no, no. Everyone plays. We need even teams." My team has Ben, Mason and Amy and this game is actually a lot of fun. Everyone is laughing and having a great time, we end up losing but it doesn't matter.

It's already after 10 pm and Mason drives Amy back to her apartment. Alex and Brittany say goodbye and head home as well. I'm sitting out on the porch steps thinking about what I am going to tell Ben when it comes to our future encounters. I hear the front door open and it's James, damn it.

So what did you think of Amy?" James asks me.

"I think she's perfect for Mason, they seem to be really happy," I say as the door opens again. It's Ben and he sits down next to me.

"What are we talking about?" Ben asks.

"Mason's new girlfriend," I answer leaning back on the steps.

"She seems nice, really funny girl. Mason seems to be crazy about her," Ben laughs.

After about fifteen minutes James decides to call it a night and says, "Enjoy your evening" while walking inside.

"Enjoy our evening, see we got his approval," Ben mumbles having a hard time keeping a straight face and I start to giggle.

"You're funny," I pause for a moment, "Hey we need to talk about something important."

"Okay, what is it?"

I take a deep breath, "Alright, here it goes. We really need to use condoms when we have sex. I know I should have said something before but I just got caught up and my mind went blank," I confess.

He smiles, "No problem. If that makes you feel more comfortable I'm on board with it. Just to ease your mind though, I don't have any diseases." Oh my god, that never even crossed my mind, I guess the responsible Layla has totally left the building.

"Um, thank you for telling me. I don't have anything either in case you're wondering," I take another deep breath, "Ben, I'm not on birth control, that's why I mentioned it. I did take the morning after pill though so everything will be fine." His eyes widen, I don't think he was expecting that at all.

"You're not on birth control?" he asks, fear written all over his face. I shake my head, I don't know what else to say. Seeing him react this way is making my eyes water a little. I look up to fight the tears.

"Layla, come here," he grabs me and holds me tight, "I'm not upset or anything, I was just a little surprised. I just assumed you were on something, that was irresponsible of me, I'm so sorry. I don't know anything about the morning after pill but the first time we had sex was more than twenty-four hours ago, do you think it's still effective?"

"From what the pharmacist explained and from my research if it's taken within three days it's should be effective. I have one more dose that I have to take at 430 am; I set my alarm so I remember.

"Well I guess I'll have to buy some condoms then," he says smirking.

"I have some. See that's why I feel like a dumbass because I always make sure I have them, it just totally slipped my mind," I pause, "I'm also going to make an appointment to get put on some kind of birth control. I never want to be in this kind of situation again."

Ben leans in to kiss me and any awkward feelings disappeared entirely. We are interrupted by the headlights of Mason's car coming up the driveway.

"Hey, I'm going to head upstairs, I'm a little tired," I say as I stand up, after our conversation I really don't want to sit here and talk to Mason. Ben squeezes my hand and tells me goodnight before I go in.

Deep in thought looking at the calendar on my phone I'm trying to figure out about when I should be expecting my period. Never ever have I been so anxious for it to arrive, I've always been regular so I should be expecting it around next weekend. A notification of a text message shows up on my screen, it's from Ben. He tells me goodnight and that he already misses me. The biggest smile comes over my face. He really has a way of making me forget everything

I'm greeted by a very cheerful Layne at work on Tuesday. I haven't seen him in a week so I'm sure he has a lot to talk about. In typical Layne fashion he has also been MIA when it comes to texting.

"Hey Layla, I've missed you. Josh said Friday night wasn't too busy, he did mention that this guy asked you out and you totally froze," Layne says with a grin.

"Wow, nothing is sacred is it," I joke, "Yeah, it was just a weird moment. How was your date with Ella?"

"You know, it was really nice. We are total opposites but I think that's what really intrigues me about her. Thursday night we are going to play mini golf, I hope I won't look like a fool. I've never played before," Layne laughs. I can tell he is head over heels for this girl, who would have ever guessed that someone like Ella would capture Layne Turner's heart.

When I get back home that night I find the house dark and quiet except for a light coming from Ben's room. I'd love nothing more than to run in and surprise him but he beats me to it.

"Hey Layla," I jump as I hear Ben's voice behind me. Instantly he grabs my waist and hugs my body, kissing my cheek. I turn around so I'm facing him and all of my thoughts have gone by the wayside. He has that devilish look in his eyes and a grin that I want to remember for the rest of my life.

Over the next week this has become our routine, when I get home from work he waits for me and that's the time we come alive. Just once I wish I could fall asleep and wake up next to him but that's pretty damn near impossible. Maybe James and Carmen will plan an overnight trip somewhere soon, hell maybe I should suggest it.

Ben

The shop door opens and Layla comes bursting in with a big smile on her face. Before saying a word she double checks that no one else is around and tells me she has good news.

"Everything's good. I got my period, you have no idea how relieved I am right now," she announces and I hug her tight, "I'm going to call my doctor on Monday to schedule an appointment."

"It's up to you, I'm fine with whatever you want to do," I lie, I really hate condoms.

"Oh I almost forgot, Carmen wants to go costume shopping in a little while, you're coming right?" Layla says.

"Yes I am. I'll meet you at the house in ten," I say giving her a long kiss before she's out the door. I really dodged a bullet there; the thought of her being pregnant has been on my mind since our conversation on the porch. What the hell would we have done? The last thing I need is a kid.

Once we arrive in Atlanta we stop at several costume shops until we reach the mother of them all. Looking through the racks it's really tough to make up my mind. Eventually I settle on a pirate costume, always a classic. James and Carmen are pretty preoccupied at the dressing room trying on several different looks so I decide to find Layla. I come up behind her and kiss her neck and she jumps, I completely surprised her.

"Ben, what are you doing? You're crazy," she giggles a bit.

"Just kissing my incredibly hot girlfriend, don't worry, James and Carmen are busy. I made sure before I came over. Did you find anything yet?"

"Well it's between these two, what do you think?" she asks holding up two costumes. In her right hand she's holding **Little Red Riding Hood** and in her left **Sexy Cop**.

"Wow," I pause, "If you're trying to turn me on it's totally working."

"Haha, focus Ben. I've already tried them on and I like them both but you choose," she demands and with the tone she just used I had to go with the Cop one, can't wait to see it on her, or even better, on the floor next to my bed.

We all meet up at the register and I see James and Carmen decided to go with a couples costume, doctor and nurse. I've got to say Carmen surprised the hell out of me with that one.

I really enjoyed the weekend. Layla and I even got to spend some alone time at the lake for a few hours. We took some fishing pole's along so it wouldn't look too suspicious, heck honestly I don't think anyone would have questioned it anyway. We've always spent a lot of time together. The Halloween party is on Saturday and I can't wait to see Layla all dressed up.

Later back at the house there's a knock at the door and I go to answer.

"Hello, I'm looking for Ben Parker," the postman says and I tell him that's me. He hands me an envelope and asks me to sign for it. I see it's from St. Louis so I am really excited. To tell the truth with everything that's happened over the last few weeks I completely forgot about this.

Chapter Fourteen

Layla

Ben has been acting a little strange today, I keep asking if everything is okay and he just smiles and assures me everything is fine. He left earlier this afternoon and still hasn't returned. I'm about to head to work and I have a weird feeling in my stomach. This has been the busiest Tuesday at the Bull but I welcome it because it's keeping me from overanalyzing Ben's behavior. Layne has been talking about Ella most of the night and I must say it's really cute to watch him gush over her. As we shut down the bar I look at my phone, no new messages. What's going on? This is so unlike Ben, I don't understand. Everything seemed to be fine up until yesterday afternoon.

When I pull up to the house I see his truck in the driveway, well at least he's back home. I walk into the house expecting to find him waiting for me like he usually does but everything is dark and he's nowhere in sight. Up in my room I grab my phone and send him a text *Goodnight, missed you tonight.* About a minute later my phone chimes and his message reads *I'm sorry babe, had some stuff to deal with. We'll talk about it tomorrow. Kisses.* In a way I'm relieved to hear back but I'm reading into the message, it just doesn't sound like Ben.

The next morning I'm up earlier than usual, surprisingly I slept well but as soon as I woke up that weird feeling returned. I walk into the kitchen and see James and Ben talking to each other over coffee.

"Good morning Layla, you're up early," James remarks. I smile and walk to the fridge to grab some orange juice. While pouring it in a glass I can feel Ben's eyes on me and when I return the glance he gives me a half smile before taking a sip of his coffee.

"Hey, Carmen and I are heading to Atlanta for a bit, we'll be back in a few hours," James says.

Carmen walks into the kitchen, saying "I'm returning the shoes I bought for the costume; I should have known the heel was just too high. I just hope I find something else. Do you guys need anything while we're out?" Ben and I both shake our heads and they get ready to leave.

I'm sitting in the living room, scrolling through my phone, I can't focus on anything. Once James and Carmen are gone Ben walks in.

"Hey Layla, we need to talk. Will you take a walk with me?" he asks, looking unsettled. Oh my god, he's breaking up with me, this is it. What could have gone wrong? What did I do?

Silently we walk in the direction of the lake. We don't take the usual path, instead walking through the trees. About halfway there he stops and takes a deep breath.

"Ben, please tell me what's going on, I'm so wor-" Ben cuts me off looking directly into my eyes and says "Layla, I'm still married."

I just stare wondering if that's really what just came out of his mouth, he's married?

"What?" I ask as if the answer is going to change, "Are you serious right now?"

"I am," he pauses, "I filed for divorce and I was hoping she would just sign the papers but I got a response in the mail yesterday and it's going to be a little more involved."

I'm speechless and not knowing how to respond I turn and walk toward the lake. I feel as if my heart has been ripped out, why would he keep something like that from me?

"Layla stop! Please talk to me, don't go," he says as he grabs my arm. Instinctively I pull away; I need a moment to process everything.

Once I get to the water I sit in one of the chairs and stare out into nothing. About five minutes later Ben sits in the chair next to me. "I need you to tell me everything Ben, no secrets. Am I just someone fun to pass the time with?"

"Oh my god Layla, no. I can't believe you would think that after everything we've gone through," Ben exclaims, "this is one of the reasons I was so adamant not to start anything with you."

"Will you tell me what happened?" I ask, realizing I really don't know anything about him.

"I got married six years ago; we dated for about a year before. We've always had our problems but things just got worse as time passed. About three years into the marriage, I found out she cheated on me and I ended up forgiving her. We went to therapy and I thought we worked it out. About a month before I got here I found her in our bed with one of her coworkers. Our fights had become out of control months before, so I should have known. When I caught them I was angry but honestly that same day I felt as if a huge weight had been lifted off my shoulder. I've been unhappy for years but didn't know how to end it and she did it for me. Before I left she told me she was sorry but she loved the guy and it would be best for us to split up. I probably sound like a fucking coward," he confesses, looking ashamed.

"No, you're not a coward. You just didn't know how to get out of it, I get it. I don't know much about divorces but you've been here for six months, how long does a divorce take?" I ask.

He takes a deep breath, "I filed about three weeks ago."

"What? So you filed after we got together?" I say shocked.

"No, I filed a few days before that. Layla, I never thought you and I would actually start dating. I had hope but didn't think it would happen."

"Why did you wait so long?"

"When I got here I just wanted a fresh start and to reconnect with everyone. As time went on I just procrastinated, put it on the back burner and didn't think about it until recently. I printed the papers, filled them out and had them sent to her. I was 100% sure it would be uncontested, I was wrong."

"So what happens now?"

"Well the papers I received yesterday state that she doesn't agree and asked the judge for counseling before hearing the case. She hired a lawyer and I'm going to have to do the same. When I left yesterday I called her to find out why she's doing this and why she won't just sign the papers. She said she doesn't want a divorce and wants us to try and work it out," Ben explains, still looking at me.

My heart feels like it's sinking to my feet, "So are you saying you're going to try and work it out?"

"Most definitely not! I don't want her, I'm done with her! This is just another way for her to make my life difficult. I spoke to a lawyer and he said more than likely the judge will grant the request for counseling since she asked for it, it's called discernment counseling. He said it would be smart to be proactive to find a counselor and set up the sessions instead of waiting for an answer which may take some time,"

That's when it hits me, "Oh my god that means you're going back to St. Louis doesn't it?"

"Yes, but it won't be for long. I will find out more in the coming week," he pauses, "I want you to know that you mean the world to me, hell, you are my world and I don't want to imagine my life without you. I also know that this is a lot to take in and you are going to need time to process and think things over. God, I don't even want to think of this because I would be devastated but if you feel that you can't trust me and you want out, then I will have to accept that," Ben says looking down.

Turning to him I touch his arm, I can't believe he just said that, "Are you serious? You think I'm just going to give up on us that easily? What you just told me was completely unexpected and yes a part of me is very hurt and terrified but the feeling of losing you is far worse," I say, feeling as if I'm about to cry.

I barely finish the sentence and he jumps out of his chair, pulling me up and holding me close. He sighs in relief and we stand there for a long time in silence. He's right, there is a lot to take in but now it is starting to make sense, more than ever I understand his reasons for pulling away in the past. Ben says he's planning on telling the others as soon as James and Carmen get back from Atlanta.

He sure doesn't waste any time and as soon as everyone is gathered in the living room he begins. The only one who seems surprised is Carmen, the guys just kind of have this '*Damn that sucks, hope it gets settled*' look on their face.

It's time for me to head to work, so I run upstairs to grab my bag. Carmen is busy in the kitchen cooking dinner and Mason and James are watching TV.

"Really James? Reality TV? I thought that was garbage," I say scrunching my forehead.

"Well, it really isn't that bad, I've gotten used to it," he chuckles and I smile and walk out the front door.

Throwing my bag in the car I see Ben walking toward me. "Hey Babe," he pauses, "Just want to make sure we're okay." Him saying that throws me a bit but then again he can't read my mind and even though I said I didn't want to lose him I'm sure he's still a bit unsure about the whole situation.

"We are totally okay, don't worry," I say grabbing his hand. I would really love to kiss him right now but it would be too risky, so I smile and let go of his hand and get into my car.

"Hey Layla, are you coming to the party tomorrow?" Layne asks while making a Martini.

"Um yeah I am," I pause and he's giving me a funny smirk, "don't look at me like that, you're acting as if I've never gone to a Halloween party before."

"Well, it doesn't really count when you're working. Are you bringing anyone? What ever happened to that Weston guy? You should have given him a chance since obviously you and Ben are never going to happen," Layne comments.

This is when I realize that Layne isn't up to speed on things. In a way I don't want to share it with him but he's been my rock and I feel I owe it to him.

"Layne, Ben and I are sort of together," I say smiling coyly.

"What? Are you serious? What do you mean sort of?" Layne bombards me with questions.
"Okay, we are together. It's been about three weeks or so. Don't tell anyone though; we are keeping this to ourselves. I don't want James or Carmen to find out."

"Holy crap, I never thought I would see the day. I am so damn happy for you Layla, is it what you imagined?"

For a moment I'm silent, thinking about the fact that he is still married and not completely available. "It's more than I imagined, it's amazing Layne," I sigh.

"Why do I have a feeling there's more to it?" Layne asks suspiciously.

I take a deep breath, "Technically he's still married and-"

"What? I can't believe this shit," Layne looks a little angry.

"Layne, calm down! He's going through a divorce but there are some complications so he has to go back to St. Louis to get everything sorted out."

Layne looks deep in thought, I know he cares about me but this is a little excessive. "I feel like it's partially my fault," he starts and I have no clue what he's talking about, "I had a talk with him a while back and told him that you're basically in love with him. Also said he really should make a choice, either he wants you or not."

"Layne, why the hell would you do that?"

"I just wanted to help Layla, you were miserable, he was unhappy. If I had known he was married I wouldn't have done that."

"He's getting divorced, so that's not an issue. We are really happy Layne. I can't even describe the emotions I feel when I'm with him."

Layne looks over at me and smiles, "Well, then I'm happy for you. I hope he can get all this sorted out quickly."

"Thanks, oh and Layne," I say with a serious expression.

"I know, I know. I will keep everything to myself."

Ben

It's Saturday and everyone is getting ready for the Halloween party at the Bull. I got a funny text from Layla yesterday saying she was no longer on her period so she may arrest me after the party. Mason and Amy won't be joining us, Amy has younger siblings that she takes trick or treating every Halloween and Mason will be going along. I have no idea what Alex and Brittany are dressing up as, I'm sure it's some sort of couples costume.

James and I are ready to go, sitting downstairs in the living room waiting on Layla and Carmen to come downstairs. I have to say James pulls the scrubs off really well and I jokingly tell him maybe he should make a career change.

Hearing voices coming down the stairs I look up and I'm totally speechless. Carmen looks pretty damn good in that nurse's outfit but holy shit, seeing Layla dressed in a skimpy outfit is getting me so aroused that I'm glad I'm sitting right now. She has the look down from head to toe, I can't take my eyes off of her cleavage and those knee-high boots that tie the entire thing together. Okay Ben, control yourself, don't be so damn obvious.

Once we get to the Bull Layne comes to meet us, he's dressed up as a cowboy minus the shirt. He really must work out all the time, seeing his abs is making me just a little self-conscious, but then again, I'm not twenty anymore.

"Holy shit, who is this and what did you do with Layla," Layne says looking her up and down.

"Haha very funny Layne," Layla responds.

Layne signals for me to step closer to him and whispers, "I think you're going to have a good time tonight if you know what I mean."

This guy is something else and by that comment I assume he knows all about us. Layne is working tonight but before heading back to the bar he introduces us to Ella and two of her friends. I feel a slap on my back and turn around to find Alex and Brittany behind me. Alex is dressed as a vampire and Brittany is wearing a belly-dancing costume. Guess I was wrong about the couple's costume.

"Wow Brittany nice costume," Layla points out.

"Thanks, I think Alex was about ready to just dress me up in a garbage bag, it was a long day of shopping," Brittany laughs and Alex rolls his eyes, "Aw Alex look at your brother and Carmen, matching costumes."

"Don't even get me started on that," Alex says looking in our direction, "I told her there's no way it would happen."

As the night goes on everyone is having a great time mingling, drinking and laughing. Randy just got everyone rounded up for the costume contest. Alex and Brittany are the only ones going up from our group. I've been staring at Layla all night and wish I had five minutes alone with her. She has had a few to drink at this point which is really fun to watch. James being mister responsible switched to drinking sodas about an hour ago, even though the house is really close we don't want to push our luck. The contest has started and everyone's eyes are focused on stage. I feel Layla touch my hand and her eyes signal for me to follow her. What is she up to?

She opens a door that leads into a small room which looks like a storage closet. Closing it behind us she pushes me against the wall and starts kissing me slowly, her hands wrapped around my neck. I run my hands from her back down to her ass.

She stops and leans back a little, "I wanted you to myself even if it's just for a few minutes. I thought since everyone is occupied it was the perfect moment."

"Good call. I like the way you think," I say kissing her one more time before we make our way back out to the crowd.

Standing at the bar talking to Layne, James comes up to us saying he and Carmen are ready to head out. Layla frowns a bit and Layne jumps in, offering to give us a ride home later.

Layla and Ella are having a great time getting to know each other and you can tell Layne is really into Ella. At one point Layne and Layla do a little karaoke, I love hearing her sing. Ella tells me that she wishes she had the guts to go up there like that and I tell her I wouldn't do it either.

When the party ends we wait for Layne to close out the register before walking out to his truck. Ella is sitting up front with Layne and we are in the backseat. Suddenly Layla leans her head on my shoulder and grabs my hand. This is a moment I never want to forget.

After dropping us off near the shop, Layla and I walk toward the house. All out of sudden Layla stops, grabs my hand and leads me in the direction of the shop. Grabbing the keys out of her bag she opens the door and we walk inside, locking the door behind us. She doesn't turn on the overhead light but instead walks over to a stool in the corner and switches on a little lamp.

She's been quite bold tonight, I wonder if it's the alcohol or being in that sexy costume.

"So," she begins, "This is where it all started."

"That's right," I answer walking toward her. She's running one hand over the edge of the workbench, unbuttoning the top of her costume with the other. I'm right in front of her now staring into her eyes, I can't decide if it's a look of innocence or mischief. Lowering my eyes to her mouth I notice that she's playfully biting her lip, she knows exactly what to do to get me going. I go for it, my tongue invading her mouth. This kiss is steamy, sensuous and wild, completely opposite from the one at the Bull. One of my hands is gripping the counter while the other is pulling down her bra, exploring her left breast. Feeling her moan in my mouth is driving me crazy. Swiftly I turn her around so that I'm pressed against her back, lifting her skirt and pulling down her underwear. I grab a condom out of my pocket and undo the drawstring on the bottoms of my costume. Using my teeth to tear the wrapper I throw it on the ground rolling on the condom. Guiding myself into place I slowly push forward resting my hands right above her hips. She lets out a loud moan and I continue thrusting steadily as she gets louder and louder. Arching her back slightly changes the sensation entirely. I slow down just a bit because I'm getting too close. Her moans are driving me wild and this is the first time we don't have to be quiet. Bracing herself on the bench I can make out two words, Ben and harder. Fuck yeah, following her direction I give it all I've got and her cries of pleasure have me at the brink.

Chapter Fifteen

Layla

I can't believe that in less than twenty minutes Ben will be leaving and I really don't know when I will see him again. He said he's hoping it won't take but a few weeks, but I have an uneasy feeling. He hasn't seen his wife in over six months and I can't shake the feeling that something may happen between them while he is there. Obviously she still wants him since she asked for counseling, I never thought it was going to be this hard to let him go. Up in my room I can't fight back the tears, I literally feel as if a piece of my heart is being ripped out. There's knock at my door and I quickly wipe my eyes before opening the door.

"Hey Babe," Ben says coming in and closing the door behind him. I stand there giving him a half smile, trying to hide my emotions.

"Oh Layla, please don't be sad, I will be back as soon as possible, I swear. I don't want to leave but I don't have a choice right now. God I hate seeing you like this," Ben says, his eyes tearing up just a little.

"I'm sorry Ben," I pause, "I just never thought it would be this hard to let you go. I just have an uneasy feeling about this."

He grabs my face and presses his lips to mine, holding on to his wrists I get lost in that beautiful kiss. He pulls back and looks directly into my eyes, "Layla, I never ever want to lose you," he pauses and takes a deep breath, "I love you."

My heart just stopped, hearing those three words was really unexpected but totally reassuring.

"I love you too," I answer, smiling from ear to ear.

Ben

Finally arriving in St. Louis I get to my buddy's house and he sets me up in his guest room. This is not how I expected to spend my birthday, driving ten hours straight to get here. I have to say I missed Chris, he is like a brother to me. I feel bad for not keeping in touch as much as I should.

"Here," Chris says handing me a beer.

"Thanks man. You are a lifesaver for letting me stay here, you have no idea how much I appreciate it."

"No worries, I'm just glad that you're back for a little while. So what's the plan? When will you be seeing Jen?"

"Our first session is tomorrow. I really hope I can talk some sense into her and we get things settled fast, I need to get back to Georgia."

"Georgia. You know I just don't see you living there, it's crazy. I know you have family there but I didn't know you were that close to them."

I look down and smirk, Chris knows me really well and I can understand that choosing a small town in Georgia over St. Louis would seem odd.

"Oh my god, you met someone. Who is she?"

I take a deep breath, "Her name is Layla. I'm completely in love and it's killing me being apart from her."

"I want to see a picture, you have one don't you?" he asks and I pull out my phone. I pull up a selfie she sent me just the other day while she was at work, I love that picture of her.

"Damn, she's beautiful. Ben isn't she a little young for you?" Chris asks raising his eyebrows.

"Well, yeah, she is a little younger than I am but it doesn't matter. I've never had such a connection with anyone before," I say feeling as if I have to defend myself.

"You should have just brought her along. She could have stayed here while you took care of business."

"It's a little more complicated than that," I blurt out and realize I don't want to explain our entire situation to him, "she has a job and just can't take a month off."

Walking into the counselor's office I see Jen sitting in one of the chairs and she's paging through a magazine.

When I close the door she looks up and smiles. "Oh my god Ben, I wasn't sure you'd make it. When did you get in?" she asks putting the magazine down.

"Yesterday," I respond.

"Oh, where are you staying? I just assumed you'd come home."

"Why would I come home?? We're getting a divorce and the only reason I am here is to get you to see there is no way we will get back together."

"Well if you go into this with that attitude then I think it's going to be a long road. Please just try to be open, it's not like these last six years meant nothing."

We are called into the office, Jen and I sit on the couch across from the therapist, she introduces herself as Mary. She starts by explaining how the process works. The first session is called the couple's session and usually lasts forty-five minutes. The others will start as individual conversations with ten minutes of couple time at the end. Mary doesn't waste any time and begins questioning us.

"What has happened to your marriage that has gotten you to the point where divorce is a possibility?"

"Her being unfaithful for starters," I say crossing my arms.

"Well I don't want a divorce so I'm not sure how to answer the question," Jen replies.

"Well eight months ago you were all for it," I reply to Jen.

"I can change my mind can't I? I have had a lot of time to think and I know I made a terrible mistake, but I am willing to work on this. I don't want to lose you Ben," Jen says, I can tell she's going to try to use the waterworks here soon.

"I've heard it all before. Even though we worked it out the last time I never trusted you again, and I was right not to."

"I'm not perfect, I'm only human," Jen snaps.

"Yep, so am I."

"So, what have you two done to try to fix these problems?" Mary asks.

"He's done nothing, he took off. I had no idea where he was until I received the divorce papers.

About a month after he left I started calling and texting him. He never responded so I had to wait until I heard from him."

"I was done, I didn't want to do anything to fix it. I never answered because I knew the only reason you would be calling was because your new boyfriend left."

"He didn't mean anything to me, you don't understand."

"Well I recall us having a conversation where you said you were in love with him and splitting up is a good thing," I reply. Here we go, now come the tears. Mary hands Jen a tissue and moves on to the next question.

"Looking back, what were some of the best times you shared together? A time when you felt the most connected in your relationship."

I sit and think for a moment, my first thought is nothing but I know that will probably make me look like an ass. "Our trip to the Bahamas, it was the first vacation we ever took. We were in a good place back then."

"Our date nights." Jen sobs, "Even though our lives were hectic we always made sure we had one night a week that we saved for each other.

Dinner, concerts, movies, those were really special times."

I notice Mary has been taking a lot of notes, she hasn't said very much but I guess it's her job to observe. First session is finally over. If it were up to me we would be doing them back to back but according to Mary it's best to space them out. God I miss Layla like crazy and I've only been here for a day and a half. How am I going to survive the rest of the time?

Outside as I unlock my truck I hear Jen's voice behind me. "Ben, can we talk?"

"Um what do you think we just did in there?" I reply.

"Let's just grab a coffee around the corner so I can explain a few things,"

"I don't think that's a good idea," I say getting into my truck. I know exactly what she's trying to do, it's her way of reeling me back in, not going to happen this time.

Layla

Ben's already been gone for three weeks but I still expect to see him downstairs after I get up in the morning. I miss him terribly and even though we talk all the time it just isn't the same. I've gotten one major thing accomplished while he's away…I'm finally on birth control. I honestly had no idea there were so many options out there. The implant was out of the question and a few of the others sounded just as bad. After much debating I decided to go with the shot because I don't trust myself to remember to take a pill every day. I was surprised to learn that I only have to go back every three months and there's a possibility that my periods will stop all together, sounds like a win-win to me.

I've been keeping busy at work, taking a few extra shifts when possible. Being at home just makes me stir crazy and Layne is the only one that I can talk to. I haven't really shared much with him though, I don't want to be an open book.

I hear my phone buzzing underneath the counter and after topping the margarita off with a lime I grab it hoping its Ben. Oh my god, he just totally made my night, a picture message of him lying in bed, shirtless with a smirk on his face saying *I want you here with me*. If I could I would just hop on a plane and fly there right now, I have toyed around with that idea actually.

"Awe, look at that smile," Layne comments, "You must really like what you're looking at right now. Can I see?"

"Nope, sorry," I say holding the phone to my chest, "For my eyes only."

"Hmm, one of those pics huh," he laughs.

Wanting to send Ben a selfie, I adjust my shirt just a bit and hold the phone up.

"Layla, are you sending this selfie to your mother? Let me help you out a little there," Layne says pulling my shirt down a little, exposing more cleavage, "Alright, now that's a selfie. You're welcome." Within a minute of sending it Ben replies, *God damn it, I miss you so much Layla. By the way, that picture is amazing. You are so beautiful*.

After exchanging a few messages back and forth we say goodnight. Great timing, because I'm all by myself at the moment, Layne is up on stage singing and a few more people have come in.

"Hey Layla, can we get a round of Jäger?"

I turn around and see Weston standing there with a few of his friends. Quickly taking a head count I grab four shot glasses, pour the alcohol and hand them over. Weston hands me his credit card and asks me to open a tab.

"So how have you been?" he asks after taking the shot.

"I've been great. Thank you for asking. How about you?" I say, wondering why I'm feeling awkward.

"Good," he pauses, "Are things going well with the boyfriend?"

For a moment I must have had a bewildered look on my face, how the hell does he know about Ben and I? Then I remember, I told him I was dating someone the last time we spoke. "Yeah, we're doing great," I answer. His look tells me he isn't buying the whole boyfriend story.

"Alright, that's good. So does he ever come in here?"

"Yeah he does actually. He's out of town for business but he'll be back soon," I respond wondering why the hell I am explaining myself to him.

"Cool, what does he do for work?" Weston asks.

"He's a mechanic," I blurt out before thinking, I should have made up something else.

"A mechanic out of town for business? That's quite unusual," he states raising his eyebrows.

"Well I didn't say it was work related," I snap back.

Directly looking at me, Weston moves his empty shot glass toward me and smirks, "Touché."

He orders a round of beer before he and his friends walk away from the bar, what a relief. He came across as a cocky jackass, something he hid very well. I am so relieved I didn't give him my number.

After Layne gets back behind the counter he tells me that he noticed Weston talking to me and I roll my eyes. That's the great thing about our friendship, no words needed.

As we close up for the night Layne asks me a question that hasn't crossed my mind. "Hey Layla, do you trust him?"

"Do I trust Ben? Of course I do, why would you ask?"

"Now don't freak out or anything," Layne explains, "I just wonder if you ever thought about the possibility of him not coming back."

"Um Layne, why wouldn't he come back?" I ask confused.

"Well you always hear about guys going back to their wives because it's the easier choice. I don't know I may just be overthinking this but I just don't want you to get hurt. Ever since you told me he was still married it's something that's been on my mind."

"Well, I do trust him and I know he's coming back for sure," I say confidently.

"Listen, I'm sorry I brought that up, I shouldn't have. I feel like an ass right now."

"Oh no, don't. You were just concerned as a best friend should be," I say giving him a hug.

I may have been able to play the cool calm and collected Layla while I was talking to Layne but being alone in my room is another story. My brain is coming up with all sorts of things that could happen and I don't like feeling this way. I know he has no intentions on staying with his wife but what if the counseling changes his mind. Obviously once upon a time they did love each other enough to get married. I have to stop thinking about it or I'm going to drive myself crazy.

Ben

I am so tired of sitting through these sessions, at least we only have two more to go. I know I can throw in the towel at any time since it's not ordered but I'm going to stick this out. I feel like we just keep talking about the same old things each time we're there. I've made it very clear that I'm 100% done with this marriage. Obviously Jen still doesn't seem to get it; she's been blowing up my phone since I arrived.

It's Thursday night and I'm sitting on the couch flipping through channels as Chris walks in.

"Hey Ben, I'm planning to have a party here tomorrow night, just a little get together. Some of our old buddies are planning to come and I know they will be happy to see you. You don't have any plans do you?" Chris asks sitting down next to me.

"Nope, not at all, sounds great. Isn't this place a little small though?" I ask wondering where everyone is going to hang out.

"Oh, you haven't seen the rooftop yet? It's the main reason I bought this place, come on I'll show you," Chris says getting up and I follow. He wasn't kidding, I think this would have sold me as well. I never thought he was a plant guy but they are everywhere. He also has a few different seating areas set up with a bar off to the side.

"See," he starts, "What did I tell you, cool right?"

"Yeah, the view is amazing," I reply, "You can see the entire city."

About ten minutes later Chris heads back downstairs but I decide to stay outside. Aside from the noise it doesn't feel as if I'm in the middle of St. Louis right now. Sitting down in one of the lounge chairs I pull out my phone to check the time. It's 11 pm here and I know Layla is still at work, I decide to send her a text. A short time later my phone starts ringing and when I check to see who it is I'm surprised to see Layla's name.

Ben: Hey! I'm surprised that you're calling. Aren't you at work?
Layla: It was slow so I got off early. I literally just got out of my car when you texted.
Ben: What are your plans tonight?
Layla: Oh nothing much, just sitting on the swing
Ben: Why do you sound sad?
Layla: Sad? I'm not sad. I'm fine.
Ben: Come on Layla, I know you pretty well by now. What's going on?
Layla: I don't know, it's stupid really. Not even worth mentioning.
Ben: Please tell me.

Layla: What if you don't come back? I know you said you were done with her but I'm just worried that something could happen. I don't know anything about therapy or counseling but talking about your time together brings back memories, not only the bad. I don't know, maybe I'm just scared that you'll fall in love with her again.
Ben: Layla, I love you. Nothing or no one is going to change that. God I hate that you have this going through your head and I can't be there. I only have about two weeks left and then I'll be home again. You have no idea how much I miss you.
Layla: Maybe it's just because we didn't have a lot of time together before you had to go. I thought I would be strong but it's the unknown that's killing me.
Ben: There is no unknown. Two weeks and I'll be with you and we'll have the rest of our lives, just you and me.
Layla: I can't wait, I miss you so much. I love you Ben.
Ben: I love you.

It's 1 am and I'm just hanging up, it so amazing that we never run out of things to talk about. I really hated hearing the sadness in her voice, I can't imagine she would think that I would suddenly change my mind and stay here. Trying to put myself in her shoes I do understand her worries, I kept this from her for so long so there has to be a little mistrust on her end. Two weeks, I'm counting down.

Some people have already arrived at the apartment and I've seen a few familiar faces. They've filled me in on everything I've missed since I've been gone. Taking my phone out of my pocket I send Layla a message. I notice that I have an unheard voicemail and I'm surprised because my phone hasn't rung all day. It's from the therapist's assistant stating next week's session is cancelled due to it being Thanksgiving Day. She also mentioned that there are no other openings next week at the moment. Just great, that pushes my stay back another week, I am so ready to get out of here.

The rooftop has definitely filled up, I know most of the people here which is nice. Some of them I worked with for years. They quiz me about what's been going on since I've been in Georgia and if I'm planning on coming back at all. About an hour later I go downstairs to grab a bottle of water out of the fridge. My phone chimes, I place the bottle on the counter and see it's from Layla. It's a picture of her and Layne with microphones in hand. That's right, she told me tonight would be karaoke night. I love this picture, they are both making funny faces and it reminds of all the funny messages we used to send each other when I first got there.

"Oh, so he does know how to check his phone." I look up in horror because I recognize the voice, it's Jen.

"What the hell are you doing here?" I ask quite angry.

"Well a friend of mine was invited and she asked me to tag along. You never told me where you were staying so how was I supposed to know," she snaps back.

I know I hadn't told her but I'm sure she knew I would be staying with Chris, the last thing I want to do is hang out with her all night. "Alright, well enjoy your night then," I say walking to the stairs that lead to the rooftop.

Back upstairs I find Chris and tell him Jen just came in and for him not to mention anything about Layla, that's the last thing I need, I know it would send her through the roof. I've actually managed to avoid her most of the night, once in a while she and her friend would pop up in the middle of a conversation but most of the topics of discussion were cars and tattoos so they would end up walking off.

It's 2 am and most people have cleared out, being a little tired I make my way to my room to get some sleep. Once I get to the living room I notice Jen standing off to the side, a glass of wine in her hand staring at a picture on the wall. She turns in my direction and walks toward me.

"Ben, listen, can we just talk for a few minutes," she asks.

"No, I don't want to talk to you, why can't you just get that?"

"Please" Jen pleads. "I won't ever ask you again."

"Fine," I sigh and we sit on the couch.

"Are you really ready to just walk away from us?"

"Yes I am. You know that we've been a disaster from the start. I obviously didn't make you happy since you had to look somewhere else."

For a moment she sits there quietly, deep in thought. "Ben, I still love you, I do. After you left I realized what I lost. I know we haven't been in a good place but we were happy at one time. I just think if we try we can get that back."

"I don't know how else to tell you. I've moved on and I'm living in a different state. I've reconnected with my family which I thought would never happen. For the first time ever I feel settled."

"Wow, it so strange to hear that, for years I was your only family," Jen says.

Not knowing how to respond I just sit there in silence. She's right, I guess I've always had a fucked up family life.

Jen continues, "Alright, well we still have two sessions so let's just keep an open mind and see where things go. If at the end you still feel the same way, I'll sign the papers."

"Thank you," is all I can manage to say. I'm actually surprised that she is being reasonable, what other choice does she have? It's not like a judge is going to force us to stay married.

Two days later I have a great idea, I am going to fly to Georgia and surprise Layla for thanksgiving. There is no reason for me to stay here since the appointment got canceled. After checking flights online, I book one that leaves Tuesday afternoon. I have the entire thing planned out and I can't wait to see Layla's face.

Chris drops me off at the airport and I give him the keys to my truck in case he needs them. After an hour and thirty minutes I finally land and pick up my bag from baggage claim. I reserved a rental car, I'm sure I could have had someone pick me up but I want to keep it a complete surprise. I stop in Macon to take care of a few things before heading to the Bull.

It's not very crowded which is to be expected for a Tuesday night. I open the door, my eyes fixed on the bar I spot Layla with her back turned talking to Layne. Wow, it feels unreal seeing her right now, I just want to go up and grab her and never let go. Layne's eyes widen as he spots me but I throw him a signal to be quiet. He gets it, keeping Layla distracted I make my way towards her, stopping as I get to the counter.

"Hey Layla, can I get a drink?" I ask with a smile on my face.

She doesn't turn around right away but when she does there's excitement written all over her face.

"Oh my god!" she says covering her mouth, "I can't believe you're here." She rushes out from behind the bar and throws her arms around me, which surprises me since she's always so cautious about anyone seeing us. She starts kissing me and I squeeze her tighter.

"Wow," Layne chuckles, "So now it's confirmed. I was beginning to think Layla was making it all up."

Layla steps back still holding on to my hands, "What are you doing here? I thought you said two more weeks?"

"I do still have two more weeks after this one. With Thanksgiving on Thursday our session got cancelled. I've missed you so much Layla, you have no idea, looks like my surprise worked," I say staring into her eyes.

"Heck yeah it did, you just made my year. This is so surreal. Did James and Carmen know you were coming?" she asks.

"No, no one did. You know I like to keep it Ben style and not tell anyone anything," I chuckle and she shakes her head.

"How long are you staying?" Layla asks with a look as if she really doesn't want to know the answer.

"I'll be here for a week," I smile.

"Are you serious? Oh my god, that is wonderful. Well, I still have a few hours left so did y-"

"No you don't Layla," Layne starts, "I just called Josh and he's on his way over so you can take off. Seriously, go. Also, I know the whole alone time thing is difficult at your place so if you want my house key I'll be happy to give it to you."

"Thanks man, I got it covered though," I smirk and Layla looks at me completely confused.

We walk out to the parking lot and I open the passenger door to my rental and Layla gets in. Once I start the car Layla's curiosity has gotten the better of her, "So, what's the plan Ben?"

"Alright, so first you're going to text someone back home, telling them you'll be crashing at Layne's tonight. Second, you're just going to sit there and enjoy the ride. You'll find out the rest soon enough," I smirk.

She agrees and takes out her phone. Once we get to Macon I pull up to a hotel and park the car.

"Wow, this place is nice," Layla comments.

"Okay, so I reserved a room for tonight, I want us to be able to wake up next to each other. For one night, all night, it's just you and me."

"I really think that is one of the sweetest things you've ever said," Layla sighs.

Layla

This place is gorgeous; I remember when they were building it last year. It looks completely out place because it's so massive. Getting out of the elevator we walk down the hallway toward the room. I think to myself, this is bringing back some memories. After walking into the room Ben places the 'Do Not Disturb' sign on the door before locking it.

I walk over to the bed and sit down taking in the sight of Ben coming my way, throwing his shirt on the floor. Once reaching me he slowly kisses my lips before moving down my neck. I lean back so that I'm lying down and he's sitting on top of me, knees on either side of my hips. I run my hands over his chest down his stomach which makes him smile. Scooting back just a bit he grabs my arms and sits me up, removing my shirt and bra, tossing them across the room. Climbing off me he lies on his side pulling me toward him, holding me tight. Parting my lips with his tongue he kisses me slowly and it just makes me realize how much I've missed him. I close my eyes and all my senses are heightened, his hand stroking my back makes we want to pull him even closer. I breathe in his scent while playing with his hair, twirling it between my fingers. For a moment his lips leave mine, "I love you Layla."

"I love you too," I answer resting my head on his chest.

Waking up next to Ben in the morning is something I've wanted to do for a long time. I look over at him and he's still sleeping, he literally takes my breath away. It just dawned on me we never had sex, I was so ready after not seeing him for three weeks but what happened last night was almost more intimate, it was beautiful. Lying on his chest listening to his heart beating is my favorite place to be. I catch myself tracing his tattoo and he wakes, kissing my head.

"So while you were gone I stopped at the graveyard to visit your dad's grave," I say still tracing his tattoo.

"Why would you do that?" he asks curiously. "This may sound completely crazy. I stood in front of his headstone for a very long time thinking about things. Before leaving I thanked him."

"My dad? What did you thank him for?"

Taking a deep breath I start, "I thanked him for making you leave twenty years ago. I know I probably sound really selfish right now but if you had stayed then you and I would have never happened. Because of his actions we eventually found each other," I pause for a moment, "You know, even if this isn't meant to last, I wouldn't trade what we have right now for anything in the world."

"Don't say that." Ben says, "I can't imagine my life without you anymore. I don't ever want to know what that feels like. You've become my entire world Layla."

After checking out of the hotel, we drive to the Bull so I can get my car and head home. The idea is that I go home first and he'll follow about an hour later to surprise everyone. Getting out of the car I see Carmen wrapped in a blanket on the porch swing having a cup of coffee, it is quite chilly this morning.

"Good morning Layla, did you have a good time last night?" she asks pulling her blanket closer to her face.

"I did, thank you. It's really cold this morning isn't it?" I respond rubbing my arms.

"Oh I know, the weather here is so unpredictable," she laughs.

A warm drink sounds really good right now, but there's no way I can do coffee. I pull out a hot chocolate mix and heat a cup of water in the microwave. After stirring in the mix I grab a blanket from the living room and join Carmen on the swing.

"Hey girls, you look really nice and warm," James comments coming up the steps, "Damn, I can't wait for Ben to get back, the shop really needs him."

I take a sip of my hot chocolate knowing that Ben will be here very soon. About twenty minutes later I see his car pull up.

"Someone else must be dropping a car off," Carmen says stretching her head out, trying to make out who it is.

James steps out of the shop, looks at the car and starts yelling, "Well speak of the devil, I was just talking about you. What a surprise."

Ben steps out and Carmen stands up, "It's Ben, I thought he still had a few weeks to go. Did you know he was coming?"

I shrug my shoulders and shake my head. Carmen gets up, placing her cup on the small table and walks toward Ben and James and I follow.

"Hey Carmen, hey Layla, I just got in. Wanted to surprise you guys and it seems like it worked," Ben laughs giving Carmen a hug before moving on to me. Very quickly he gives me a little peck on my shoulder while embracing me which was pretty slick. The four of us walk into the shop, Shane and Mason are surprised by his arrival as well.

"Hey James, we have to leave here in about an hour," Carmen says looking at her phone. I completely forgot that Gio is flying in to spend thanksgiving with us. Carmen mentioned that he's bringing his new girlfriend along as well.

"Damn, where has the time gone? Hey Ben do you mind replacing the brakes on the Chevy in there? Mason and Shane are in the middle of working on some bikes," James says looking at Ben.

"Yeah of course, I'll be here for a bit so I'll help out as much as I can," Ben smiles.

I walk in the house and head upstairs to take a shower. My life feels complete again and I'm going to enjoy every minute of it, only two and a half more weeks and Ben will be back for good. A few hours later everyone returns from the airport and we get to meet Gio's girlfriend, Isabella. She is quiet and soft-spoken but I suppose you have to be if you're dating Gio, that guy loves to hear himself talk. Normally I should be at work right now but Layne arranged shifts with the other bartenders so I won't have to return to work until Monday, he really is a great friend. Carmen made eggplant parmesan and lasagna for dinner tonight, apparently those are Gio's favorites and he wastes no time digging in. This is the first time he's ever come for a visit and he seems to fit right in. He and Mason are getting along great, through conversation I find out that Gio has kept in touch with Mason and Alex since the wedding.

"So, I was wondering if anyone wants to go to the movies tonight?" Ben asks. This comes as a surprise, in a conversation quite some time ago I remember him saying he's not really into movie theaters.

"Well, we kind of made plans for tonight. Gio, Isabella and I are heading to Alex and Brittany's. Amy is meeting us there too, otherwise I'd be down," Mason explains.

"I still have a lot of things to prepare for tomorrow, I'm sorry. James why don't you go?" Carmen suggests.

"Nah, I'm too tired. Must have been that drive to Atlanta," James yawns.

Ben looks over in my direction and gives me the slightest smirk, "Layla, do you want to go?"

"Sure, I'll go, why not," I answer nonchalantly and after helping clear the table I grab a jacket and my bag and we head out the door.

While driving to Macon Ben looks over at me chuckling, "You have no idea what I just did there do you? You are too damn cute."

"Well I remember you saying you don't care for movie theaters so it made me wonder. Are we not going to the movies?"

"Oh, we are definitely going to the movies. This is going to be our first date."

"Wait. Did you plan this?" I ask.

"I sure did," Ben replies.
"Well how did you know that we would be alone? You asked everyone else to join," I inquire.

"I knew that Mason and Gio had plans, overheard Mason talking to Shane in the shop. Carmen and James? It was a given that they wouldn't go. Not bad huh," Ben explains.

"Wow, I have to give it to you, that was a smart move," I say.

When we get to the theater I let him choose the movie and he picks a slasher film. We still have about twenty minutes before it starts but we go inside anyway to get some good seats. To my surprise there are only a handful of people so far but I'm sure it's going to fill up quick because the movie just came out last week. Ben leads me all the way to the top seats. As soon as we're seated Ben lifts the armrest so it's out of the way and holds my hand, inside of me butterflies are having a field day right now. Wait, why do I have butterflies?

"I can't wait to be back, you don't understand," Ben says sinking into the chair.

"How are things going?" I curiously ask.

"I don't know, I feel as if we're not really getting anywhere. Like you know we still have two appointments left. I suppose after that it's up to the judge," Ben says.

"She probably finally realized what she lost," I point out.

I'm really proud of myself, I just sat through the entire movie without holding my hands in front of my eyes. It was quite gory and I know I'll be checking my closet and under my bed before going to sleep. As we walk out of the theater doors I stop to take a selfie, I definitely need to capture our first date. Ben is standing behind me, arms wrapped around my waist and his chin resting on my shoulder. Telling me to take one more picture he squeezes me tighter and kisses my cheek. I click the camera roll to see how they came out and just as I figured I'm totally in love with them. We really do make a cute couple, maybe a little unusual, but still cute.

Once we get to the car before opening my door he pulls me close and within two seconds we are in full make-out mode. At this point my mother could be standing there and I wouldn't care, he drives me crazy.

Ben

Our date couldn't have gone better, I'm so glad that I was able to pull it off. I really hate having to hide our relationship, it makes what we have seem so wrong but I know it's not. After arriving home, we kiss goodnight and Layla goes upstairs. A perfect ending for our first date.

The next day I hear a lot of noise coming from the kitchen. Carmen is busy preparing the thanksgiving feast. Layla, Isabella and Brittany are helping out as well. For a moment I stand in the doorway watching them, it seems as if they are having a lot of fun. Looking for the guys I walk toward the living room but there's no one in sight. I open the front door and find everyone lounging on the porch.

"Hey Ben, want a beer?" James asks handing one over, it's a little early but what the hell.

"I can't wait to eat, it smells amazing," I comment, popping the top off the bottle.

"Yep, that's why we are out here. I got yelled at for stealing a bite a few minutes ago," Gio laughs, "Mom doesn't play when it comes to preparing food, you think I would know by now,"

"How did you like the movie? I'm kind of jealous now because Layla told me what you saw," Mason mentions.

"It was great, you all should have come along," I say grinning.

"I don't know how you coaxed Layla into watching that movie but good job man," James says giving me a high five, "I was kind of surprised that she didn't have to work last night."

"Her shifts have been completely out of whack the last few weeks, Randy probably figured she could use a few days off since she's been working nonstop. Last week she looked like a zombie walking around here…well when she was here," Mason comments. I know Layla told me she was volunteering for more shifts while I was away but I don't want her to kill herself. She said sitting around at home without me is just depressing and just wants to stay busy.

"So Gio, when did you meet Isabella?" I ask taking a sip of my beer.

"Oh we met about two months ago in school, I noticed her before but we didn't hang around with the same crowd. I saw her sitting in a coffee shop with her laptop and I decided to talk to her, so glad I did. We've been together ever since," he explains smiling.

The front door opens and Carmen comes out, "Hey guys, everything is in the oven and the rest will just need a quick reheat before we eat. What do you say we all go out to the lake and enjoy the day? Layla said she would stay in the house to make sure it doesn't burn down."

"Great, come on Ben. Let's grab the fishing poles, Gio do you like to fish?" James asks getting up from the steps.

"I've never attempted it but I'm game," Gio laughs.

The girls join us at the lake and within ten minutes Gio has already caught his first fish. I've spent the entire time thinking of an excuse to go back to the house.

"Oh hey guys, I forgot my phone, I'll be back in a few," I say handing my fishing pole to Brittany.

I walk in the front door and head toward the kitchen. Layla is leaning on the counter holding her phone. I sneak up behind her and wrap my hands around her waist kissing her neck.

She giggles, "Wow your ears must have been ringing, I was in the middle of texting you."

"Well, I'm glad you didn't send it. I told them I was coming back to get my phone, really would have sucked if it started chiming in my pocket."

She turns around, facing me and her lips are on mine. Gently her tongue grazes my lip before investigating further. Damn, I've really missed just being able to walk into a room to find her standing there, it's going to be so hard flying back. Her hands are at the back of my neck, my hair twisting between her fingers. My phone keeps chiming in my pocket, hastily I rip it out and throw it on the counter. Slipping my hands under her shirt I find the clasp of her bra, at this point I just want to tear it off. Suddenly I hear the front door open and Layla jumps back fixing the clasps.

"Fuck," I groan and I hear footsteps coming in our direction. Layla grabs two glasses out of the cabinet and heads toward the fridge.

"Hey Ben, James sent me to grab another case of beer. He texted you a few times but figured you were still looking for your phone," Mason says walking to the fridge.

"Oh Ben, here it is," Layla says picking up my phone and handing it to me, "I thought I heard something but with this crazy mess all over the kitchen I'm not surprised you couldn't find it.

Hey Mason I was just about to pour us some lemonade, do you want some?"

For a moment Mason stands there staring at us, "No thanks, I'm going to stick with the beer. You ready Ben?"

I nod and Layla hands me the glass of lemonade she just poured before we make our way back to the lake. That was way too close. I know Mason didn't see anything but the way he was staring at us just gives me an uneasy feeling.

"You okay Mason?" I ask while walking on the path.

"Do you think Layla is acting a little weird? I don't know what it is but there's something off about her," he answers and I'm a little relieved.

"Not sure Mason, I haven't been here for a while. She seems fine to me."

"Yeah you're probably right," Mason agrees, "I haven't been around a whole lot either since Amy and I started dating."

"Why isn't she here today?" I ask.

"Thanksgiving is a big thing in her family so she's spending it with her parents and some family that came in from out of town. She invited me but I

haven't met her parents yet. I think I'd rather meet them one on one and not have a ton of extended family around," Mason snickers.
Back at the lake I get a message from Layla, *I love you.*

Finally it's time to eat, Carmen leads with a prayer which strikes me as kind of odd. This is the first time we've ever prayed before eating. Either way I got to hold Layla's hand so if she wants to make this a reoccurring thing, I'm for it.

"Oh Ben I can't believe I let this slip my mind," James starts, "My buddy had a rental come available, he texted me two days ago. The tenants already moved out and it just needs to be cleaned. I told him you were back in town for a few days and he said he can meet us there tomorrow if you want to see it. It's right in town, actually really close to the Bull."

"Yeah that would be great, awesome timing man," I say and I feel Layla tensing up next to me just a bit. I just remembered that I hadn't told her about my plans to get my own place, must have come as a surprise to her.

We all spend the evening outside sitting around a bonfire, it's gotten pretty chilly out so the fire gives off just enough heat to make it comfortable. Mason runs into the house and returns with skewers and marshmallows, what a great idea, I must have been around ten the last time I did that. Layla is sitting in the chair next to me wrapped in a blanket, staring at the fire.

"Now all we need is chocolate and graham crackers," Gio laughs.

"Unfortunately I don't think we have any, I can run in and check but I really never buy them," Carmen says.

"Nah, it's ok mom, this is fine," Gio says.
After about an hour Alex and Brittany say their goodbye's and drive home.

"The last thing I needed was marshmallows on top of that dinner we had. I feel like you're going to have to roll me in the house Carmen," James jokes.

"Don't worry, you'll work it off in Atlanta on Saturday, "Carmen smiles and turns to me," Gio and Isabella are flying back on Sunday so we're driving to Atlanta a day before since they haven't seen anything but the inside of the airport. I got us a hotel in the middle of downtown so we should have a great time."

"Sounds great. Gio you'll love it there, it's not quite New Orleans but it's fun," I remark before glancing over at Layla. She has the tiniest little smile on her lips and I know exactly what's going through her mind.

A few minutes later everyone heads inside leaving Mason, Layla and me out by the fire. Grabbing her phone out of her pocket Layla suggests that we look to see if we can find any constellations.

"And I'm out," Mason says getting up from the chair, "That shit is so boring, you know Ben is just being polite when he sits here and does that with you. I'm going to be inside watching TV, Ben can you handle the fire?"

"Really Mason? You think I don't know how to put out a fire?" Layla says sarcastically.

"You'd probably just end up burning yourself, let Ben handle it," Mason laughs before walking in the house. Layla rolls her eyes and sighs.

"Well for what it's worth, I know you can handle it," I smile grabbing her hand.

"You're so sweet," she smiles and squeezes my hand, "Do you remember the 4th of July barbeque we had?"

"How could I forget, it was a blast. I remember a certain someone starting a little war by pouring water down my back," I say raising my eyebrows.

"That's right. I thought I was being so funny and then I ended up in the lake, drenched from head to toe," she giggles.

"Hey at least I was nice enough to pull you back out, "I smile, pausing for a moment, "You know, when we were lying in the grass looking at each other, I swear that was the day I fell in love with you."

"Ben you're going to make me cry, that is the sweetest thing ever," Layla sighs

"Did I just make your year again," I say

"I'm not sure anything can top you surprising me like you did the other day, but it's very close."

"Oh I'm sure I can top it, actually I know I can, just wait," I grin

She leans in to give me a kiss on the cheek before sitting back in her chair.

"So hey I know I hadn't mentioned getting my own place before but it's something I really need to do," I explain.

"Why do you want to move out?

"Well, I'm forty-two years old and I can't keep living in my brother's house," I continue, "I really love it here but I need to be on my own."

"I get it," she pauses, "It just makes me sad that I won't get to see you all the time."

"Actually you'll see it's going to be better, we will have our alone time, no disturbances. Anyway, I'll still be working at the shop so you'll see me all the time."

I'm really excited to see this place James has been telling me about, it's actually a house and not an apartment. As we pull up I'm already loving the exterior, it's a two story with two small porches, top and bottom. As we get out of the car we're greeted by James' friend John.

"Hey so glad you guys were able to make it, like I said it just needs to be cleaned and then it will be ready. It was built in 1892 but the inside is completely renovated. Anyway it's a three bedroom, two bath about 1800 square feet. As you can see you're pretty close to everything here, the Bull is around the corner, Betty's is right there and town square is about three blocks away. The previous couple that lived here is going through a divorce and moved out unexpectedly so I'd love to get someone in as soon as possible."

I am completely surprised by the inside. It's totally updated with carpet throughout. I really don't need three bedrooms but the price and location are spot on so there's no way I can turn it down. I can't wait to show it to Layla, I wish I could just move her in here with me.

Chapter Sixteen

Layla

I have been counting down the hours for James, Carmen, Gio and Isabella to go to Atlanta. Just have to get Mason out of the house and we will be set. "Hey Mason, what are you plans today? Are you doing anything with Amy?"

"Yeah she's coming over here so if you guys want to hang out we can find something to do."

Not exactly what I wanted to hear, damn it. The sexual tension between Ben and I is out of this world right now, it's been building up since our encounter in the kitchen. After hearing us having the house to ourselves I was cheering inside, but now there's Mason and Amy. I could have just snuck in Ben's room on either of the nights but with more people in the house the possibly of being found out was greater. Maybe Ben getting his own place is a smart idea. He told me about the house and I know exactly which one he is talking about, it's literally a block from my job. Ben put down the deposit earlier today and will be getting the keys before going back to St. Louis. Mason suggests that the four of us watch a movie that he picked up at the store a few days ago, hell why not, we're not doing anything anyway.

Mason and Amy make themselves comfortable on the couch while Ben and I sit in the armchairs. Every once in a while I look over at them and it's really sweet seeing them cuddling on the couch but it also depresses me a bit since Ben and I can't be carefree like that.

About half way through the movie the front door opens and Alex and Brittany enter. They sit on the floor and Brittany starts talking about a flea market they visited earlier in the day. My phone buzzes and I check to see who it is; the message is from Ben. I look over at him wondering why he is sending me a message. After swiping to the right it reads *So much for some alone time.* Returning my glace to him I smirk and raise my eyebrows and he smiles, god that smile still makes me weak in the knees.

"Hey guys, let's play a game, what do you say? I bought at the flea-market and we have it in the car. Alex can you go get it?" Brittany asks, "You'll love it, it's a card game where you finish each other's sentences, I've played it at a party before, such a hit."

After about three hours I check the time and it's past 11 pm, we've been playing this card game the entire night. It's been great though, at some points I laughed so hard that I was on the verge of tears. Everyone heads upstairs to bed and I stay behind clearing away a few things left in the living room.

"Guess everyone is staying over," Ben comments while helping with the cleanup.

"Yeah, probably a good idea since everyone was drinking," I pause, "I pictured this day just a little different."

"Hey is Brit's phone down there?" Alex asks coming down the stairs passing me, "Oh Ben good you're still up I wanted to talk to you about something."

I hand Alex the phone and he asks if I can take it to Brittany on my way up. Well so much for a good night kiss too, I'm just going to write this entire day off I guess. Up in my room I change into my shorts and a tank top and get ready for bed. Lying in the dark I wonder why Alex needed to talk to Ben, that was kind of odd. Placing my phone on my nightstand I turn on my side and attempt to go to sleep. A few minutes later there is a knock on my door, I heard Mason laughing in the hallway a little bit ago so I wonder what the hell he could want now. Turning on my lamp, I push the covers to the side and get up to answer the door.

A huge smile comes over my face, it's Ben. Quickly slipping in my room he closes the door and locks it.

"What are you doing here?" I whisper

"Staying the night, what do you think?" he says, removing his shirt.

"You're kidding right? There are people across and next to us."

"Well then I suppose we will have to be very quiet," he smirks, unbuttoning his pants. Sitting on my bed he removes his pants and slips under the covers signaling for me to join him. We lie there for a while just staring at each other, talking about silly things. For a little while Ben is quiet and just stares directly into my eyes.

"Layla, come to St. Louis with me."

"What? You know that's impossible Ben."

"Is it?"

"If I was able to pull it off you know I'd be right there with you, but what would I tell everyone here? *'Hey guys I've always wanted to see St. Louis and since Ben is going there anyway I figured I'd just tag along'.* I'm sure that wouldn't raise any questions at all," I say sarcastically.

"Hey that sounds pretty good to me," he chuckles, "I know, you're right. It's just a few more weeks anyway. I would just love for you to meet my friend Chris, he's a really cool guy, you'd like him. He's the one who did my dragon tattoo."

"Don't talk about leaving right now, I don't want to think about it. Just kiss me and make me forget everything."

"Oh I can definitely do that," he says pulling me closer kissing me gently and slipping his hand under my shirt.

I'm at work waiting for Ben to stop by before driving to Atlanta to catch his flight back to St. Louis. I told myself to smile and stay positive but as the hour gets closer I feel as if I'm about to lose it. The door opens and my heart stops, it's him. Walking towards him I lead him to the back office and squeeze him really tight.

"Ben, I'm going to miss you so much. Please be safe and come back quick. I love you so much."

"I love you more, I already miss you," Ben counters.

After a long beautiful kiss, he disappears and I take a deep breath and head back to the bar.

"You okay Layla?" Layne asks.

"Not really. Why does it hurt so bad?" I sigh.

"Oh come here, I'm sorry you have to go through this but that's love for ya. It's not all sunshine and butterflies, sometimes it fucking sucks." Unfortunately, Randy doesn't have any extra shifts to offer so I'm back to the regular schedule. At home everything has returned to normal and I'm counting down the days until Ben returns.

It's Saturday night and we're about to sit down for dinner, tonight it's just James, Carmen and myself since Mason is out.

"Layla, is everything alright?" Carmen asks looing concerned.

"Yeah I'm great. Why?" I respond a little surprised.

"You just don't seem like yourself lately, you've just been very quiet."

"I think I'm just recovering from all of the extra shifts I worked, I don't know what I was thinking. The money is great but I'm not sure it was worth it," Thinking to myself, *'come on Layla, pull it together. You don't need everyone questioning your state of mind, it's only one more week'*.

I get a text from Layne asking if I have plans tonight, I reply that I don't and he says he will be over in a bit. Twenty minutes later Layne shows up at the house with a smile on his face.

"Hey Layne, what's up? Do you ever work anymore?" I ask jokingly.

"Haha, you're funny. I'm off today. You and I are going to have some much needed friend time," Layne replies.

"What about Ella?" I ask.

"Ella is at my place studying for her finals, she told me I was driving her crazy."

We get into his truck and drive to Macon and stop at a coffee shop, since neither one of us are coffee drinkers we order hot chocolates.

"So Layla I want to run something by you, I'm thinking of asking Ella to move in with me," Layne surprises me.

I choke on my hot chocolate and start coughing, "What? Are you serious?"

"This is exactly what I thought you would say, but after the initial shock, what do you think?" Layne inquires.

"Um, I think it's completely surprising but I know you love her, so why not?"

"I knew I could get an honest answer out of you. I was flip flopping and just couldn't make up my mind," he pauses, "so any news on the Ben front?"

"Not really, same old stuff. He signed a lease for a house in town so when he gets back he'll be moving in."

"Well that's awesome, you'll have your own secret love nest. I can't imagine how it's been with you all living under the same roof. At some point you're planning on telling everyone, right? I mean, you can't keep it a secret forever," Layne says.

I haven't really thought about it; sure I'd love to be able to just kiss Ben in front of everyone or hold his hand while watching TV but I have no idea how I would even begin to explain our relationship.

Ben

Last therapy session today, I really feel that this whole thing is a big waste of my time. Jen is still living in her little dream world of the two of us having a happily ever after. I talked to Layla last night and she is so excited for me to be home on Sunday. Originally I planned on leaving directly after therapy but Chris asked if he could put together a going away dinner Saturday night since he won't know when he will see me again.

Once I get to the office I see Jen sitting in the waiting area with a smile on her face, great, wonder what she is going to pull today. Once Mary opens the door to call me in Jen gets up and asks if we could start with couple time. Yep, I knew she was up to something.

After an hour we finish and I still can't believe what I heard in there. Jen decided that she agrees to the divorce; I thought I was going to fall out of my chair. We also discussed dividing our belongings, another surprise; I just figured she was keeping everything.

In the parking lot Jen walks up to me asking when I would like to come by the apartment to choose the things I would like to have. We set up a time for the next day.

Back at home I grab a beer out of the fridge, lounge on the couch and call Layla to tell her the great news, she is beyond excitement. She's at work so we can't talk long and I need to fill out these papers so I can have them served as soon as possible.

I rent a small trailer and pickup Chris who is coming along to help load up my belongings. Walking into our old apartment feels familiar and foreign at the same time. Nothing has really changed, furniture is still in the same spots, same pictures on the wall. The three of us sit at the dining table and Jen and I discuss who gets what. I'm actually quite thankful because I end up with the living room set, the entire guest bedroom and a lot of the paintings on the wall. There are also a few sealed boxes sitting at the door that Jen said she packed up for me, just a few odds and ends. Once Chris and I move everything out into the trailer I run back upstairs to tell Jen goodbye, I figured it's the right thing to do.

"I guess this is it, I was hoping for a different outcome but now I see that you would never be happy," she sighs as she leans in to hug me.

I know all I wanted was for her to sign the papers so I can move on with my life but I have to say it does hit me just a bit. Maybe it's just being in this place and seeing her a little emotional, it's just striking a nerve and I really need to get out of here.

"Thank you Jen, this is the right thing. I wish you all the happiness in the future, I really do," I say and she squeezes me tighter. She tells me to drive safe and I go downstairs and get into my truck.

On the way home Chris and I stop by the courthouse so I can file the divorce papers. After paying the filing fee the clerk informs me that a copy of the papers will need to be served to my wife and he gives me the three different options. He also tells me that Missouri has a thirty day waiting period after filing the petition before the courts can grant a divorce and that I will be notified of a final hearing. Great, sounds like I'll be making another trip here. After finishing at the courthouse I opt to send the papers via certified mail again to ensure I get a receipt of acceptance. Alright, now I'm back in the same boat I was a few months ago, I just pray things go smooth.

Layla

Looking out the window I see Ben's truck pulling up the driveway and it takes everything I have not to run out there and jump into his arms. James walks up behind me, "Oh good, he's here, perfect timing. Carmen just finished cooking."

James walks to the front door and opens it, "Hey, it's great to have you back, brother. Hope you're hungry."

"Hey man, I'm starving. It's good to see you," Ben says giving James a hug. I stand there, frozen staring at him, I have no idea how to greet him. Kissing him is obviously out of the question but what about a hug? This was so much easier at the Bull. Maybe I'm just overthinking this.

"Layla," Ben smiles and leans in for a hug. Okay I totally overthought this, there's nothing wrong with hugging him in front of everyone. My eyes are closed and I take in his smell, god have I missed his scent. I know it's only been two weeks but it feels like months.

"We're really glad to have you back," I say as we pull away from each other. Carmen walks into the living room to say hello before we make our way into the dining room for dinner.

"Where's Mason?" Ben asks looking around.

"Take a wild guess, he's with Amy," Carmen starts, "Most of the time it's just James, Layla and I. Amazing how things change over a short period of time."

"It's a good thing, it was about time for him to finally meet someone. He was always such a homebody I really thought he would be here forever. I get the feeling by next year he and Amy will be moving in together," James pauses and looks at me, "you know with Ben getting his own place now we just have to get rid of you and then we're all set," he jokes.

"Hell, Layla can move in with me," Ben responds quickly, "I mean, my place is big enough." I can't believe he just said that, my heart is pounding and I can't come up with a response.

"Sounds great, let's bring her stuff over tomorrow," James continues, "I'm just teasing sweetie, you can stay here as long as you want."

"You guys are so bad, you're making her blush," Carmen says playfully pushing James' shoulder.

After dinner, Carmen and I clear the table while James and Ben head out to the shop. While drying the dishes I look out the window and see Ben and James sitting on the picnic table. I remember the time when the guys were fixing the shop's roof and I was so engrossed in watching Ben that I broke something, can't remember what it was now.

"So when are you going to meet that special someone Layla?" Carmen asks, handing me a plate.

"Who knows? It will happen when it's supposed to I guess," I respond, feeling terrible for lying to her.

"I was honestly pulling for you and Layne, really thought you two would get back together," she adds.

I giggle, "I think everyone did. Most people don't get our friendship, I guess it may look a little unusual. I am so happy that he found Ella, he is completely in love with her. You know, you can't choose who you fall in love with, it just happens."

"You're absolutely right," Carmen smiles.

After finishing the cleanup I head in the direction of the shop, Ben has been back for about two hours and I still haven't had the chance to have him to myself. As I open the door Ben and James are sitting on the workbench in the middle of a conversation. When James sees me he asks what time it is, pulling out my phone I tell him it's just a little after 8 pm and he jumps down rushing past me.

"What was that all about?" Ben asks walking toward me as I shut the door.

"Oh, there's this TV show he and Carmen started watching that comes on Sunday's at 8 pm. It's a singing competition and they really get into it and when I say really get into it I mean they don't want anyone to talk while it's on."

"Well, I guess it's good we're out here then," he says grabbing my waist and pulling me close. I wrap my arms around his neck and pull him towards me kissing him slowly.

"God if I died right this second I would die a happy man," Ben mumbles between kisses.

I pull back slightly giving him a little smirk, "Well I was about to kill you at dinner. You were crazy for saying that."

"What, that you can come live with me? I was serious about it," he grins.

"I'm sure you were but there's no way we can pull that off, you have to watch what you say," I add with a worried expression on my face.

"About that, I really think we need to start coming up with a plan," Ben says.

"A plan for what?"

"A plan on telling them that you and I are together," Ben responds.

I step back and lean against the workbench, "Ben, I'm not ready for that."

"Why? What's the matter? Are you ashamed?"

"God no, never. I'm scared, I don't know how they are going to react," I explain.

"Well, that's why I said we need to come up with a plan, I know it won't be easy but the longer we wait the harder it gets. The fact that I couldn't just walk up to you and kiss you when I got back fucking killed me."

"Okay, let's not think about it right now though. I have other thoughts that are running through my mind that involve less talking, if you know what I mean," I say biting my lip and by the look in his eyes we are on the same page.

The next day is bittersweet, Ben is moving into his new house and James is helping with the unloading. Carmen was very generous and gave Ben most of her kitchen items, they've been sitting in boxes upstairs since she moved in. Walking into the kitchen I stop at the doorway to Ben's room, wow all of the personal touches are gone and it looks like an ordinary guest room. I walk in and sit on the bed, running my hand over the comforter. I think back on when we first got together, that night has never left my mind. I also remember the horrific week that followed, all I can say is thanks to the person who invented the morning after pill. I get up and notice a box in the corner with some of Ben's belongings, he must have missed it when he loaded the truck. I pick it up and take it out to my car figuring I have a good excuse to head over since James is there as well. On the ride over I actually pass James near the Bull, he stops and rolls down his window.

"Hey Layla, where are you off to?"

"Ben left a box at the house so I was bringing it over."

"You're lucky, we just got back from dropping the trailer off in Macon. Maybe you can help him unpack a little if you're not busy today," James suggests

I nod and continue on to Ben's house, now I'm really glad that I decided to bring the box over. I pull into the small driveway and park next to his truck, getting out I look around and suddenly everything feels foreign. I knock on the door and a few seconds later Ben answers.

"Special delivery," I say handing him the box. "Layla, come in. Screw the box, you're the special delivery," he says grabbing the box and placing it down inside next to the door.

"Wow," is all I can manage to say, I never thought that the inside was this nice.

"I know right? It's a little bigger than I wanted but we'll make it work."

I turn to him with a confused look, "We'll make it work?"

"Yeah," he says taking a key out of his pocket, "here's your key. Come here whenever you want, even if I'm not home but definitely when I am. Eventually you will be living here, I'm thinking sooner than later. Let me give you a tour."

The house is gorgeous and very spacious. The living room and bedroom are already set up. I notice a slew of paintings resting against the wall waiting to be hung up and quite a few boxes needing emptying. I'm guessing this is the furniture he had in St. Louis, I'm loving the couch, it's an L-shape, grey in color with a chaise. The bedroom set is really beautiful as well, a sleigh bed with matching nightstands and dresser. I wonder if his Ex was the one who chose these things, on second thought I don't want to know.

I spend the next hour helping him unpack boxes, placing books in the bookshelf while he starts hanging some of the paintings. I stumble across a box with photographs, I sit on the floor and look through them. There are a lot of pictures of Ben with who I believe is Chris. Ben's told me what he looks like and this guy fits the description. Ben comes up behind me, "Wow, I haven't seen those in a while. I was in my early thirties in that picture."

"You had such a baby face. That's exactly how I remembered you. Your hair was much shorter," I comment holding the picture, "It looks good but I like it long."

"I think you just like to play with it," he laughs and I grab the next stack of pictures. He and Chris must have been friends for a very long time, it seems as if they did everything together. There's even a picture of Ben getting tattooed by him. Moving on to the next picture it shows Ben with his arm around a woman.

"Is this her?" I ask and Ben seems a little uncomfortable.

"Yeah, that' Jen. I'm sorry Layla, I didn't know those would be in there," he answers.

"She's pretty," I pause looking at the picture, "It's weird, she didn't seem real before but actually seeing her, I don't know, I guess she is real," I add placing the picture on top of the others.

"Here," Ben says holding out his hand, "I'll get rid of the pictures, no reason to keep them."

"Don't do it because of me, I don't have a problem with them. It's your past and it has made you who you are today, the man that completely swept me off my feet and continues to do so every day," I say smiling.

"I can't believe just how lucky I am, how the hell did I deserve you?"

"I've asked myself that exact same question a time or two," I say and he leans in to kiss me.

Ben was totally right about getting his own place; it has been amazing spending so much time with him without the fear or someone showing up. I know I had my reservations since I thought I wouldn't see him as much as before but it's been working out great. I just hate lying to everyone at home. I'm an adult and I really don't have to tell anyone where I'm going but for some reason I feel as if I have to justify my absence. I've come up with everything from shift changes to overnight stays with Layne and Ella, whatever gets me to spend more time with Ben. I even keep my car parked behind the Bull, I don't want anyone to see it in Ben's driveway. Ben absolutely hates being so secretive and has been telling me it's time to set the record straight. He's right, the more time goes by the more anxious I become.

Chapter Seventeen

Ben

It's a typical Saturday night, Layla and I are sitting on the couch watching a movie. She's spread across the chaise with my head in her lap. These are some of our best moment together, so close, not a care in the world and completely in love. The way her fingers run through my hair is so relaxing and puts me to sleep every time. With Christmas and New Year's behind us I'm hoping to hear news from St. Louis sometime soon. I received a delivery receipt two days after arriving back here and I also got a text from Jen saying she signed everything in front of a notary. I guess now we are just waiting on a date for the final hearing, it can't come soon enough. We are really close to the thirty-day mark so I'm actually surprised that we don't have anything scheduled.

Layla wakes me, telling me the movie has ended and we make our way to the bedroom. Who would have thought that standing in the mirror brushing our teeth together is something that would have ever happened? I love seeing her toothbrush in the holder next to mine, even more I'd love for her to live here with me. Removing my shirt and tossing it into the hamper I climb into bed enjoying the view of Layla changing into her tank top.

"What are you smiling about?" she says scrunching her forehead.

"I'm just debating on what exactly I want to do to you tonight," I say grinning from ear to ear.

"What? I thought you were beat, you were sound asleep downstairs," she scoffs walking to my side of the bed.

"Just recharging," I smile grabbing her arm and pulling her on top of me.

The mornings always come way too fast, Layla is already up and dressed and leans in to give me a kiss, "I have to go but I will see you at dinner tonight, I love you babe."

Sunday dinners have become a tradition in the Parker home, an idea Carmen came up with. I really like the idea, it's really crazy but it's one of the only times we get to see Alex lately. We all live in the same town but Alex and Brittany are always on the go. They did stop by to see my place last week. Brittany said she has been inside it years ago when she thought about renting it herself with two of her friends, instead decided on her one bedroom minus the roommates. Layne has also become a frequent visitor, stopping by for an occasional beer on the porch. I can now say that we have officially become friends. Honestly I think our friendship started the night he told me to get my shit together.

I have a few hours to kill so I drive to Macon to do some grocery shopping. It's the middle of January so it's quite chilly outside but I love it. Stopping by the hardware store I pick up a few tools to replace some of the old ones in the shop. If it were up to James, he would use them until they fall apart and then find some way to fix them. I've come across a few of the '*rigged by James*' tools and a some of them are just plain dangerous.

While putting the groceries away my phone chimes and I assume it's a message from Layla. Taking it out of my pocket I'm shocked because it's from Jen, what could she want now? I swipe the screen and her message reads ***Hey Ben, sorry to bother you. Just wondering if you've gotten any word about a court date***. I reply letting her know that I haven't heard anything either. I'm sure it has something to do with the holidays, our divorce is pretty straight forward so that should be the only reason. Thinking about it a little more in depth, I hope we included all of the necessary paperwork since we decided to forgo the lawyers in the end. I'll give it another week, if we don't have a court date by then I'll just have to make some calls.

Straightening up the house a little I notice it's getting close to 6 pm so it's time to head to James'. Alex and I pull up at the same time and I notice he's riding solo today. He said Brittany is meeting some of her girlfriends for coffee tonight but she may stop by a little later.

Walking into the dining room Layla is setting plates on the table, "No Brittany tonight either? Guess it will be like old times," Mason said

"Amy can't make it tonight," Layla comments as she retrieves the plate she had set out for Brittany.

"You guys must have a sixth sense, we're ready to eat," Carmen says as she walks in and sets a big pot of Jambalaya on the table. Layla was right, it's just like old times, really brings back some memories.

Once we finish eating we sit around the table and talk for a while, Alex mentions that Brittany's parents will be visiting next month and are really looking forward to meet everyone. Even though they are only a state over, owning a successful family business doesn't give them a lot of time to get away.

"Yeah so we've been pretty busy working lately," Mason starts, "not that I'm complaining, I like the money. I've noticed a lot of new clients too; must be because of all those developments they are building in Macon."

"I guess word has gotten around that we have the best prices," James chuckles, "speaking of new clients, Ben do you remember the woman that came in on Wednesday with the Forte?"

"Um, vaguely," I answer knowing exactly who he is talking about, she kept mentioning that she was recently divorced and moved here with her kids.

"Oh come on, you have to remember her. She was blonde and very friendly, just moved here recently," James says before pausing for a moment, "She was checking out your bike outside and told you that she used to ride when she was younger." Where the hell is he going with this? Moving my eyes to the right I notice Layla looking a bit confused as well.

"Oh yeah, I remember," is all I say.

"Great, well Carmen and I ran into her in Macon and we talked for a little while. She really took an interest in you and asked if you were single. I told her you were and she gave me her number and asked me to pass it on to you," James announces and Carmen smiles. Layla lets out a little cough and grabs her water. Fuck.

"James why would you do that?" I demand.

"Ben I think she is a really nice woman and you are single so why not just call her and go out and see how it goes," James responds, looking at me like I'm unappreciative.

"James, that was not okay. I appreciate you looking out for me but I'm not interested," I reply hoping that is the end of that conversation. The entire table is eerily quiet, Mason decided to try to strike up a conversation with Layla but she doesn't seem to hear a word he is saying.

"Ben, I just don't understand. I mean, I know your marriage didn't work out and that may be a factor but just get back out there, I did and I'm happier than ever," James maintains, clearly he isn't letting this go and I'm starting to feel as if I am being backed into a corner. By the way Layla is sitting I can tell she is tense, I hate seeing her that way.

"Just don't worry about it, it's my business. I really don't mean to be an ass about it but I'm done talking about this."

"Well I think you are being ridiculous, sorry but you are," James scowls and Carmen grabs his arm telling him to let it go, "No Carmen, I just want to understand why he's getting so upset about this. Ben come on, just give me one reason why you won't even consi-"

"Because I'm in love with Layla," I yell out, and suddenly I feel relieved. Looking over at Layla her expression has turned to fear and she lowers her eyes and stares at the table. Instinctively I grab her hand under the table and she squeezes it tight and I notice she is shaking. A part of me feels terrible for not being able to just cool down and make up some kind of story.

"Layla? Layla who? What are you talking about Ben?" James asks and I can't believe he hasn't caught on. My eyes make a quick run around the table and by the look on everyone else's face they know exactly who I am talking about. Carmen leans in close to James and points out the obvious.

"What? This is a joke right? You can't be serious, Ben come on man," James chuckles nervously before studying Layla's body language, "Oh my god, you are serious. How long has this been going on?"

Alex interjects," Come on James just co-"

"No, I want to know how long this has been going on," James interrupts, his voice carrying an angry tone. I can tell Layla is at the verge of tears, I take a deep breath, "Since early October."

For a moment James sits there staring straight past us before getting up and walking out.

Mason and Alex are yelling after him but Carmen says he just needs some time to cool off. Fuck that, I get up and follow him outside.

I see him walking toward the path leading to the lake, "James, stop! Come on this is ridiculous. Stop!"

He stops and turns around to face me, "I don't get it, how did this happen?"

"It just did; I don't even know how to explain it."

"You're not even divorced yet; don't you think you're jumping into something a little too soon?" James argues.

"Well that is kind of hypocritical coming from the guy who was so adamant to set me up with a total stranger," I counter.

"But, there are almost twenty years between the two of you. Is this just some fantasy you're living out? I mean, she's a beautiful girl, I can see the attraction." James says.

"Absolutely not James. I didn't just jump into this headfirst. I battled with this for months before I broke down and realized that she is everything I've always wanted. I love her."

For a moment James just stands there quietly, you can tell he is processing everything right now.

"I'm sorry for freaking out like that in there. I'm just worried," he pauses, "I'm worried that you are going to break her heart Ben. I don't want that for her, I know she won't be able to handle that."

"What would make you think I would break her heart?" I ask.

"Let's face it Ben, you've always been a runner. Things get tough and you're gone. I'm not just talking about here and St. Louis, I'm talking about the times when we were teenagers. Stuff didn't go as planned and you took off for a few weeks here or a month there. I don't mean to throw that in your face but it's a fact." James says.

"I understand your concern but I won't abandon her," I reply.

"Oh I know you don't have intentions to abandon her right now, you've only been together for three or four months, it's still exciting, no big problems, everything's great. We all know that's not the way life goes," James says.

He's right, he does have good reason to doubt me. In the past I have made some questionable decisions.

"Listen Ben, in the end Layla is an adult and she can do what she wants. I'm not her father, I have no right to tell her what's right or wrong. All I can do is voice my concerns and let her choose which path she wants to take."

Layla

My heart is pounding and I have no idea what to think right now. I wasn't ready for this, hell, after witnessing James' behavior tonight I don't think I could have ever been ready for it. I get up from the table and move into the living room and sit on the couch. Mason and Alex follow, taking a seat on either side of me. Mason wraps his arms around me and tells me to cheer up. I can't help but wonder what is going on outside right now, I don't want them to fight, especially not because of me.

Carmen walks into the living room and sits on the edge of the coffee table in front of me grabbing my hand, "Don't worry, Layla. Everything is going to be fine. He's just shocked that's all, it was something so unexpected."

"Not that unexpected," Mason says, "I had my suspicious but I honestly thought I was crazy. Nice to know that I can trust my gut." Leave it to Mason to try and throw a little comedy into it.

"You really love him don't you?" Carmen asks.

I look up staring directly into Carmen's concerned eyes, "You have no idea, he's my world."
She smiles and a moment later I hear the front door open. Seeing Ben and James walking in together gives me a small sense of relief.

"Layla," James pauses, "can you come take a walk with me please?"

This is the moment I was afraid of but I don't really have a choice. Slowly rising from my seat I take a few steps toward him stopping next to Ben before proceeding. Looking at him I hope to find some kind of answer as to what went on outside. Ben reaches for my hand, squeezing it before leaning in to kiss my forehead, instantly I feel about sixty percent better.

Once outside James begins, "Layla, first of all I want to apologize for my behavior, it was uncalled for. I can't say I am completely convinced that this is a good idea but it's not my place to make that decision. I love Ben to death, I really do but Layla, I love you more. I've watched you grow up and go through so many ups and downs, I consider you the daughter I never had and the last thing I want is to see you hurt. Ben has always had demons; he's been fighting them for a very long time. I know people change but some things are just ingrained in us. Let me ask you an important question, Layla do you want kids?"

Wow, that came out of nowhere, "Um, I don't know, sure, maybe. I really don't know James, why?"

"Ben is so much older than you are and the likelihood of him wanting kids is slim. It's probably something that hasn't ever crossed your mind but it's important to think about before you get too invested. I want to make sure that you won't be the one making all of the compromises in this relationship. From talking to Ben I know he deeply cares for you and seeing the look he gave you just before we stepped outside reassured me. All I want is for both of you to be happy and if it's with each other, then that's how it is. Just know, I am always here for you no matter what."

"Do you regret not having kids?" I ask

"I wouldn't say regret. You know Cheryl wasn't able to get pregnant, it was never a deal breaker for me. I'm not going to lie, there have been times I've wondered how it would have been if I had the chance of being a dad. I'd like to think I would have done a decent job."

"So looking back knowing what you know now, would you change anything?" I ask.

"Probably not, if I did I would have never met Carmen," he pauses giving me a smirk, "How did this get turned around on me? You have always had a way of deflecting from the issue at hand."

"So it's still an issue?" I joke.

James leans in to give me a hug, "No, I have faith that you will do the right thing for yourself, you're smart. I'm guessing this means that you will probably want to move in with Ben?" Looking up at him I give him a cute little grin and he squeezes me one more time before we head back inside.

It's crazy how many things have happened in the last two months. Ben is finally divorced, he didn't even have to go back to court, I guess a judge just signed it. I've been living with Ben since the night everyone found out about us and I couldn't be happier. I can't believe how easy things have been and being so close to work is definitely a big plus. We still spend just about every Sunday with the family for our traditional dinner. Alex and Mason are slowly warming up to the idea that I am dating their big brother. Anytime Ben is affectionate towards me Carmen just sighs as if she's watching a romantic movie, time and again she has told me how she thinks we are perfect for each other. It took James a few weeks to be convinced that this wasn't just a fun idea we had, now he even comments that he's never seen Ben this happy in his life. I feel like kicking myself, had I known that things would run this smooth I would have come forward a long time ago. Well, maybe not. Even though things were a little challenging, those three months were some of the best times of my life.

It's another typical Friday night at the Bull, Ben just walked in the door and my heart skips a beat.

"Hey Babe, long time no see," Ben says leaning over the bar to give me kiss.

"Oh it's been what, like four hours?" I grin.

"Four hours too long if you ask me," Ben says in a flirtatious tone.

"Alright guys, break it up, you know some of us have a job to do here," Layne jumps in, "Hey man what's going on? Cool that both of you are here right now. I was talking to Ella last night and we are planning a trip to New Orleans. We're wondering if you guys would like to come along, like a mini vacation. What do you say?"

Ben and I look at each other, getting out of town for a little while would be nice and I loved New Orleans. "Hell why not," Ben says giving Layne a fist bump, "I think it's a great idea, I'm always up for New Orleans. We are going to have a great time."

We just landed in New Orleans and the weather is gorgeous, it's the end of March and much more comfortable than it was in July. On the taxi ride to our hotel Ella and I have been talking nonstop, she and I have become very close friends. Once we come to a stop I look out the window and we are parked in front of the same hotel that we stayed at when James and Carmen got married.

"Are you kidding?" I ask a little shocked, "This place is crazy expensive."

"Come on Layla, you only live one, besides I really wanted to see that famous swim up bar that you showed me pictures of," Layne grins

"It's a little too cold for that Layne, it may not be open," I reply.

"That would be my luck wouldn't it," Layne says.

We check in at the front desk and get our room keys. Walking down the hall it feels so surreal being here, so many memories. Layne and Ella's room is a few doors down from ours and we make plans to meet in the lobby to go to dinner in about an hour.

Our room looks a little different than the one I stayed in last time. For starters, it has a King size bed and not two doubles. The room has its own little balcony that overlooks the pool area and the bathroom is ultra-modern with a giant garden tub in the middle. I don't think I'll ever want to leave here. After dinner, we head to a few bars and Layne has completely fallen in love with Bourbon Street.

"Ella, what the hell are we doing living in shithole Georgia? This is where it's at. I think I see a move in our future," Layne broadcasts, looking happy as can be.

"I don't know Layne, I like small towns. I bet this gets old after a while too," Ella says shaking her head.

"I tend to agree with Ella, I'm sure that the people living here don't see it as we do," I answer smiling at Ella.

"I lived here for a while and I never got bored," Ben adds, "You guys want another round before heading back?"

A few minutes later Ben comes back with a round of shots and we talk about all the places we want to visit tomorrow. Before leaving Georgia, Layne suggested that Ella and I each bring a semi-formal dress for a dinner at a fancy restaurant. This will be interesting; I have never seen Layne dressed up.

Back at the hotel after dropping Layne and Ella at their room we continue on to ours. Ben takes the keycard out of his wallet but freezes for a moment.

"What is it Ben?" I ask.

"Hmm, I just had a flashback. This time I can go through with," he says and before I know it I'm up against the door and his lips are on mine. This really brings me back to the night everything started and excitement is shooting through my body. While kissing me he maneuvers the card in the door and guides me into the room.

I start to unbutton his shirt while his hands find the zipper of my pants. When I reach the last button, his shirt falls to the floor and we move onto the bed, losing my top in the process. While removing my jeans he plants kisses all around my navel, moving his tongue down the inside of my thigh. Changing direction, he slowly makes his way up toward my mouth, stopping at my breasts, teasing me with his tongue. At this point I am begging him to rip off my G-string and fuck but he just smirks and tells me to be patient. Removing his pants and boxers, his lips move up my neck until they reach my chin. I can feel his erection pressed against the inside of my thigh, this is madness. Finding his lips, my tongue invades his mouth. Gently using my nails I run my hands from the middle of his back all the way up to his shoulders and down the sides of his arms. He lets out a slight groan and now I have him exactly where I want him. Hooking my leg around his waist I pull him closer to me and his kiss picks up intensity. His right hand starts moving down my body and within seconds he's buried inside me. Slowly thrusting forward, he kisses my neck and reaches for my hand, squeezing it tightly. Resting his other arm at my side he continues moving in a slow but steady pace. Feeling the pressure building inside me I place my hand on the back of his neck and pull him towards my lips. This kiss is beyond anything I can describe and feeling him groan against my mouth is taking it to a whole new level. Placing my hands on the sides of his hips and pulling him harder against me he picks up momentum and within thirty seconds the intensity that has been pooling inside me is released. Crying out in pleasure Ben continues pushing forward until he can no longer hold back. The sight of his body quivering is something that makes my heart pound every time. Resting his forehead to mine, catching our breath I whisper *'I love you'* and he softly kisses my lips while stroking the side of my face. We lie in each other's arms and I notice him drifting and a few minutes later he is sound asleep. I could stare at him all night long, he looks so peaceful. Once in a while I still can't believe that this gorgeous man is mine.

The next day is spent giving Layne and Ella a tour of the French quarter; to me it's just as breathtaking as the last time. Maybe Layne wasn't so far off with the idea of possibly moving here. Ben and I are walking hand in hand just enjoying the sights, no need to take pictures this time around, except for the occasional selfie. While walking down Decatur Street, Ben suddenly comes to a stop.

"Layla, remember this," he says pointing to a shop on the corner.

"Oh my god yes, the voodoo shop. Let's take them inside," I reply. Inside we find the same old woman sitting behind the counter, again, trying to entice us with her potions. After browsing for about fifteen minutes we pick up a few small trinkets before heading back to the hotel.

Back in the room Ben and I get dressed for dinner. Ben is looking so sexy wearing black slacks and a matching black button shirt. Standing in front of the mirror he rolls the sleeves up to his elbows. He turns around to look at me.

"That's the dress you wore to the wedding isn't it?" he asks with a smile on his face.

"It is, I had another one I bought but after much debating, this is the one that made the cut."

"God you look so beautiful; I love that dress on you. Hey we still have about ten minutes before we have to meet them, you want to make good use of them?" Ben asks and before I can answer there's a knock on our door.

Ben sighs, "Well, scratch that."

I open the door to find Ella standing there, Layne is nowhere in sight.

"Hey guys, sorry to bother you. Layne wanted to know if Ben could come by the room really quick, he's having issues with his tie and I have no idea what I'm doing," Ella confesses with an embarrassed look on her face. Ben leans in to kiss me before heading out the door.

"Come on in Ella, I just have to finish my makeup and I'll be ready," I say.

"Sure," she says walking in and shutting the door behind her, "Wow, look at this place. Now this is a room."

"Yeah, you should see the view from the balcony, it's amazing," I say applying my mascara.

I join her on the balcony, the sun has already set and the pool area is lit up with lights. Ella mentions that she and Layne went to check out the pool earlier this morning because he really wanted to see the bar, but just like I had assumed, it was closed. My phone buzzes and I walk inside to see who it is, it's from Ben and it reads *Hey Layne and I are already downstairs. We had the front desk call for a cab, meet us at the fountain when you guys are ready*. That's odd, why would they be at the fountain? It's not anywhere near the front desk. After grabbing my purse Ella and I head out of the room towards the elevator. When we reach the courtyard I see Ben and Layne sitting on the rim of the fountain. Just like last time, the entire area is lit up by strands of lights, just beautiful.

"Wow Layne, you clean up really nice," I comment with a smile.

"Why thank you Layla, I'm kind of digging this look. May have to dress up more often," Layne smirks grabbing Ella's hand, "Hey Ella, I have to show you this ballroom, they are setting up for an event, it's seriously awesome."

"Okay Layne, lets hurry it up though, we don't want to miss the cab," Ella says as they walk through the French doors.

"Layla, come sit," Ben says grabbing my hand, "Remember the last time we were here?"

"Of course I do, I know we were drunk but I remember it like it was yesterday. I still have the picture on my phone; it's always been one of my favorites."

"It's one of my favorites too. Who would have thought that you and I would be sitting here today," he pauses staring into my eyes, "You know, I still can't believe how lucky I am to have you. I love you so much and I can't picture a life without you anymore. You're smart, beautiful, kind and you keep me grounded. There's only one thing I'd like to change about you."

"Oh," I hesitate for moment wondering what he could be talking about, "What would you change?"

"Your last name," he reveals before grabbing my hand, "Layla, will you marry me?"

Ben just asked me to marry him, I can't believe it. My entire body is trembling and I can feel happy tears pooling in my eyes.

"Yes! Yes! Yes!" I cry, wrapping my arms around him and kissing him as if we were the only two people left in this world.

"I love you Layla," Ben declares, moving a strand of hair out of my face.

"I love you too."